Taking a chance, a huge chance, Grant leaned forward and slowly lowered his head. He gave Lynn every opportunity to move away or say something, but she stayed still and finally lifted her face. He placed a gentle kiss on her luxurious mouth.

Her lips warmed under his in intoxicating seconds. Her breath quickened. He sensed her fighting the urge to pull away, and rejoiced silently when she stayed with him, panic and all.

He slowly let his tongue trace the corners of her mouth. First one, then the other. A swipe of his lower lip against hers gained him a small gasp.

With the lightest of touches, he skimmed his fingers over her eyebrows, her cheekbones, her silky jaw. His blood sang with desire. She was sweet, so sweet.

Pressing the fullness of his mouth against hers, he drank in the nectar of her, fighting back the overpowering need to enfold her in his arms and hold tight . . .

Silver Threads Golden Needles

PAULA McKINLEY

JOVE BOOKS, NEW YORK

As always, to Bart. With all my love.

This is a work of fiction. Names, characters, places, and incidents are
either the product of the author's imagination or are used fictitiously,
and any resemblance to actual persons, living or dead, business
establishments, events, or locales is entirely coincidental.

MAGICAL LOVE is a registered trademark of Penguin Putnam Inc.

SILVER THREADS GOLDEN NEEDLES

A Jove Book / published by arrangement with
the author

PRINTING HISTORY
Jove edition / November 2000

The Penguin Putnam Inc.World Wide Web site address is
http://www.penguinputnam.com

ISBN: 0-515-12953-4

A JOVE BOOK®
Jove Books are published by The Berkley Publishing Group,
a division of Penguin Putnam Inc.,
375 Hudson Street, New York, New York 10014.
JOVE and the "J" design
are trademarks belonging to Penguin Putnam Inc.

PRINTED IN THE UNITED STATES OF AMERICA

10 9 8 7 6 5 4 3 2 1

Prologue

~~

England, 1097

Jeanette's fading spirit felt the pull of the sweet darkness as shadows rose to meet the night. The hiss and crackle of the fire was as lovely as a troubadour's song, the quiet sigh of the wood as it was consumed by the flame fitting her mood.

She wished she had the strength to open the shutters to the moonlight, but she was too weak to withstand Anna's apoplexy if she returned to find the evil evening air wafting into the room. Justin had loved the stars, and when Jeanette looked at the night sky, he seemed closer somehow.

"Justin," she whispered, closing her eyes and smiling faintly as she lay in the warm cocoon of furs.

She heard a rustling just past her door and felt impatience with those who waited outside. They were kind folk who had pitied her maiden and childless state . . . even as they had benefited from her time not taken by husband and child. She did not mean to cause them sadness, but she was anxious to cast off this mortal coil. What was Death waiting for? She was ready. She'd been ready for thirty-one years . . .

A bright light tortured her.

"Anna, remove the candle, please."

"Jeanette, your journey has reached its end."

The voice was warm, serene. Certainly not Anna's harsh rasp.

Jeanette shielded her eyes with a soft, smooth hand that did not seem to fit the rest of her frail frame. Even now, if her body would cooperate, her fingers would be nimble in plying her needle, a needle she'd used every day since Justin had been taken from her.

She squinted. The room was lit as though by a hundred candles. No, more than that. Many more. Jeanette could see each frame of her tapestries as if in the brightest sunshine.

Her eyes sought the face of the man stitched into every panel. *My beloved . . .*

After a moment, she could make out a tall body, seemingly clothed in the very glow around her, else the gown was of a fabric unlike any Jeanette had beheld. The long dress was radiant, holding the light the way glass captured a flame.

Rays of brilliance fanned out like wings behind her. Behind him? Although the ethereal face was beautiful, filled with serenity and compassion, she could not decide if her visitor were male or female.

In a way, the messenger reminded her of the tapestry she had done in honor of Justin's death. She had stitched a host of angels guiding him to a warrior's reception in heaven. Her visitor looked much like the fair, golden beings she had imagined taking her beloved to God's arms.

"Who are you?" she asked, straining to see the figure hidden in the light.

"A simple herald."

"Are you here for me?" she whispered hopefully.

The messenger glided closer. "Jeanette," the voice said with gentle reprimand, "you have chosen to withhold your heart from those who would have cherished you."

"But, how could I? My beloved—"

"All the trials set before you were lessons, but you refused to consider any other paths open to you. You had many chances to have love again, but you kept your pain close to your heart."

"I'm . . . I'm sorry," she whispered.

Jeanette wanted to refute the truth being told her, but it was as the messenger said. Many a man had courted her, especially when she'd been young and still beautiful, but she had turned them each away, choosing instead to hold on to the image of Justin she had engraved in her mind.

"Yes, Jeanette, you bestowed tremendous compassion to those around you, yet you withheld it from the person who needed it most: yourself. But be at peace, child, for while you kept yourself from love, you gave it to others freely. In doing so, you have imbued your needle with that greatest of all powers."

The light in the room intensified.

"From this day," the voice continued with authority, "the needle will find its way to a special woman who has much love to give, but a soul much wounded. If the person guided to the needle has enough courage, she will find happiness again. And love. Then she shall pass the legacy on."

"Help them," Jeanette whispered, a tear rolling slowly down her cheek. "Don't let them make the same mistake I made."

"The choice is always up to the individual, Jeanette, but your gift may help some avoid a life of loneliness and pain. Rest now. Your journey is over."

Sighing, Jeanette closed her eyes again, nestling back into the furs with a blissful sense of peace, and went to her final rest.

One

The present

Grant Major squinted against the bright winter sunshine and eased his foot a bit off the accelerator. Fueled by too much coffee and frustration, he was driving too fast, and had let anger make him reckless. He'd been in the middle of chewing out a subcontractor for delivering the wrong roofing joists when the maps that would take him to his sister had been delivered.

It had taken almost a week, but when he finally found this Lynn Powell lady, he intended to give her a piece of his mind. And it sure wouldn't be a pretty piece. What the hell did she think she was doing, hiding his sister? Betsy's journal claimed this Lynn person ran an underground railroad for abused women. That was all well and good, but Betsy wasn't an abused spouse; she was a spoiled brat. And once again Grant had to spend valuable time chasing after her, time he could be spending on his own ranch training the new cutting horse he hadn't even seen yet because his work schedule had been so tight lately. If he didn't love the little ditz so much . . .

He'd already lost one day off the job site scouring the

small town of Winterhaven, but no one seemed to know a Lynn Powell. One man had mentioned a Leonard Powell who used to live outside of town, but he'd died five, maybe six, years ago. One woman at a quilt and antique shop had jumped suspiciously when he'd asked, but had denied knowing anyone by that name.

It had taken a lot of digging, and help from a surveyor he knew in the area, but now he knew exactly where to find Lynn Powell's ranch . . . and where Betsy had run off to this time.

Grant twisted a dial on the dashboard and cast a quick glance at the brilliant blue sky. Only in Texas did one need to crank up the air conditioner with Thanksgiving less than a month away. It was difficult to imagine that by nightfall the temperature would be dropping like a stone and by morning, coats and caps and mittens would be in order. Then, no doubt, they'd be back to shorts and t-shirts before turkey day arrived.

Texas weather . . . just wait an hour—it'll change.

On a normal day, he would have enjoyed the drive through the rustic hill country. The juniper were in full bloom, their berries casting a purple hue to the trees from a distance. As one of the lucky few unaffected by cedar allergies, he could look out over the scrub-covered hills and appreciate their rough beauty. Today, though, he concentrated on the asphalt before him.

He pulled into the long driveway that would, he hoped, be the end of his search. A sea of potholes reminded him that he had roads on his own property that needed to see the blade end of a grader. He just hoped the neglect before him didn't mean he was on another wild-goose chase, and that all he'd find when he came to the dead end was a dead end.

Stopping his SUV just as the house came into sight up a long hill, he got out and quietly shut the door. Sound carried a long way in the quietude of country, and he didn't intend to announce his arrival until the last

possible second. Sneaky, yes, but there was no sense
giving Betsy time to spot him and then having a footrace
with her through the surrounding hills. With the way his
luck had been running, he'd trip and fall face-first into
a bed of cactus and come out looking like a human por-
cupine.

Jamming his hat onto his head, he stayed within the
shadows of the huge oak and pecan trees lining the road.
As he made his way toward the porch, a brisk breeze
offered the scent of columbine and wisteria. He silently
neared the woman seated in a rocker, apparently asleep.
Her head was relaxed back and her eyes were closed.

She certainly wasn't Betsy. He assumed she was the
reclusive Lynn Powell since there didn't appear to be
anyone else around, but the delicate features framed by
fiery auburn hair didn't look like the face of a woman
running an underground railroad. He supposed he'd been
expecting an old battle-ax, a harsh-faced, ball-breaking
harridan who had lost any trace of femininity.

Grant winced at his sexist conception. The thought
was so stereotypical he was ashamed of himself. Oh, he
was certainly no "sensitive" man of the new millennium,
but he wanted to believe he wasn't a Neanderthal, either.

He guessed he was wrong . . .

After edging closer, he could tell she was much
younger than he'd anticipated, probably in her early thirties. Grant stared at the sleeping woman, surprised to
find just about all his assumptions incorrect.

Her auburn hair was pulled back in a no-nonsense
style, dispaying high cheekbones and flawless skin. Her
T-shirt was plain white and clung to her curves in a way
that made a man's mouth water. The waistband of her
blue jeans peeked out above a large quilt covering her
lap, part of it encased in a wooden hoop, but she clearly
dressed for function, not fashion. Yet, it didn't detract
from her beauty. In fact, Grant guessed her spared-down
attire only served to accentuate it.

He was no expert, but it was clear the blanket in her lap was beautifully crafted. He seemed to remember his grandmother having a wooden contraption like that, but she'd never put shades of purple, green and turquoise together in any of her creations.

A gold needle had slipped from her hand and lay tethered to the quilt by a length of thread. Sunshine glanced off the sliver of metal and shot a beam right into his eyes. He jerked his head away in reflex, but looked back again, unable to keep his attention off of her. He'd certainly seen women more beautiful, more striking, but she had, even in her simple attire, an ineffable quality that captivated him.

She had a fragility that surprised him. He hadn't been anticipating a woman who ran part of an underground railroad for battered women to look even the slightest bit vunerable.

Grant couldn't help it. He was a student of the old school, despite the fact that he was still on the near side of forty. His father and grandfather had laid down the example of how women were to be treated and no feminist manifesto could stop the urge to protect and defend. If that's what it meant to be a "modern man" then he guessed he would never fit the mold.

He told himself that her incredible good looks had nothing to do with his feelings, although he did have to admit he would label her a classic beauty. Her face was devoid of makeup, but her skin was flawless, her features delicate, and her lips an inviting red.

The serene picture before him made him painfully aware that he was an intruder, and he wanted to look away. But he couldn't. She slept on a sun-dappled porch, a basket by her side piled with the tools of her trade. A pitcher of tea sat on the porch railing, and a walkie-talkie lay on its side next to a tall glass graced with a sprig of mint. Her face held a peace that defied description, and it touched a place inside him he knew he wasn't ready to explore. Right now he was angry and tired. He had no interest in figuring out why the quiet stillness made him uncomfortable.

Yet his thoughts gave him pause, as well as an excuse to keep watching her while he formed a greeting. Miss Powell was doing something he found admirable—helping people when the system failed them. But what in the heck was she doing aiding and abetting one of Betsy's schemes?

Once again he shook his head. He needed to get Betsy home to their parents so he could return to work. And possibly find time to decide if he had any interest in salvaging what was left of his relationship with Veronica. She had made her dissatisfaction with his lack of attention quite clear.

The demise of the relationship had, at least in Grant's mind, been inevitable once Veronica had become demanding and possessive. Still, he had his campaign to consider. His first bid for the city council was going to be difficult enough without antagonizing his campaign manager. He should have listened to that little voice in his head that warned him not to date someone who worked for him. He had no one to blame but himself for letting his hormones overtake his common sense, no matter how persuasive Veronica's political and . . . social skills.

When they'd met, he'd found her interesting, intelligent, and incredibly sexy. All powerful reasons to opt out of the stretch of celibacy he'd been racking up. It was small salve to his conscience that he'd been up-front with her from the beginning about being gun-shy in the commitment department. One horrendous divorce was enough for him. Veronica had insisted she wasn't looking for a ring, but her possessive attitude of late sang another tune.

Grant forced Veronica out of his thoughts. He had too much to do to be analyzing the vagaries of romance.

What he needed, instead, was to be grateful he only had to cross one county to retrieve Betsy from her latest shenanigans. One memorable trip had taken an international flight, a trip by ferry, and a burro ride. At least this time he was only losing hours instead of days. Hopefully.

Grant retreated several feet to lean against the trunk of a towering oak, deciding as he watched the sleeping woman that he would announce himself . . .

In just a minute . . .

Lynn was lost in a dream, a vision really. She knew she was on her porch, with her needle and quilt, but she felt powerless to resist the images playing as clearly as a movie in her mind. This had happened a few times over the years, but the visions and the voices had never been as vivid as the ones she was seeing and hearing now.

. . . A red-haired woman sat in a straight-backed chair by a blazing fire in a room that looked rough and poor. The woman sitting in a rocking chair across the small living area had raven-black hair, and wore a high-necked dress of pale blue wool. She had a length of white fabric in her lap and was carefully stitching on the edge.

"Oh, Moyra," the redhead said, clearly exasperated, "ye should be embroiderin' christenin' gowns for wee babes of yer own, not mine. Nor your brothers. Or any of the others in this village. Ye may have a way with the needle that would make the Virgin Mary weep, but it's still no' fair."

Moyra smiled, but didn't look up from her task. "Mary Catherine Mulgrew, if ye gi' me that speech one mur time, I think I'll take me needle and go home."

Mary's foot began to tap on the dirt floor below her worn slipper. "Aye, and spend yer night alone with that daft cat. You need a mon of yer own, Moyra McKee."

A tear dropped to the pristine white cloth. Moyra

wiped her cheek with the back of her hand, then deter-
minedly returned to her task.

"I had a mon," she whispered.

Slipping to her knees beside her friend, Mary put a
gentle hand on Moyra's arm. "I know, love. We lost too
many good men at Culloden. But it's been years."

Moyra looked up, her eyes bright. "How long is too
long to mourn a mon who put the sunshine in the sky
for me? How can I betray me Ian by bein' with another
mon?"

"Ian would understan'. He'd be wantin' ye to go on."

With a determined shake of her head, Moyra focused
on her stitches, refusing to look into her friend's plead-
ing eyes. Then the wail of an unhappy child broke the
moment.

"Just go on and get the babe from her nap, Mary Catherine. I've go' to get this finished so my goddaughter
can look beautiful in the kirk on the morrow."

Mary couldn't ignore her child's cry, but her face was
filled with sadness as she hurried to the tiny, rough-hewn
cradle next to the seat she'd just vacated.

"Excuse me? Miss Powell?"

Startled out of her dream, Lynn jerked awake with a
disappointed gasp. Instantly alert, she dove her right
hand into the basket beside her as her eyes came open.
With the comforting reassurance of her nun-chaku in her
grip, she slipped the weapon into her lap under the cover
of the quilt.

Bless the stars for Leonard, she thought automatically
as she assessed the tall man standing uncomfortably near
under the oak tree that stood sentinel at the edge of her
porch steps. She assumed this was the stranger Nan said
had been asking about her in town last week, and taking
in his imposing height and broad shoulders, she was
thankful she'd never let her training slip. She had been

especially careful these last few days to keep herself prepared.

She was more than a little angry with herself for falling asleep like that and putting herself in such a vulnerable position. But what was done was done, and Lynn studied the man she could only assume was Betsy's brother. He certainly fit the description, although she had smiled indulgently at the time Betsy had used the words, "tall, dark, and too damn gorgeous for his own good."

Now Lynn understood.

"Are you Lynn Powell?" he asked curtly, as if uncomfortable with her bold scrutiny.

"Who are you and what are you doing on my property?" she countered, hoping her voice did not betray the resentment and fear she felt at letting this stranger catch her unaware.

She had to stay cool and collected. As if he were standing beside her, she heard Leonard advise, "Never let the enemy make you mad or you've lost the upper hand."

"My name is Grant Major. I asked if you're Lynn Powell."

"And I chose not to answer," she said calmly, but firmly.

The man seemed startled by her terseness. He was undeniably handsome, and obviously used to being given deference. *Well, too bad, buddy. You can try to intimidate me with those beautiful blue eyes of yours, but it won't work. I'll open a popsicle stand in hell before I'll ever defer to a man, handsome or not, ever again.*

"Then I'll get right to the point. I'm looking for my sister, Betsy. Where is she?"

"I'm afraid I can't help you."

When he took a step toward her, Lynn sprang out of the rocking chair and backed away, tossing the quilt free from her legs.

She noted the surprised look that crossed his face when he saw the nun-chaku in her fist, and felt a surge of confidence run through her. He obviously had no idea what he was up against. *Serves him right*, she thought, *for sneaking up on me like that.*

He put his hands up and backed away a few steps. "Hey, take it easy. I'm not going to hurt you."

She gave him a small, cold smile. "You've got that right."

"Look, I'm gonna take a guess here that you're Lynn. And it appears you have unwelcome visitors from time to time. But as much as I respect what you're doing, and admire your courage, I'm out of patience. I know my sister is around here, and I need to find her. You can either choose to help me or I'll go around you."

Lynn shook her head, amazed at the man's arrogance. Was there something hard-wired in the Y chromosome that let this guy actually believe that just because he'd said, "Jump," she'd ask, "How high?"

"No, *you* look. This is private property and you're trespassing." She pointed to the POSTED—KEEP OUT sign. "Can't you read?"

She waited with pseudo-patience as he stalled for time, his attention fixed on the chair slowly rocking to a stop.

He gave a deep sigh. "If I may, I'd like to start over. It's vitally important that I find my sister, and I know she's here. Or she came through here. Either way, I need your help."

Lynn, kept her face expressionless. It didn't matter where he measured on the gorgeous-meter, she would never be fooled by a pretty face or smooth voice again.

"Betts . . . er . . . Betsy is under a doctor's supervision and medication. When she took off last week, she left a journal in her room with your name and a reference to the hill country. It took me a while to find you, but I have every reason to believe she's here. And I will find her."

Lynn fought the urge to cuss. Loudly. But he had satisfied one curiosity, at least, explaining how he knew of her operation. She had wanted to ask him that when he'd first mentioned that he was looking for his sister, but hadn't for fear of giving anything away.

The success of any underground railroad depended on secrecy. It was patently unfair that the person jeopardizing the setup wasn't even a battered woman. When Betsy had appeared at her door, explaining that she needed help in escaping her "oppressive family," Lynn had agreed to help despite the uneasy feeling she'd had. Now she regretted not trusting her gut that things weren't usual.

Not that helping women whose faces and bodies were black and blue, and whose spirits had been crushed could be considered *usual*, but all things were relative . . .

In the end, though, Lynn hadn't listened to her inner voice and hadn't questioned the oddity. She had no explanation for how, once or twice a year, a battered woman found her way to Winterhaven and sought her help. She considered that an act of providence, just as she'd been found and given help when she'd been thrown into a ravine and left for dead. There was no logical reason for Leonard and Jake to have discovered her, so she didn't search for logic in the stories of those who had found her.

There had been something magical in the process, from the very beginning some five years ago. Those who came had bruised and battered bodies; some had self-confidence nearly pulverized but bore no outward scars . . . but all had souls that had seen a darkness that seemed too deep to survive. Each woman had reached one last time for the sunlight, made one last plea to whatever force ruled the universe, and had been led to this rustic place.

Belinda, Lynn's first "visitor," had said she'd found the directions on a scrap of paper in her purse. She couldn't explain how it had gotten there; she'd just known an overwhelming urge to find this haven against a heavy, drunken fist.

Lynn had been petrified that first time, scared to the soles of her feet to risk her precious safety. But a dream that had seemed too real for sleep, too amorphous to be real, had showed her that she had a chance to do something special, and she'd awakened with an unshakeable conviction that she had a job to do.

Each subsequent guest had had similarly vague explanations, and Lynn had soon simply accepted there was no logical answer. They might not come often, but she never took lightly her duty to the women who appeared at her door. She moved heaven and earth to help them, and with each successful wresting of a human soul from the depths of despair, her own was healed a tiny bit more.

To say she was part of an underground railroad wasn't exactly right. She wasn't part of an organization, per se. She called her own shots, improvising to meet the need at the moment. Mostly, she gave these wounded women a place to recover, and then helped them get out on their own. Then she went back to her own routines until the next needy soul appeared.

Betsy had broken the pattern by claiming a need to escape something other than a violent boyfriend or husband.

Worse, she'd changed everything by leading her brother—if that's who this man really was—to the ranch. Lynn had never had to face a single one of the abusers, for no one had ever found her.

Before now.

From the stories she'd been told over the years, as

well as her own experience, she knew that a man with a twisted mind could appear perfectly normal on the outside and lie with a perfectly straight face. She had no way to know if Betsy needed medical help, or if Mr. Major was simply running a con.

The indecision was making her nauseous. What if she believed him and led an abusive bastard to a fragile young woman who'd only asked for help? What if she sent him away . . . and Betsy *did* need help?

What scared her even more was a sensation she'd been ignoring up to this moment. Attraction. Something she hadn't felt in a long, long time, and certainly not toward a complete stranger who'd startled the hell out of her.

With more than a clinical eye, her feminine side catalogued his six-plus feet in height, his black hair with distinguished streaks of gray at the temples, his dark blue eyes both clear and piercing, his broad shoulders and trim waist.

And she could tell he just as quickly logged in her grand total height of five feet, four inches, and her un-fashionably curvy figure outlined in a plain white t-shirt and comfortable jeans. She may not have had much dealing with men these past few years, but even her rusty radar could register his interest. Could he be one of the few men left on the planet who wanted a woman with more than skin stretched over bone?

She snorted at that particular flight of fancy and hid a grunt of disgust at the current messages from Hollywood that were as abusive to woman's self-esteem as any man's fist. When a size four was considered borderline, and a size six or over fat, there was something incredibly sick going on in society. As for herself, she had vowed long ago to never starve herself into a single-digit dress size again.

Lynn gave herself a mental shake. What was she

thinking? It didn't matter what kind of figure this man preferred!

Was she slipping? Could her highly defined sense of self-preservation be fading after all these years? The very thought made her mouth go dry, and she tightened her grip on the nun-chaku. She couldn't let something as simple as a handsome face and incredible physique make her lose her edge.

She forced the disconcerting thoughts away and concentrated on her current dilemma. The intuition that he was indeed merely a concerned brother remained strong. Maybe she'd made a mistake. Maybe . . .

With a shake of her head, she dismissed her indecision. Even if he was exactly who he claimed to be, he was still trying to make Betsy live her life as *he* wanted her to. What was wrong with her—she had never hesitated in her resolution to protect any woman who asked for her help before today. *Got to be a surge of rusty hormones making me so uncertain.* Betsy had made a choice and Lynn would never betray her.

"I'm sorry, but I can't help you. I'm sure your sister will come home when she's ready."

The momentary softening that she had witnessed in Grant fled as soon as the words were out of her mouth.

"That's not good enough. I'm afraid you've given me no choice. I'll search every inch of this property—"

"Try it, Mr. Major, and I'll—"

"Call the sheriff? Go ahead. I have a court order declaring my sister unstable and a doctor's statement verifying her need for regular medication. And while you're on the phone, ask him to form a search posse."

Cold, hard fear jelled in the pit of Lynn's stomach. The last thing she needed was a troupe of lawmen stumbling around her property, and the undoubted notoriety that would follow. What if her picture was splashed in the newspaper, or God forbid, over television? It wasn't just *him* seeing her, it could be any one of his minions

who might recognize her despite her new figure and return to her natural hair color. One glimpse could spell
disaster.

She fought the absolute, mind-numbing terror that
threatened her resolve and struggled for a way to diffuse
the situation. "Your sister doesn't want to be found, Mr.
Major. Can't you just leave her alone?"

"This is really none of your business, but for what it's
worth I'm sorry my sister has conned you into believing
her poor-pitiful-me act. This isn't the first time I've had
to locate her and get help for her, Miss Powell. I'm just
praying it's going to be the last."

Lynn forced her hands to relax. She was squeezing
the nun-chaku so hard her fingers felt numb. Tension
had her so wired she wondered why she didn't crumble
like brittle paper right then and there.

"Betsy is an adult, you know." With difficulty, she
managed to make her voice sound calm. "You can't
force her to live the way you want, no matter how wrong
you think she is and how right you are."

"What I can't do is stand by and let my sister get
away again, maybe get involved in another cult, and
perhaps end up in a morgue this time. There's not a
whole lot of room for argument after she's dead."

Behind the irritation, Lynn heard the fear and love in
his voice. She accepted what her instincts had said all
along—he was clearly angry . . . and clearly worried.
Still, she couldn't give him the answer he needed. Her
very purpose was to keep women in jeopardy alive. And
to do that, she had to honor their trust.

"Would you take my word that I'll talk to Betsy and
try to convince her to go home? I hear your concern,
but I can't betray her. It would be a violation of a duty."

"Then I'll find her myself."

Despite her best intentions to remain composed and
soothing, she couldn't resist shooting a mocking glance
at his attire. "You're going to walk two thousand acres

in cowboy boots? Your denim shirt may be crisply starched, Mr. Major, but it's no protection against the rain. It's about to get very wet and very cold when that blue 'norther moves through here."

Her blood chilled when he nodded toward her bannister. "The way I figure it, the mate to that walkie-talkie is with my sister, and probably has a maximum range of five miles. Her journal said something about a cabin, and most people place cabins by water. I have a survey map of this area showing Bitter Springs cutting through the eastern portion of the property. So my bet is, if I follow the creek until I find a cabin, I'll find Betts."

Methodical. Logical.

And correct.

Which limited her to one choice—give Betts time to get away. That meant Nan's help. Lynn's brain worked furiously as she fought to keep her expression tranquil.

"All right, Mr. Major, you win. I'll take you to her, but I only have one horse available. There are no roads to the cabin."

"I have an SUV—"

"Not even a Land Cruiser would make this trip."

"Then we'll walk."

She gave him an exasperated huff. "You might be willing to walk two hours in, and then face an equal walk out in the cold rain, but I'm sure not."

He stayed quiet for a long moment, his jaw working. His eyes were hard when he said, "I can be back in an hour, maybe two, with a horse."

"I realize I'm repeating myself, but you really should consider the weather. The sun is already going down and I can just about guarantee we'll be forced to stay at the cabin when the front hits. Even with the horses, it'll be too dark to make it back. It would be better to wait until morn—"

"I'm not waiting, and I'm certainly not going to give you the chance to warn her and let her disappear again.

I can survive a little rain." With two quick steps, he reached the porch and to Lynn's surprise, grabbed the walkie-talkie. "I'll be back in two hours with a horse. And I'll just hang on to this while I'm gone."

Without another word, he turned sharply on his heels and strode away. He stopped abruptly right before the bend in the road and called out, "Don't even think about not being here when I get back. I wouldn't hesitate to have your cute little butt tossed in jail."

Lynn maintained her rigid posture until she heard the sound of his car fade away. Collapsing into the rocker, she dropped the nun-chaku from her cramping hand and picked up her quilt. She clutched it to her racing heart until a semblance of her normal pulse rate returned. Except for the odd noise or creak that occasionally made her start in alarm, she hadn't felt this type of fear in years. She had held a hope that the gut-wrenching terror of the past was gone, but Mr. Major's appearance proved that theory woefully inadequate.

She pushed her resentment and regret aside as she sat in the dappled sunshine. She let the cool breeze bathe over her as she gathered her courage, her conviction, and her determination, pulling them around her as if they were battle armor.

The act of reclaiming her center, her fortitude, galvanized her into action.

Without thinking, she took her needle from the quilt and slipped it along the edge of her shirt collar. There were days she felt silly needing to keep her needle so close. Then there were days like today when she needed to be able to touch it at any moment and gather strength from this symbol of her transformation into a new strong woman. Then she took her supplies inside the tiny, two-bedroom home that had been her haven, her refuge.

Let him threaten all he wanted. She was in control again, and would remember her training.

Wait a minute . . . Cute little butt? She twisted to

glance over her shoulder. No one had ever called it cute
before, much less little . . .

Shaking her head to clear yet another odd and exasperating thought, she considered her options. She could
take her horse and race to Betsy, but at the rate the
temperature was dropping, it would hit freezing by sun-
set. They'd be stuck there like sitting ducks for Grant to
find. Or, even more likely, he'd intercept them as they
made their way across to Nan's place. Lynn's rough and
scrub-filled acreage meant there were only so many trails
she could use to lead Betsy away, making Grant's job
all that much easier.

No, the best bet would be to lead Grant on a round-
about route to the cabin. By the time they arrived, Nan
would have gotten Betsy away. Of course, this plan
meant she might get caught with him in the storm, but
she wouldn't fail in her duty.

Lynn headed for the second bedroom that served as
both her office and her sewing center. She took her survival knife and boot holster out of the rustic armoire,
and stared at the wicked-looking blade that was tangible
evidence that her peace had been shattered. Oddly, she
wasn't afraid for her safety. There was no logical explanation for her conclusion, but she was absolutely certain
that while he would be mad as hell when he discovered
she had tricked him, Grant would never turn his anger
on her.

How in the world she could know that after a two-
minute conversation defied description . . . and sanity.
Still, she had been wrong before, so she tossed the knife
and holster onto the bed to strap on after she changed
clothes.

Lynn keyed the microphone on the CB radio on her
desk with shaking fingers. "Nan, come in."

"Nan here. What's up?"

"We have a problem. Saddle Hot Shot and get over
here. Now."

In less than an hour, although it had seemed like three, Nan thundered into the yard atop her gelding. Lynn stepped outside to meet her friend.

"What in the world is wrong?" Nan asked as she dismounted. "Ted was mighty curious when I ran out just now."

Lynn accepted Nan's hug, for she had been the demonstrative type from the day they'd met. They seemed total opposites, yet Lynn thanked the stars for her friend. Nan stood all of five-feet-two, but the petite brunette with soulful brown eyes was a whirlwind of energy, and Lynn loved her dearly.

She stepped back and gave Nan an arch look. "Ted our illustrious sheriff? That Ted?"

Nan blushed furiously. "Um, yes."

"And what was the sheriff doing at the shop, hmmm?" she teased. "He doesn't seem like an antique browser to me."

Reaching self-consciously to smooth back the hair that had escaped from her ponytail, Nan looked over Lynn's shoulder.

"He . . . uh . . . just came by for a cup of joe. No big deal."

Although everyone in town knew Nan kept a fresh pot of coffee ready at all times, Lynn hadn't heard of the sheriff coming by for a cup.

"I see," Lynn said suggestively. "The coffeemaker at the station broken?"

Nan's face turned an even darker shade of red. "Lynn, stop teasing me."

"Sorry. I just don't get much of a chance, so I couldn't resist. I like that you have a new beau."

"He's not a beau. We've only had a few lunches together. Hardly dates. Besides, he's just being the sheriff. A few windows have been broken lately, and he thinks some local kids are into mischief. He just came by to take a report."

"Um hum. I find it interesting that our busy sheriff took the time to take your report personally."

Nan gave her a stern look. Lynn held up her hands. "All right, all right. I'll quit."

"So, what did you need me for so frantically?"

All the amusement died instantly from Lynn's expression. "Nan, I'm really sorry to get you involved—"

"Hey, missy, haven't I been asking for years to help?"

Lynn blushed with appreciation. "I know you have. You've been one hell of a friend, but I never wanted to put you in the thick of things unless I had no choice."

Nan nodded soberly. "I take it that time has come?"

With a wry grin, Lynn nodded in return. "You know that girl at the cabin? Betsy?"

"Yeah, you said she was young, and not the type that usually needs your help."

"Exactly. Well, her big brother just showed up."

Two

Following Lynn into the house, Nan sputtered in surprise. "How does he even know she's here, much less about the cabin?" she asked, undressing to change without question into the clothes Lynn tossed her way.

Lynn stripped out of her jeans and tugged on long johns. "The dimwit put my name in a journal, which she oh-so-conveniently left behind! Can you believe someone running away could be so stupid?"

She closed her eyes and offered a silent apology. She'd made more than one bone-headed move in her lifetime, so she could hardly judge another person's mistakes . . . no matter how frustrating they were.

They'd moved to the kitchen as they tucked almost identical turtlenecks and flannel shirts into their jeans. Lynn ran the brush she'd grabbed through her long hair and began to twist it into a simple braid down her back.

Nan tugged at the tight neck of her shirt. "Why don't you let me call Ted and have him detain this guy. Betsy isn't a minor—"

"Bad idea on two counts. One, it would reveal my operation to the sheriff, even if Betsy isn't a runaway spouse. And two, Mr. Major has a court order and a doctor's opinion backing him up, or so he says. I think

I could be in some serious hot water with this one."

"Of course. I don't know what I was thinking."

Lynn put a comforting hand on her friend's shoulder. "You were thinking one tall, lanky lawman has cast his eye in your direction and would jump at the chance to do something for you. And you're right," she said with a gently teasing smile.

"Maybe, but it was awfully silly of me to even think about blowing your cover . . . to the county sheriff of all people. Whether I like him or he likes me is irrelevant."

"Your hormones just got in the way for a minute. No big deal."

"Still, I'm sorry."

Nan looked so dejected, Lynn said brightly, "Would you quit! There's no harm done. Besides, I'm delighted you're even thinking about our handsome sheriff in a . . . shall we say . . . romantic light."

"Okay, I surrender. What's the plan."

"The plan is for you to do as little as possible. I'm having a huge dilemma that I've involved you at all. You have a business, a son, a new relationship . . . all things I could be putting at risk."

"Now *you* quit, and tell me what I need to do."

"Well, Mr. Major reasoned it out that the cabin would be by the only creek on my property. If he's smart enough to figure that out, it wouldn't take him long to find it. Bitter Springs isn't that long of a creek anyway. He could follow it end to end if he wanted to."

Lynn paused for a moment, making some mental calculations.

"Here's what I thought would be the best plan. You get to the cabin and take Betsy away. I'll lead her brother on a round-about trip, so by the time we get there, you should be able to get her to town and on a bus. Or a plane. Or whatever she chooses, so long as she's away from here."

Taking a can of flour from the shelf, Lynn slipped off

the false bottom. She thrust a roll of bills into Nan's hand.

"Here's enough money to get her just about anywhere in the States. If she wants to leave the country, she'll have to do that on her own."

Nan tried to hand the money back. "This is wrong, Lynn. You do amazing things to help women in need, but it isn't fair for you to give up your own safety net. I'll get her away, don't worry."

Lynn stopped her frenetic packing of dehydrated food into a saddlebag. A wave of overwhelming sadness rolled over her, making her clutch the leather satchel to her chest as a single tear slid down her cheek.

"I guess today proves that there's no such thing as being safe, doesn't it?" She heard the despair in her own voice and chastised herself for her self-pity. This wasn't about her—it was about helping someone who was in need. Sniffing, she straightened her shoulders and said, "That's not all the money I have, Nan. Don't worry. Here's food if you guys get stuck, and some water purification tablets. I know it's ten miles in the wrong direction, but head for your cabin if you can't get back to town. If the weather turns bad, just stay put at mine. I'll hole up at the big cave where you and I camped last summer."

"I'll take care of her, Lynn. You just take care of you, hear me?"

Lynn managed a weak smile. "I promise. Now go."

Armed with a jacket, slicker, hat, and the saddlebag, Nan hurried out of the house with Lynn following close behind. As she watched her friend mount, Lynn thought to ask, "Where's Jeremy?"

"My darling son, who's grown over an inch in the last month without my permission thank-you-very-much, is down in Houston with the 4-H club showing his lambs. He won't be home until this weekend."

"Good. I'm glad Jeremy's safe since I'm asking you

such a big favor, and on such short notice."

Nan tried for a smile. "Hey, I'm just proud you've finally asked me to do something really worthwhile."

"You don't consider being my friend, my confidant and my sounding board worthwhile?" Lynn teased.

"You know what I mean," Nan scolded. "How many women does this make that you've risked your own safety for? Eight? Ten? And you do it all by yourself."

Lynn waved away the sentiment. It made her uncomfortable. She was only doing what she had to, giving back in some small part what she had received. It wasn't the battered women's shelter she had dreams of opening, but it was a something.

Nan gave an aggrieved sigh. "You know, some day you're actually going to accept a compliment." She tilted her head to the side. "You know what else? This is the first time we've ever had to go into James Bond mode. It'll be good training for me in case you might actually accept help in the future."

Nan's frivolity caught Lynn unprepared. She'd been in "James Bond mode" before, and, contrary to what Nan thought, it was anything but fun. Time had barely begun to ease the fear she'd lived with since waking up in Leonard Powell's house to find her ex-husband hadn't managed to kill her after all. Trey had come close, no doubt, but he couldn't have anticipated a man and his dog discovering her unconscious while out for one of their very long hikes into the hills. Lynn chided herself for her reaction. Nan had only been trying to lighten the mood.

"Hey, now," Nan scolded again. "None of those faces. You've got angels watching over you, remember?"

She didn't believe in angels, but arguing would only hurt Nan's feelings so Lynn remained silent. Nan was unshakable in her belief that a miracle had happened when Leonard and Jake had found Lynn's pummeled body at the bottom of the ravine. To Nan, there was no other explanation for why Leonard and Jake had hiked some ten miles through rough country in the opposite direction of their normal route.

There had been days after the attack when Lynn struggled to appreciate the rescue, miracle or not.

But she had eventually recovered, with Leonard's kind help. Nan had gone on to extrapolate that the theory of divine intervention applied to the quilts Lynn produced as well. Nan would not be dissuaded from believing the quilts had magic qualities, helping those who bought them.

Like the time Nan swore a woman had come back to the shop after buying a child-sized comforter for her autistic son. The lady said the child had begun saying "momma" and "daddy" after sleeping under the Heart's Ease pattern Lynn had done in deep blue and cream-colored fabrics. Nan said the mother had danced around the store with tears in her eyes.

Or the young woman who'd bought the gold and red sun star for her grandmother with rheumatoid arthritis. Within a month, the woman had supposedly returned to work on her own creations. Her doctors had been amazed for they had told her she'd never hold a needle again.

Or even the trapunto quilt she'd done that a mother had bought for her son when he'd lost his young wife. The young man had been in a deep depression for months, but just a few weeks after she'd wrapped the quilt around him, he'd been able to release the tears that had been dammed up for the last year. The mother had cried her own tears that her son was finally on the road to healing.

Lynn wasn't so sure she believed the fantastic stories, but she kept her mouth shut and continued to quilt because it soothed her, and provided her the modest income she needed for her basic survival. If Nan wanted

to believe in fairy tales, Lynn was the last person who
would take someone's dream away.

What Nan couldn't know was the paralyzing fear that
came with abuse, or the emotional scars that made believing in miracles nigh onto impossible. Lynn knew she
was one of the odd ones—she had refused to stay and
be a voluntary punching bag. But for all her bravado, a
divorce decree and restraining order hadn't stopped him
from kidnapping, beating, and leaving her for dead.
Even now, almost eight years later, a nightmare that included Trey's face was guaranteed to have her heaving
over the toilet.

She shook her head to stop the reverie. Trey wasn't
her problem any longer. Right now it was time to help
Betsy.

She flashed a joking grin up at Nan and lightly
punched her friend in the leg. "Well, double-oh-seven,
get on with it. I've got less than thirty minutes to pack
my stuff and be ready when Mr. Major gets back. If I
don't have anything packed, he'll know I'm jerking him
around."

With a salute, Nan kicked her bay into a trot and
disappeared into the woods. Lynn returned inside and
stocked another satchel, then hurried to the stable to saddle Nothin' But Trouble. As she entered the warmth of
the barn, she inhaled the comforting scents of horseflesh
and hay.

A nose appeared over a stall door and bright brown
eyes looked at her as the mare offered a whicker of
welcome. Lynn gave the soft nose a rub, and offered
Sassy an apple from the bucket on the bench.

She'd lied to Mr. Major. She had two mounts, but
with Sassy close to foaling, Lynn wasn't about to subject
the mare to a harsh trek across the property.

Besides, she needed time to prepare. Time to prepare,
and to get this most disconcerting attraction under control. She couldn't seem to wrap her mind around the fact

that she had noticed, viscerally, that the man was pulse-poundingly attractive.

Lynn rubbed her eyes wearily. She didn't need this added dilemma right now. She really didn't . . .

"I appreciate you letting me borrow one of your horses, V. T. I'll be there in a few minutes."

Grant hit the end button and tossed his cellular phone on the seat next to him. It grated mightily to ask anyone for help, but it truly irked him to have to ask a potential business associate. V. T. Murdock had all the appearances of being a good businessman, and the joint venture to build a master-planned community on some of the most expensive land on Lake Travis was certainly intriguing. But there was something ineffable about him that made Grant uneasy. And until he could figure out why V. T. set off his internal alarms, he wouldn't commit himself to to anything.

Which made it doubly aggravating to have to ask a favor. It gave Murdock an edge in their negotiations and Grant gritted his teeth in frustration. God knew he loved Betts, crackpot schemes and all, but this escapade of hers might cost him more than time away from his job and the attendant loss of income. She was risking his business reputation. If her shenanigans forced his hand with Murdock, Grant would be royally ticked off.

When he had accepted the job of building Murdock's new ranch house, he'd known good and well the man was hoping to sway a decision on the joint venture. Murdock had also been spending an inordinate amount of time on the property. Grant had received the impression he only spent a week or two in the hill country during hunting season. As the project had progressed, it had been clear the man was more interested in schmoozing Grant than overseeing the construction.

Then again, Grant should be grateful. If V. T. hadn't been so involved, he would have had to go all the way into Austin and get a horse from his own place, adding at least an additional hour's delay.

He pulled into the yard and carefully backed up to the horse trailer waiting in the front yard. It only took a few moments to get the trailer hitched, and by the time he was done, Murdock had come out of the house.

Grant moved forward and extended his hand. "I appreciate the help. Especially on such short notice."

"Glad to do it," Murdock said magnanimously, shaking Grant's hand with a hearty pump. "I know this area pretty well, so why don't you come inside and show me where you're going. Perhaps I could be of some help."

Grant retrieved his survey map from the truck and followed Murdock into the nearly completed showplace home. Despite his urgency, Grant gave the room a satisfied glance. With only minor inconveniences, as were inevitable on any job, Grant had pulled off some stunning design work in this house.

Spreading the map on a huge, ornately carved desk when they reached the office, Grant pointed to the creek.

"I'm looking for a cabin along here."

"You're looking for your sister, I understand," Murdock said, ringing for his housekeeper.

Grant nodded tersely. "As I mentioned on the phone, she pulls stunts like this every now and then. Last time I had to fly to Boise to claim her."

"I understand how troublesome women can be, believe me—"

A small, older Mexican woman appeared at the doorway interrupting their conversation. "Yes, Mr. Trey?"

"Juanita, bring Mr. Major some hot coffee, and fill a Thermos. Herbal tea for me."

"Si, señor. Right away."

"My stomach just won't handle coffee lately," Murdock explained, as though embarrassed. "Stress I guess. Anyway, I wish I had my helicopter here to offer you.

My partner has it and won't be back until tomorrow sometime."

"I don't think that will be necessary."

"Well, hopefully you will find her today, but if not, call me tomorrow. I'd be glad to fly out and help. So show me again where you're headed?"

Grant pointed along the eastern edge of the property where a stream was marked by blue lines. "I think it'll be right along here somewhere."

Murdock's eyes widened for just an instant before a shuttered expression came over his face.

"Isn't this dog-leg piece of property yours?" Grant asked, pointing to a diamond-shaped section that tear-dropped off the rear of the area marked "Vernon T. Murdock, III." His nearly ten thousand acres were east of Lynn Powell's, and "fronted" on the little town of Hewitt. Lynn's property "fronted" Winterhaven, almost thirty miles away by the highway. The two properties had no borders in common, but the little section dipped close.

"Yes, that's mine. When I bought this place last year, I included that little piece because a geologist friend of mine said the area showed promise of oil. It's a really rough patch of land, filled with ravines and limestone outcroppings, but maybe it'll be the next Spindletop, who knows?" He gave a too-hearty laugh.

Murdock had given a lot more explanation than Grant had been looking for, and he struggled with a sense of unease. A simple yes or no would have sufficed.

Juanita brought in coffee and Grant thanked her. He drank his cup quickly, not wishing to be rude but he wanted to get back on the road.

"I appreciate the help. I'll bring your rig back as soon as I can."

"No hurry at all. Safe Bet is a great mount. Very strong and he has an easy temperament. When my partner returns, I'll bring the 'copter over."

"I'm sure I'll be back with my sister before that's

necessary, but thanks. I'll call you if I need anything further."

As he headed for the highway again, Grant struggled to contain his anger and impatience. He had little doubt that Lynn had been planning something. Her expression had been placid, but he'd seen her mind working behind her beautiful green eyes. He didn't dare take any more time getting back or she'd find a way to contact Betts, walkie-talkie or no walkie-talkie.

Grant put his sunglasses over the visor as he drove. The clouds blowing in on a healthy wind made them unnecessary and gave him a moment's concern. Lynn was right. The storm was definitely on its way. It was supposed to be the first real cold snap of the season, and the forecasters had warned about sleet or hail in the hill country. And since this was the dead middle of the hill country, there was a good chance it was going to be a pretty miserable ride to the cabin.

But that couldn't be helped. Betts needed to be back under Dr. Richard's care. Even though Grant had concerns about the medication that had been prescribed, he believed Betsy's doctors had her best interest in mind. He couldn't risk her slipping away again, both figuratively and literally.

His cell phone chirped, interrupting his thoughts, and Grant keyed the console so he could talk hands-free. He grimaced at the number on the display.

"Hello, Veronica."

"Grant, darling, where are you?"

"Near the job site. Long story."

"What time will you be picking me up?"

"Pardon?"

"For the mayor's party? You want his endorsement, remember?"

Grant heaved a sigh. "I won't be able to make it. Give him my apologies, would you?"

"What do you mean, you won't make it?"

"I'm going to pick up my sister, and I won't be back until I find her."

"Darling, I worked very hard to arrange an invitation to this event. It will look bad if you're not there." Her voice was clipped.

"It can't be helped." His voice was equally terse.

"Can't the little brat wait . . . I mean, can't this wait until tomorrow at least?"

She posed it as a question, but he could hear the demand in her voice.

"No." He refused to offer explanations.

"I must tell you I don't like going stag to these things, especially considering the trouble I've gone through for you."

Grant let a lengthy silence speak for him.

"I'm sorry, darling, I didn't mean to sound bitchy."

He wasn't fooled by her sudden conciliatory tone. She fully expected him to buckle under her icy displeasure. He had news for her.

"I need to go, Veronica. Give my regards to the mayor."

"Call me—"

He disconnected, forcing his hands to relax on the wheel while he put Veronica from his mind. He intended to set a few things straight as soon as he got home, but for now, it was best to not think about anything but the task at hand.

As he drove, he wondered again how Betts had gotten Lynn to assist in this latest scheme. She had seemed like an intelligent, reasonable gal. The fact that she was a one-woman underground railroad—or so Betts had written in her journal—said she was pretty gutsy. And the way she'd stood up to him spoke volumes. It might have aggravated him, but he respected people with backbone. And he had the feeling she had a very nice backbone indeed, if her backside was as equally attractive as her

front side. He'd never considered a white t-shirt and
jeans especially sexy . . . until now.

Grant shook his head and gave himself a mental
scolding. Wasn't his life complicated enough? It
wouldn't matter if Lynn Powell was a supermodel, he
had no time for sexual attraction. Especially with a
woman who had the temerity to scold him for doing
what had to be done. Come to think of it, he'd had just
about enough scolding from women as he was going to
put up with.

He sighed as he finally pulled up to Lynn's house.
She'd changed clothes and indeed, her back view—from
firm shoulders to full hips and down long, strong legs—
was definitely as attractive as her front. She'd put on a
turtleneck and a flannel shirt, and he had to admit that
he could remember lingerie less sexy than the red plaid
she had tucked into her jeans.

Grant sighed. He had the feeling it was going to be a
long night.

Just as Lynn was tightening the cinch on Trouble, Jake
raced into the yard, tongue lolling, eyes bright and
happy.

"And just where have you been, oh terror of the
woods?" Lynn scolded lovingly, bending down to ruffle
his ears. "I could've used your ferocious growl about an
hour ago, ya' know."

Not that Lynn believed Grant would have been intimidated. Still, as an indiscriminate mix of German Shep-
herd, black Lab, and something else along the way, Jake
was no small furball. When he was in protective mode,
the few people who had trespassed on her property over
the years had taken good notice.

Jake's tail wagged wildly as he turned his head to get
the best angle for a scratch. With his eyes closed in bliss,
he looked anything but ferocious.

"Come on, mister," she said, leaving Trouble in the

yard and signaling toward the house. "You need to eat 'cause we've got a long walk to the cabin."

At the word "cabin," Jake barked and raced to Trouble, to her, and back to Trouble. He looked at her expectantly as he danced in place.

"Jake," she said sharply, "inside."

With his tail drooping, Jake slowly walked to the porch as ordered, and she struggled not to laugh and spoil her stern demeanor. Jake had the energy of ten canines, it seemed, but he tended to forget that he wasn't a pup anymore. The gray on his muzzle made Lynn's heart ache, and Jake was always stiff after he'd been zipping around without a pause. Lynn was especially worried with the weather getting colder. It took longer for Jake's joints to warm up these days.

But age in no way impaired Jake's eagerness to accompany her. As soon as he'd finished his dog food, he headed for the door, ready to go.

Lynn shook her head and opened the screen so he could escape. In a flash, he took point by Trouble's front hooves and cast her impatient glances as though saying, "Head 'em up, move 'em out!"

The sound of an unfamiliar engine caught Lynn's attention, as well as Jake's. Instantly, he was by her side on the porch, the fur on his neck bristling while a low growl emanated from his throat.

As soon as Grant stepped out of his truck, Jake stopped growling. Lynn looked down in amazement as he stared intently, and then cocked his head to the side for a long moment. Without another sound, he bounded off the steps and ran to greet Grant, dropping onto his front paws, his rump in the air in the doggie signal for "let's play!"

Lynn couldn't put words to how betrayed she felt. Jake had abandoned her to go make friends with a stranger! Even worse, she hated having to admit her own pulse had raced as soon as Grant's tall, trim form appeared. He'd put on a gray cowboy hat, and it irked her to realize she'd noticed immediately how well it suited him. A lot of men looked like geeks in a hat.

Grant Major looked anything but geeky . . .

He looked confident and handsome and sexy as all get-out.

Lynn shut her eyes and struggled for control. She hadn't been attracted to anyone in a very, very long time. And to have it inexplicably rearing up at a time like this was simply not acceptable.

Then again, as soon as he found out Betsy had escaped he'd be boiling mad at her. She had no doubt her raging hormones would dry up like dust. Without realizing it, she checked for the nun-chaku she had secured under her belt, and felt the reassuring weight of her knife in her boot. She'd drape the chucks over the saddle horn when she mounted, not that she really believed she'd have to use them, but she knew better than to assume. And she intended to be sure Grant knew she meant business.

Unaware of her inner struggle, Grant smiled as he tussled with the dog. "Hi, boy. What's your name?"

"Traitor," Lynn said, frowning at them both.

He seemed surprised. "Really?"

"No, it's Jake. Who's supposed to be a guard dog," she said, directing the last part at the unrepentant mutt. "In all the years I've had him, he's never gone to a stranger like that."

Grant gave her an aw-shucks, Harrison Ford kind of grin. "I'll consider myself flattered then." He glanced at her horse and then back. "I see you're ready to go."

"I told you I would be," she said with a straight face.

He looked at her for a long moment, as though taking her measure. She raised her chin a notch, daring him to challenge her. Another of Leonard's instructions included keeping her head up. To drop her chin meant submission.

Grant chose to break eye contact by retrieving his jacket from the backseat and moving to the trailer. In no time, he expertly backed a beautiful sorrel gelding out into the yard. He checked the saddle and tack, adjusted the stirrups, and then signalling he was done, secured the rig.

Lynn took the cue and locked her house before heading toward Trouble. She shrugged on her sheepskin-lined jacket, but left it open. It wasn't quite cold enough yet, but at the rate the temperature was dropping, it wouldn't take long before she was snapping it up all the way to the collar. She had a muffler in one pocket, throwing stars in the other, and her brown felt cowboy hat on her head.

She was tugging on her leather gloves when Grant led his mount next to hers.

"What's his name?" she asked, curiosity overcoming her reluctance to talk.

"Safe Bet. Yours?"

"Nothin' But Trouble. Trouble for short."

Grant chuckled. "Trouble for a horse and Traitor for a dog. Does this say something about your life?"

Normally Lynn had a great sense of humor, but this day had already been too long, and was about to be much longer. Her funny bone seemed to be missing at the moment.

Instead of answering, she checked her cinches and her stirrups one last time. No one had used the saddle except for her, but it gave her a decent excuse to refuse to look at him.

"What's all that for?" Grant asked, nodding toward the full saddlebags, and the quilt rolled and tied to the back.

"I told you that if you insist on riding out, we're gonna get stuck. I'm not willing to freeze my butt off, or starve, if we don't make it all the way to the cabin.

It's going to be an uncomfortable ride any way you look at it, and it doesn't hurt to be prepared."

He caught a bundle that looked much like hers and didn't argue as he tied it to Safe Bet. He hadn't thought to ask Murdock for camping gear, and the thought of sleeping with a mere saddle blanket for warmth hardly sounded appealing. Once again he was indebted, and it grated on his last nerve.

They mounted simultaneously. Grant looked at the sky, then his watch, and then to her. "I find it hard to believe the ride is that arduous."

"Believe, don't believe. I don't care either way."

"Then I'll choose to believe that if the ride in is less than two hours, we can be back out by dark."

"Not a chance. Not with the clouds coming in. And just what are you going to do if Betsy balks? Tie her up and throw her over your saddle? I guarantee I won't help."

Her question seemed to surprise him. "Will she need to ride double?"

"No, she has a horse. I never leave someone stranded, but that doesn't answer my question."

His mouth set in a hard line. "I'll deal with it in a couple of hours. Betts is usually pretty reasonable when I manage to find her. Maybe because by that time she's feeling guilty for what she's put me through."

"And will you feel guilty for what you're putting me through?"

His face went cold as his jaw worked. "Let's just get going, shall we?"

Leading the way, she nudged Trouble into a trot as they headed into the setting sun. The ground was forgiving for a half of a mile or so, then they slowed to a walk as scrub oak, cedar, and cacti began to crowd the trail. More often than not, they had to ride single file, but at least it kept her from having to hold a conversation.

An hour into the journey, with clouds now completely obscuring the sky, she was startled by a loud expletive behind her. She turned to see Grant reining his horse. She did the same.

"What's the problem?"

Grant dismounted. "I think he took a stone." Lifting Safe Bet's foot, he cursed again. "Nope, threw a shoe."

Lynn hid a surge of relief. She wasn't happy that Safe Bet would have to walk without a shoe, but it was the perfect excuse to terminate this little excursion without it being her fault.

"Well," she said in an even voice, "you can't ride a horse—"

"I've been riding since I was old enough to sit upright," snapped Grant. "You don't have to tell me you can't ride a horse that's thrown a shoe."

"Excuse me!" she said with a huff, moving back toward Trouble, surprised at the harshness of his tone.

She heard him sigh.

"Lynn, I'm sorry. I'm just frustrated."

She turned and gave him an arch look.

"Okay, so we're both frustrated."

Without responding, she took Trouble's reins and started to turn him around.

"What are you doing?" he asked sharply.

"Heading back, what do you think?"

"Like hell we are. Let's keep going."

She looked at him like he'd lost his mind. "Just what do you plan to do once we get there? You'll have to walk all the way out again."

"Then I'll have to walk," he said tersely.

"You," she said with her teeth clenched, matching his clipped tone, "have to be the most stubborn man I've ever met!"

"You aren't the first person to make that accusation. Now, let's go."

Lynn refused to say another word as she remounted

and started forward again. She had to slow Trouble due
to the vast difference between a horse's comfortable
walking gait, and a human's. It also meant that they
would be caught in the inclement weather long before
they reached the cabin.

After thirty more minutes of tense silence, she made
a decision. When a fat drop of cold rain plopped onto
her glove, she stopped Trouble and dismounted to face
Grant.

"Look, this has reached the point of ridiculousness.
It's now officially cold, it's about to rain and possibly
sleet, and we've got at least an hour left at this pace.
You can go on if you want to, and try to find your way
in the dark, but I'm stopping. About ten minutes that
way," she pointed to the right, "is a terrific limestone
cave. Follow, or don't. It's up to you."

Without another word, she remounted and changed
directions.

Grant watched her lead Trouble away, ignoring the
raindrop that hit his shoulder.

Damn that woman . . .

He'd been watching her very fetching backside for
almost two hours now, and the colder it had become,
the more he'd had stray thoughts about what it would
be like to slip his hands inside that coat and wrap himself around her. Conversely, wrapping her around him
seemed an equally pleasant alternative.

On the heels of such thoughts came a reminder that
the last thing he should be doing was playing a game of
mental footsie with a woman who was mad enough at
him to nail his hide to a wall. She undoubtedly had several things she wished to do with said hide, none of
which included lots of hot, mind-blowing sex.

With a grunt, he started walking before he lost sight
of her. As if to spur him, Jake came tearing down the
path, slid to a stop, barked, and took off again.

Maybe he could find the cabin and maybe not, but it

would be foolish to risk getting lost in the freezing rain. He felt a moment's guilt about starting this trek in the first place, but then he reminded himself that they would have made it to the cabin if Safe Bet hadn't thrown a shoe. Having attached a horseshoe or two in his day, he'd been surprised when he'd examined Safe Bet's hoof. The farrier who'd shod him had done an excellent job, so it seemed odd that this one had come off.

He shrugged the thought away. It didn't matter why it had happened.

As darkness descended faster than he'd expected, Grant was thankful for Jake's check-ups. Lynn had made no attempt to let him keep up, but with Jake's kind guidance he wasn't worried about losing the way.

By the time he made it to the cave, and ducked inside, he saw that Lynn had been a busy girl. Trouble stood free of his saddle, contentedly munching on a pile of grass at his feet. Grant led Safe Bet over next to Trouble, noting she'd built a fire inside a stone ring that had obviously been there a long time. He could only assume the logs had been previously laid because he hadn't been that far behind her.

Moving into the cave, Grant noted there was enough light thrown against the white stone walls for him to see almost all the way to the back. He could just barely stand upright without knocking his head, although the far corners were too dark to see where the rock started sloping. She'd been right; it was a great place to stop. There was plenty of room for the horses on one side of the fire, and two humans on the other. Although there was no way to keep out stray gusts of wind, it was certainly warmer than being outside.

Lynn purposefully ignored him. When she went back into the far shadows, he followed her with his eyes. Her flashlight clicked on and he stared, amazed, as she rummaged in a metal footlocker. Jake's eyes flitted back and forth between them from his position near the flames.

"Isn't this just a tad convenient?" Grant asked when she turned around with a plastic gallon jug of water in one hand, and a saucepan in the other.

"Yes," she said, putting the items down and returning to the locker, her back to him.

"Did you intend to stop here all along?"

"No."

He waited.

"You're not going to tell me why you have a locker of provisions in a remote cave in the middle of your property, are you?"

"No."

"And you accuse me of being stubborn?"

Lynn refused to take his bait. Instead she finished getting what she needed out of the locker, closed the lid and came back with packages of what he assumed was dehydrated food.

Deciding two could play at this game, Grant took care of Safe Bet and sat on one end of a huge log placed near the fire.

Finally, he gave in. "So do you have food and water in every cave on your property?"

"No."

He thought for a moment. "Have you provisioned any other caves on your property?"

"Yes."

He watched as she set up a tripod and began heating water in a battered pot. He watched dispassionately as she dropped two tea bags into the waiting water and sat back, staring at the flames.

There was something so lost in her expression, he had to say something to break the solemn mood. He'd already tossed off six or seven questions . . . why not a few more?

Clearing his throat, he asked, "If I reach twenty questions, do I win a prize?"

Lynn glared at him and began working with her saucepan.

"Okay, is there something I can do to help?"

"Get more wood," she said, holding out the flashlight.

The stack off to his left seemed plenty for the night, but he didn't argue. Not when it was his fault they were stuck there in the first place. Grabbing a hatchet that had seen better days, he left.

To Grant's surprise, Jake stepped outside with him.

"You know what, boy? Your mistress is one exasperating woman."

Jake barked, and Grant laughed out loud.

It was either that, or kick a tree . . .

Inside the cave, Lynn threw a small branch onto the fire with unnecessary force. A shower of sparks rose to the ceiling, dying quickly in the cool air.

Without thought, she reached up to check on her needle, although in all the years she'd carried it with her like this, she'd never misplaced it once.

She gasped as she touched the needle. It felt almost hot under her thumb. She barely had time to sit down before a vision overtook her . . .

. . . A young woman sat on a rock, her stark black dress and pristine white collar a sharp contrast to the pale rock. She watched the shore below her, where the waves crashed against the sand with ceaseless rhythm, with sad eyes.

"Patience?"

Patience quickly wiped the tears streaking her cheeks and took some deep breaths. When she felt composed, she straightened her prayer cap and called back over her shoulder. "I am here, Charity. I will be directly down."

"Stay. I'll join thee."

"No!"

But it was too late. Charity had already scrambled up the cliff, and Patience felt a moment of panic as her friend struggled with her balance, her body ungainly with the imminent birth of her first child.

"Are thee daft? In thy condition—"

"A bit of risk is a good thing, now and again."

Patience rolled her eyes at her friend. "I sense a message in thy words."

Charity folded her hands primly in her lap . . . what lap remained . . .

"Thou hast been hiding of late."

Patience turned her head to look back out to sea. "I have need of solitude."

"Thou hast need to accept Brother Matthew's proposal and become a bride and mother as the Lord intended."

A shudder overtook her before Patience could shake her head in denial. "I will never—"

"Thou must stop this brooding, Patience."

"And thou dost not understand," she whispered.

"Agreed," Charity said, surprising her friend. "I have never suffered under the hand of my husband. Though a husband has authority over his wife, a good one understands that he must love his wife as Christ loves the Church. Husbands and wives are commanded to submit one to another."

"A pity not all husbands understand the Lord's command."

"True. But Lucas was not thy husband. His treachery was revealed before thou took vows before God, and he has been banished. Now thou must not hide thy heart anymore."

Patience took a deep breath and turned to her friend. "Charity, thou art as kind as thy name, but I must ask thee to keep thy counsel. It is well-intended, but hear me: I will never submit to a man again."

Charity struggled to her feet and prepared to return.

"Then thy stubborn heart dooms thee to loneliness. My heart grieves that thou suffered such hurt, but if thee refuses to live again, then Lucas Easter has won. And thou hast lost."

Patience watched her friend to make sure she got down safely, then turned her face away.

"Thou dost not understand," Patience said, but only the wind off the waves heard her tear-filled words . . .

Lynn snapped out of her reverie suddenly. Had Grant returned? She looked around, and listened, but the cave was silent.

With shaking hands, she added wood to the fire. What was happening? There was no rhyme or reason to when the dreams would hit her, but she had never had two in one month, much less two in one day. Nan would probably say she was getting messages, but Lynn didn't believe in such stuff and nonsense. Her mind was merely overstimulated from all the excitement, and she was simply playing out scenes from novels she had read in her head. She had always had an active imagination.

Yes, that was it. Although these flashes had been awfully real, and quite startling, they were nothing more than the product of too much adrenaline. In fact, if she went home and searched through all her books, she had every confidence she'd find stories with characters matching her odd visions. There was nothing mystical about all this.

Lynn wrapped one arm around her shins and rested her chin on her knees. Absently, she ran her thumbs along the tiny ridge created in her collar where the needle lay.

Nothing mystical at all . . .

Three

In the waning twilight, and with the aid of his flashlight, Grant found an oak tree that had given up its fight with the Texas heat and sun. Even with the rain that had been falling, it would be hot-burning wood. The hatchet was a bit dull, and he'd had to use as much brute force as skill to loosen a limb, but he finally won the battle. Dragged a section of the trunk closer to the cave, he went to work turning it into manageable logs.

Soon Grant was breathing heavily from exertion. He didn't mind, though. It felt good to have something to do to vent his anger. Normally when he was frustrated he had any number of job sites to inspect, or chores to do on his own ranch. He definitely disliked the forced inactivity, on top of feeling awkward. It was a rare occasion when he felt out of his element, but today certainly qualified.

Once he had finished his chore, he began dragging the logs into the cave. He sniffed appreciatively as he deposited the wood near the rest of the pile. Lynn was crouched beside the tripod stirring something in a pot. "That smells amazingly good," he said as a peace offering.

"Watch out for snakes," she said without turning around.

Grant was glad she couldn't see him jump, nor how white his face had surely grown.

He hated snakes.

She laughed at her own taunt, and he glared at her back.

"Don't worry, tough guy. Snakes are lethargic this time of year, and I rattled the stack when I came in. It's always wise to check for critters when staying outdoors."

He had recovered his composure by the time he moved to sit on the log, being careful not to crowd her. "I'll have you know I've camped a time or two."

"Yeah, I'm sure you're a proverbial Boy Scout."

He wasn't about to bring up his being an Eagle Scout, not with that tone . . .

She filled two dented cups with steaming soup, and handed him one. "Bon appetit."

He started to take a sip and then paused. "Thank you."

"It's just rehydrated soup."

"Not for the meal—for not taking my head off for being a fool."

"They guillotine for that now?" She glanced up at Grant with a look of mock surprise on her face. "Goodness, it's a miracle there are any men left on the planet."

He chuckled, pleased that she had finally said more than a clipped one-word response. "Touché." He took a careful sip of the hot bouillon and vegetables. "I don't suppose it would do any good to tell you that most days I'm level-headed, and anything but impetuous."

Lynn blew into her own cup and seemed to consider his statement. "Nope."

Grant rolled his eyes and concentrated on the food he'd done nothing to deserve.

"So what do you do on the days you're being level-headed and non-impulsive?" she asked after a while.

"I'm a custom home builder."

"Do you build around here?"

"No, not usually. I concentrate on high-end homes around Lake Travis."

"My, my, we are certainly a step above your basic tract home, I'd say."

Grant laughed. "A bit, but I started out building tract homes, and I make no apologies about where I came from. I have to confess though, I like the freedom building custom gives me."

"Frees the artisté?"

"Something like that. But then, you'd know about that since you're an artist yourself."

"Me? Hardly."

"Oh, yes, hardly. I might not be an expert, but I can recognize talent. And the quilt you had spread over you on the porch this afternoon was absolutely beautiful. It made me think of my grandmother, and all the quilts she made before she died. I have to tell you, though, she never put colors together like you have."

Lynn finished her soup and moved away to top off Jake's water bowl, which was nearly full. She seemed uncomfortable, and that surprised him. After drinking the last drop from his own cup, he stood.

"Lynn—"

"I hate to interrupt our little mutual admiration society, but we need to get beds ready."

She busied herself at the trunk, accepting his offered cup and putting it beside hers. She tossed him a sleeping bag and carried another for herself. He took her cue and made a pallet from the sleeping bag, covering it with the quilt she'd given him earlier. With their saddles for pillows, it would make a tolerable bed. Nothing he'd recommend for constant use—he'd slept with a saddle for a pillow before—but it would get them through the night.

"Is it my imagination, or are you limping?" she asked as he settled with a small grunt.

Grant shrugged as he rubbed the offended joint. "Just the ubiquitous football knee injury. It bothers me when it's cold and damp, but I'll live."

"College ball, right?"

He took her ribbing good-naturedly. "Right. Except I played many more downs on the bench than on the field. I was a definite wanna-be. I got cut after my freshman year, but not before a senior nailed me good one day in practice."

"Ouch," she said with sympathy.

"I'm not complaining. I did then, of course, but it was the best thing that could have happened. I gave up the ridiculous dream I had about starting for the Cowboys and got busy on my degree. But enough about my less-than-illustrious football career. It's a boring story."

"No, it's not. I'm always fascinated by the events that bring people to certain turning points in their lives. It's almost always something unplanned and unexpected. If we're lucky, we can look back and see that what we thought was the worst thing that could happen caused good things in the end."

She seemed suddenly agitated, as if she'd revealed far more than she had intended to. Ducking her head down, she busied herself pouring a cup of tea and blowing over the battered rim.

"Tell me about your quilts," Grant prompted, wanting to fill the silence. "I seem to remember my gran giving them names."

Lynn looked extremely ill-at-ease. Then she squared her shoulders. She tipped her head toward the quilt he was using. "Some names are factual, those from well-known patterns. Some are my own monikers. Like yours. I call it Heart of Mine. It's a pieced design intended to look like interlocking hearts."

"It certainly accomplishes its goal, then. These look like hearts to me."

She seemed grateful he didn't offer anything except his bland comment. Under other circumstances, he might have made a joke, but considering he hardly knew her, he chose the safe path. He didn't want her to stop talking again.

"Curved pieces, for things such as hearts, are often appliquéd. I prefer the challenge of making straight lines bend. Betsy has one with her that I called Spiral Fantasy."

"And yours?"

"Mine's called Flying Geese. It's one of my favorites."

He wondered if that was due to the metaphor of flying away, or because of the colors, but again, he felt he shouldn't ask. And just as strangely, he was pleased his sister had the comfort of one of Lynn's fabulous creations.

"They are beautiful, Lynn. You have an extraordinary talent."

She cut him a glance. "I thought you said you weren't an expert."

"I don't have to be to recognize talent. I meant the compliment sincerely. I'm sorry if I've made you uncomfortable."

Lynn gave a self-deprecating laugh. "I have a friend who scolds me all the time about not knowing how to take a compliment. Let me try and save face by simply saying thank you."

"You're welcome."

She ran her hand over the triangles that made up the quilt by her leg. "Quilting is my passion. When I'm working, I can lose entire days as I play with designs, colors, textures. I've been known to get a bit obsessed."

"I can certainly understand. I do the same thing when I'm starting a new house."

Lynn swirled her tea and blew before she took a sip. "It sounds like we're both anxious to get back to our projects. If we're lucky, we can strike out at first light."

If the storm ever stopped, that is . . .

As if to mock his thoughts, a crash of thunder rolled overhead, and a few moments later, the rain began in earnest. He imagined if he'd been home he could hear the tapping of sleet against his windows. The cave insulated against any sounds, but the opening admitted blasts of icy wind. He was grateful for his jacket, and the hot cup Lynn handed him.

"You're probably not a tea kind of guy, but I'm not big on coffee unless I'm really tired. Then I love a big mug of decaf."

"I've got a thermos, but I don't mind tea. Beggars can't be choosers, and all that."

"That wasn't an apology. I'm just trying for conversation since we both seem to be far from sleep."

Grant settled back against his saddle, putting his drink beside him to stack his hands behind his head.

"What would you like to talk about next?"

Lynn studied his open expression and tamped down the flutter in her stomach. What did she want to talk about? Something safe. Something that would distract her errant pulse.

"Tell me about Betsy," she said, settling herself on her pallet. Jake came over and made himself at home between them.

Lynn stroked Jake's damp fur as she waited for Grant to begin. Jake's presence comforted her, putting her a bit more at ease. Not that she could feel truly comfortable being trapped with a total stranger. Yet Jake scampered about with Grant as though they were bosom buddies, and that hadn't happened in all the years they'd been together. He tolerated some men better than others, but he'd never been so friendly, even with Nan's son.

She wondered if dogs suffered from senility. Maybe
Jake was going through a phase. Maybe he thought
Grant was Leonard. After all, Leonard had been tall and
dark-haired. She felt guilty that her next thought compared Leonard's gruff appearance to Grant's handsome
features. She didn't want to be noticing the way the fire-
light gleamed in his black hair. Or that his eyes were
deep and intelligent. Or that his chest was broad and
inviting.

"Betsy is the most exasperating, frustrating, impulsive . . . adorable person on this earth."

Lynn heard the affection in his voice, and relaxed just
a notch. He clearly loved his sister, even if she made
him traipse around the countryside trying to find her.

"I take it she . . . um . . . disappears rather regularly?"

It was better to keep him talking. And keep herself
distracted.

Grant snorted. "Betts was a late-life baby for my
folks, and maybe that's part of it. For all intents and
purposes, she was an only child. And incredibly spoiled.
But she can't seem to find her niche. Let's see, five years
ago her thing was astral projection and she had to go to
the Andes Mountains and find some guy who'd written
a book on it. Then it was channelling, and she followed
some nutcase all around the country. Then it was Catholicism, of all things, and my parents were pretty
hopeful that one would stick."

"I'll hazard a guess that it didn't."

"When she couldn't get a personal audience with the
Pope she decided any religion that out of touch with its
people wasn't for her."

Lynn hid a grin behind her hand. She was getting a
picture of Betsy that made her previous instincts make
sense.

"So what happened after the Pope?"

"She decided to be a great painter. I might add here
that she'd never held a paintbrush before, but my folks

were so delighted she'd picked something in the realm
of normal, they went for it."

"Let me interject. Paris?"

Grant touched the tip of his nose. "Apartment on the
Seine, black beret and all."

"Okay, what next."

"Men."

Lynn winced. She should have seen that coming.

"I guess we should be grateful she didn't end up with
something incurable, but before too long she decided
that she needed to be a nun. But she didn't want to go
back to Catholicism, regardless of the fact that you don't
just pop in and take vows. She decided she'd be a Bud-
dhist nun."

"I didn't know the Buddhists had nuns."

"I didn't either. And Betts found out they require quite
a stretch of devotion before taking someone seriously.
So instead, she found this crackpot cult in the northwest.
And I do mean a cult, not just some folks with a few
weird ideas."

"I'm so sorry. There always seems to be those who
will prey on the innocent and lost."

"You got that right. It took some serious skullduggery
to get her out of there and deprogrammed, but she still
isn't happy. She wants so badly to master something,
but she can't seem to stick with anything, even something farfetched, long enough to feel accomplished before she jumps to the next scheme. And of course, the
doctors think this pill or that is the answer."

Grant paused, studying the fire, his thoughts full of
his beautiful if ditzy sister. "To be absolutely honest,
I'm not sure that she needs to be on any medicine. I'm
no doctor, of course, but she doesn't seem sick, just . . .
lost."

Lynn raised one eyebrow. "Which is probably why
she keeps running away, yet needing you to find her. In
her heart she knows that no matter how frustrated you

get, you'll always love her. And come after her."

He shrugged one shoulder. "I don't know about that. In the notes she left, she included me as one of the people who was smothering her, and that she was going to disappear forever this time."

"But left a notebook giving you some pretty big clues where she went? She obviously didn't want to disappear too completely," Lynn said with a wry chuckle.

Once again, he touched his nose. "I'm just not sure what to do this time. I have every confidence she'll come home, and perhaps even stay in therapy for a while. But I'm afraid that one of these days she'll devise a scheme I can't pull her out of."

Playing with the corner of her quilt, Lynn's fingers itched to hold her needle, as they always did when she was nervous or upset. With Grant watching her, though, she forced her hand away from her collar. She felt silly enough about her connection to the tiny piece of metal without advertising her odd habit.

The fire crackled and the horses shifted their hooves. The smell of leather and burning oak created a marvelous, rustic aroma. It made her think of Leonard, and all the times they had spent camping in the wilderness. He'd taught her how to live off the land, to take care of herself, even disappear if she had to. But for all his skill, he hadn't been able to fight the cancer that had ravaged his body. And he'd left her, bereft.

Lynn pulled her thoughts back to the present. "Have you considered that you shouldn't rescue Betsy this time? Maybe she needs you to stop facilitating her behavior."

Grant looked at her long and hard. "And could you sit by and let your sister die when you could do something about it?"

"I don't have any siblings, but I know that's not your point. And the answer is, I probably would do the same thing. Theory is all well and good until someone you love is in jeopardy."

He nodded solemnly. "You are absolutely right. I want to be tough with Betts, but I want her alive more."

"You're a good man, Grant. Your heart is in the right place."

She caught a gleam in his eyes, one that said he saw her, truly saw her, and it made her immensely uncomfortable. She hadn't seen desire in a man's eyes in so long she'd almost forgotten what it looked like. But not so long that fear didn't coil its way up her spine to make her shoulders freeze painfully.

The fact that a simple glance from a handsome man could make her go cold with terror was a reminder that she was still broken, unlikely to ever be fixed.

Grant reached out to touch her face. Lynn scrambled back so furiously she kicked a rock into the fire, which sent Jake to his feet with a sharp bark.

"Hey, I'm sorry," he said, pulling away.

"Don't do that," she said between clenched teeth. "Don't ever do that."

Grant shook his head, looking bewildered. "I know it doesn't make it okay, but you had this lost expression on your face. I didn't mean to scare you. I just wanted to make sure you were okay."

Lynn stood and dusted off her jeans. She nodded, then headed for the opening to the cave.

Grant stood as well. "Where are you—"

She gave him an arch look. "I don't need an audience right now. I'll be back in a minute." And with that she stalked away.

Grant watched the mouth of the cave, waiting anxiously as Lynn and Jake disappeared from sight. He didn't relax until Jake trotted back in, with Lynn right behind him. She stoked the fire and added a healthy pile of logs to keep it going through the night. He would have done it, but he doubted she would appreciate his interference, especially at the moment.

They didn't speak again as they took to their bedrolls and settled down to sleep. There wouldn't be any more conversation this night.

Grant rolled into the beautiful quilt Lynn had given him, and traced the tiny indentions the stitches had made. The threads seemed warm under his touch, as if they'd absorbed the heat of the fire. There was something elementally feminine about her work.

He pretended not to notice when she reached out to pull a wicked-looking knife from her boot near her bedroll. It upset him that she felt the need to place it at her side and keep her hand wrapped around the hilt.

What caused a woman to panic at the thought of being touched? What made her learn survival skills of this magnitude? And why did it bother him so deeply that she had those fears, and needed such training?

She'd obviously been profoundly hurt, and it rallied every protective instinct within him . . . even for a woman he barely knew. He was glad Lynn *could* take care of herself, it simply angered him that it was necessary.

Yet it was equally clear that he'd like to get to know her better. Their meeting had been less than auspicious, but maybe after Betts was settled, he could find a way to meet Lynn on less rocky ground.

Grant shifted, pulling a stone out from under his back, and tossed it aside.

Figuratively speaking, of course.

His eyes drifted shut. Exhaustion had taken its toll.

Lynn was lost in that no-man's land between sleeping and waking. If her internal clock was right, she had slept for several hours, which amazed her. When she was keyed up, a two-hour nap was usually all she could manage.

She heard Grant stirring the fire, but didn't want to open her eyes just yet. With Jake still and warm by her side, and her knife under her hand, she felt safe. Safe enough to ignore the pull of the new day.

Truth be told, she knew Grant watched her, and incongruously, that made her feel even more secure. She should have felt trapped, threatened, but instead she'd drifted into a half-sleep. She knew she'd never get back to dreamland, and still she resisted rising. For that meant facing Grant, and she was reluctant after her inelegant display last night.

She felt so guilty. He'd only been trying to be nice. She'd seen that in his eyes, yet the moment his hand had reached for her face, she had been assaulted by memories, and she had instantly expected the bruising sting of a slap, or the mind-numbing pain of a fist.

To her consternation, in that instant she'd reacted as the old Lynn, the untrained Lynn, the helpless Lynn. Where had her hour upon endless hour of training gone? She could take down a man twice her weight and had the skill to break arms and legs if she needed to. Yet she'd scurried away from Grant like a frightened mouse, not a tae kwon do blackbelt.

God, how she hated this feeling! Leonard would have been ashamed of her.

Lynn cancelled that thought. Leonard would have never been ashamed of her. Ever. His gentle love and boundless patience had been a gift she felt certain she didn't deserve. She had wanted to love him the same way he had loved her, but her heart had been too scarred.

Leonard had never pushed, never demanded more from her than she could give. He'd survived her bouts of gut-wrenching sobbing, her fits of uncontrolled anger, her lengthy silences when she had been lost within herself. For those much-too-brief years, he had been father, brother, and friend to her, comforting her when needed, pushing her when necessary, and always a model of inner peace.

A peace he'd said had been hard won.

He'd nearly let bitterness overwhelm him, he'd explained, after his wife had been killed by a drunk driver. He'd even fallen in love again, but that woman had run away, afraid of the power of their feelings for each other. Yet, instead of giving in to the blackness of despair, he'd channeled his energies in a new direction and the martial arts had become his passion. His sensei had been a master of survival training as well as tae kwon do, and teacher and student had become close friends. They spent weeks in the mountains, living off the land.

It had seemed incongruous in a man who'd worked for the government all his life. But put the man in a karate uniform and another side of him appeared. If she believed in reincarnation, she would have suspected he had the soul of a karate master inside him, awakened when the call of kata or weapons practice came.

After their sessions, the quiet, learned man returned as if the warrior had never been. Leonard had never let her slack with him. He had demanded her all and she had tossed him to the ground many times with untempered force. If she could do that to Leonard, she could do that to anyone.

Yet none of that knowledge stopped the nausea, the utterly helpless feeling that had overwhelmed her when Grant had attempted to touch her. He had seemed to tower over her, and she had been thrown into a complete state of panic.

He hadn't been towering over her, of course. In her fear, it had simply felt that way since he was so tall, his shoulders so broad. It hardly seemed possible that moments before his chest had seemed warm and inviting, not huge and threatening.

And then she'd gone and insulted the blue blazes out of him when he was simply being kind.

When she looked back into the past, she recognized that she had known when Trey had begun to change, and had ignored her instincts that told her darkness had taken residence in his soul. Now she was feeling foolish for keeping her knife in her hand and not trusting her instincts telling her that Grant was a good, decent man.

Would she ever be normal? Was it possible for her to be around a member of the human race who carried a Y-chromosome without abject terror making her act like an idiot?

She felt Jake stir, but bless his furry heart, he stayed right by her side. And if Grant was aware she was awake, he was being kind enough to leave her alone.

Lynn threw her arm over her face to hide the tears sliding down her cheeks. She wanted that again . . . to be normal. Whole. To feel need and desire, to laugh from the bottom of her soul, to twirl in the sunshine like a little girl with pigtails flying.

She'd actually been tossing around the idea of going dancing with Nan at the monthly fish fry at the volunteer fire station. Now Lynn knew what a drastic mistake that would have been. The first time someone asked her to dance she'd have either tossed him to the ground like a rag doll, or dissolved into a pitiful puddle. Either reaction would hardly have earned her a slot on the desirable bachelorette list.

When she realized her humor was returning, weakly maybe, but returning, she decided to quit playing possum. She sat up, rubbing her eyes and wiping away Jake's sloppy good-morning swipe on the cheek. As soon as she stood, he took off like a shot.

Lynn gave Grant an awkward smile. "I think I'll join him," she said, edging toward the entrance of the cave to hide the knife in her hand.

The weak dawn was hardly enough to see by as she headed out for her walk. Despite the frigid temperature, she took her time, needing to gather her courage as much as she needed to stretch her legs and take care of her full bladder. She waited until she was well out of sight before she bent and put her knife back in her boot, then she glanced around at the trees. Guessing the temperature hovered in the twenties, she turned up her collar and pulled the jacket closer together against the wind coming out of the north.

When she returned, rubbing her hands briskly against the chill, she was amazed to see Grant had given the horses water and had tidied the cave.

"Thanks." She picked up her gloves and tugged them on.

"Not a problem," he said. "I have that coffee I mentioned yesterday, if you'd like some. It's not as hot as I'd like, but it's drinkable."

"No, thanks." She attempted another smile. "I'll fix tea."

"I figured as much, so I started some water."

She looked at the tripod appreciatively. "I appreciate that."

Grant swiveled his cup between his palms, studying the dark depths as though seeking divine inspiration. When he looked up, Lynn read the apology in his eyes before he opened his mouth.

"Lynn, I'm very sorry for all this. I'm not sorry for my determination to get my sister home, but I do regret what I've put you through."

Lynn nodded an acceptance, unsure how to reply. Words weren't coming too well this morning.

He busied himself with finishing his coffee. "I think we should head back to your place as soon as we can. Do you think we can make it out this morning? Or is it too icy?"

She cut him a sharp glance. She had the feeling he could read the weather just as well as she could, but was trying to be diplomatic. "Why the change of heart?"

Grant met her eyes frankly. "You were right. It was

foolish to strike out so late yesterday. I let my anger rule my actions, and look where it got me. Besides, it wouldn't be fair to push Sure Bet and risk injuring his leg, so we'll head back, get you safe and warm. I'll find Betts on my own."

"You could call her on the walkie-talkie and ask her to meet you there." If they were lucky, Betts and Nan would still be within range.

His cheeks heated. "I ... uh ... must have dropped it on the trail somewhere 'cause it's not in my saddlebag anymore. I looked while you were gone."

Lynn laughed, a reluctant cough of amusement.

"I'll replace it as soon as I get back to town."

She waved her hand, dismissing the issue. "I'm not going to argue your change of heart. By the time we get the cave in order and get something in our stomachs, it'll already have warmed up a few degrees. I bet it hits the forties by noon."

Grant nodded. "It's too early in the year for a prolonged freeze, even in the hill country. We'll probably be back in shorts tomorrow."

Lynn managed a chuckle at the all-too-true statement. "Don't you just love Texas weather?"

Grant's wry smile in return was answer enough.

Fixing a cup of tea kept her hands busy while she found the courage to make her next offer. "We can ride double on Trouble. He's big enough to handle us both. That'll get us back in just over an hour."

Grant nodded, and then it seemed to strike him what she'd just offered, considering her reaction last night.

"Lynn, I can walk. I'll be okay."

She took a deep breath, fortifying herself. "No, that's silly. We'll get there a lot faster without you on foot."

Before she could change her mind, Lynn turned to rummage in the trunk and pulled out two food packs for breakfast. Then she brought out a gallon container, and moved to the horses. Grant watched her divide the grain between the two animals and pat each one with a gentle hand.

"That's really not enough for both of them, but it'll have to do until we get them back to my stable."

"Great," he muttered to himself. "One more thing to feel guilty about."

Lynn returned to the fire and offered the packages for inspection. "Would you like lentil soup or beef stew for breakfast?"

Grant pretended to play eenie-meenie-minie-moe and ended up with the stew. After a few minutes of silence, they were once again sharing a rehydrated meal from battered cups. But it was warm, and filling, and had them just about ready to make the cold trip home.

Grant took the clean-up chore and Lynn relinquished her empty cup. She sat on her pallet watching the flames, reluctant to douse the fire. It was more than a lack of desire to leave the warmth and coziness of the cave. She had to admit, in the secret part of her heart, that she'd enjoyed the time in Grant's company. It had been awkward at moments, but it had made her realize how much she missed male companionship. Especially the companionship of a man who had feelings . . . deep feelings. Grant loved his sister and even if he had been a bit high-handed, he was motivated by caring and concern.

Leonard had promised that someday she'd want to be around men again, to be with a man in every sense of the word. She'd scoffed. Now that feeling had returned, and had reared its head with a vengeance.

She was afraid of just how right Leonard was proving to be. And where would that leave her? She didn't believe for a second that her reaction to Grant consisted of anything deeper than physical attraction. As soon as he found Betsy and was gone, she had no doubt he'd be out of her mind in a second.

What was bothering her was more a sense of frustration that she had something new to deal with. She'd just gotten over her grief from losing Leonard. Now she had to face deep, aching loneliness? That wasn't fair.

She thought she had come to terms with being alone, but Grant had unwittingly reminded her of her isolation. She couldn't say she'd chosen the healthiest of relationships, even before Trey, but still she missed the feel of a man's arms around her, a strong chest against her cheek, tangy aftershave in her nose . . .

She was startled out of her thoughts when Grant finished wiping out the cups and saucepan, and cleared his throat.

"Lynn, it's none of my business, I know, but . . . what happened?"

She watched the flames devour the dirty paper towels and struggled with the instant tightening in her stomach. A predictable reaction, but still a feeling she would never get used to. She pulled her knees to her chest and wrapped her arms around her shins, trying to decide what to say. While she certainly didn't owe him any explanations, she felt she should say something after the way she'd been acting.

"It's not a matter of whether it's your business. It's a matter that you're a complete stranger. You already know far too much about me, and that makes you dangerous."

He raised one of his eyebrows in obvious surprise. "I guess that wasn't the response I was expecting. I give you my word I'm no danger to you, Lynn. Despite my frustration with my sister, I admire what you're doing."

"Really?" she asked with little conviction. "Most men would find me irritating, or meddlesome."

"I'm not like most men."

"I can see that. You've surprised me, especially when you apologized."

He tilted his head. "I hope I can restore the male image in your eyes. It's obviously a tad tarnished."

She gave a dry chuckle. "A tad."

"Would it be odd for me to say I'm surprised no one has found you before me? Aren't abusers usually stalkers as well?"

"That's absolutely true. But I've been lucky, I guess." She brushed her cheek against the collar of her jacket. "The women I have helped have been ready to make a clean break. I did have one woman go back to her abuser, but she never betrayed me. I visit her grave every time I'm up around Kerrville."

Grant's grunt as he tossed a twig onto the fire could have meant many things, but she chose to believe he indicated disappointment in that particular story's ending.

"Do you do this often?"

He undoubtedly meant her underground activities, not camping in a cave on the spur of the moment. "Once or twice a year is about the average."

"How do they find you?"

Lynn shrugged, resting her chin on her knees. "I've gotten a lot of odd answers but without being able to give details, they tell me that someone gave them my name. When pressed, they can't seem to remember who that someone is exactly and since most abuse victims are skittish, I don't press."

"Did you ask Betsy?"

An amused if skeptical smile tugged at her mouth. "She said a psychic told her how to find me. I'm not sure I bought that one, but what could I do? Call her a liar?"

Grant opened his mouth as if to reply, then pressed his lips together for a long moment. Finally, he said, "Does my finding you change things?"

Lynn tossed a few twigs of her own onto the hot coals and watched the flames greedily consume the offering.

"I don't know," she answered honestly. "I haven't thought about it. I don't want to move. I've made a home here, but I also refuse to live in fear again."

"Is this the fear that has you keeping karate weapons in a quilting basket and a knife by your side?"

"Pretty much," she confirmed tersely. She resented the reminder of her needed vigilance, and suddenly was no longer content to sit and chat.

She stood abruptly and began folding her bedding. She put the sleeping bag back in the trunk and rolled her quilt with loving hands. She traced the triangles of blue, green, and gold, noting it was showing signs of wear. The fraying didn't bother her, though, because she'd never made her quilts for just-for-pretties. They were meant to be used.

Grant handed her his sleeping bag, neatly tied. "Thank you for letting me use the quilt. However you made it, it sure was cozy. In fact, I was expecting to be stove-up like an old man this morning, but my knee feels great."

Lynn picked up her saddle and headed for Trouble. "I'm glad you were warm. It was actually tolerable in here, as the horses give off an amazing amount of body heat."

Grant put the saddle on Sure Bet and adjusted the saddlebags. Jake, sensing they were leaving, danced in and out of the entrance. Lynn shook her head.

"It's a long walk home, boy. You should save your energy."

Jake just looked at her and barked, then raced out again.

She watched his antics with a twinge of envy. For Jake, the trip home would be an adventure. For her . . . torture.

Grant laughed when Jake pranced back in to bark at them, obviously wanting them to hurry, before disappearing into the sunshine again. Then he noticed the tight cast to Lynn's shoulders, and his smile faded. Guilt surged through him once more, but he forced it down.

Maybe he had acted spontaneously, but he still had Betsy to worry about.

He struggled for something light to say. "That's some dog you've got there, Lynn."

Her rigid posture eased a bit. "Yeah, he's some mutt all right. I don't know what I'd do without him."

He'd watched Jake while Lynn slept that morning. He had seemed as conscious of her fitful rest as Grant had been, but the dog hadn't so much as lifted his muzzle from his paws until she'd opened her eyes.

Jake's vigilance pleased Grant. He was comforted that she had Jake close by for her peace of mind. He just wished his own presence wasn't so disconcerting to her.

Glancing over at her, he watched while she tightened the saddle cinch and lowered the stirrups. She was a gorgeous lady, there was no doubt about that. Even with her hair a bit mussed and her clothes rumpled, she looked sexy in a wholesome, real-woman kind of way. The only thing wrong with the picture was the sadness and wariness in her face.

And it bothered him more than he could say that he'd added to the fear that never seemed to leave her luminous green eyes. He had never hurt a woman in his life, and to remember the absolute terror in her expression as she'd scuttled away from him tore at his heart.

It also made him incredibly angry at the man who'd put the fear there. It made him want to be entirely uncivilized and beat the crap out of the jerk who could hurt such a beautiful woman. Hell, *any* woman. Beauty had nothing to do with it.

Grant patted Sure Bet's neck and busied himself putting the fire out. Lynn hadn't finished her tea so he poured what was left onto the coals and stirred them, spreading out the ashes to be sure he left no hot spots, and added some dirt for good measure.

He stood and dusted his hands off. Turning, he saw

Lynn locking the trunk, and his dark thoughts were swept away as he smiled.

"Get much thievery out here?" he teased.

She gave him an arch look. "Yes, as a matter of fact. The masked bandits that live in these woods are remarkably adept at opening latches. But I've yet to meet a raccoon who can work a combination lock."

Grant chuckled, and addressed a bow to her superior knowledge. When she finished and dusted off her hands, he took Sure Bet's reins and led the way outside.

Lynn and Grant stood side by side, staring up at the milky sky. When he let his eyes trail over her face, there was something so lost in her expression that he felt compelled to touch her, to let her know she wasn't as alone as she felt.

"Lynn," he said to get her attention, determined that he wouldn't scare her as he had last night.

When she looked at him, he reached out slowly and placed his hand on her shoulder. Between his gloves, her jacket and her clothes, the touch was hardly intimate, but he could tell she had to steel herself not to pull away. It gratified him when she didn't.

The magnetism between them amazed him. The mere fact that she was willing to stay close to him, despite her fear, spoke volumes about her attraction to him, even if it was a reluctant attraction. He didn't want to let go of her. What had started out as a reassuring touch had become much more, and he was as confused as Lynn appeared. He could see emotions warring in her eyes, and smiled when she conquered her fear to watch him with curiosity and interest.

Taking a chance, a huge chance, he leaned forward and slowly lowered his head. He gave her every opportunity to move away or say something, but she stayed still and finally lifted her face. He placed a gentle kiss on her luxurious mouth.

Her lips warmed under his in intoxicating seconds.

Her breath quickened. He sensed her fighting the urge to pull away, and rejoiced silently when she stayed with him, panic and all.

He slowly let his tongue trace the corners of her mouth. First one, then the other. A swipe of his lower lip against hers gained him a small gasp.

With the lightest of touches, he skimmed his fingers over her eyebrows, her cheekbones, her silky jaw. His blood sang with desire. She was sweet, so sweet.

Pressing the fullness of his mouth against hers, he drank in the nectar of her, fighting back the overpowering need to enfold her in his arms and hold tight. That might be what he needed, but it certainly wasn't what she needed.

When he felt her begin to quiver, he reluctantly stepped away. He'd made her afraid of him last night; this morning he wanted to leave her with the knowledge that he desired a much different reaction from her. And he wanted to leave her with a memory of him that wasn't tainted by terror.

He watched as she seemed to gather herself together, as if she'd been coming undone, and with a shudder, she pulled her shoulders back.

"Grant—"

"Lynn—"

They both laughed with shaky, husky voices.

They looked at each other for an endless moment. Then she shook her head as if there weren't any words for what she was feeling. Instead, she reached for Trouble's reins and held them out.

His brow furrowed. "It's all right, Lynn. I'll take the back."

"No, it's better for Trouble if you're in the saddle. You're heavier."

"That may be true, but—"

"Please don't argue with me. I want to get home, and we're wasting time."

Grant mounted silently, biting his tongue to keep from snapping at the stubborn woman. He'd done enough of that for one twenty-four hour period, he supposed.

She'd guessed well when she'd adjusted the stirrups to accommodate his longer legs, so he settled into the saddle and held out his hand to her. Placing her foot on top of his boot, she swung up behind him onto the blanket she'd left long over Trouble's hindquarters.

She took Sure Bet's reins and with Jake barking to urge them to get moving, the group hit the trail once again.

Grant couldn't help but notice her reluctance as she wrapped her arms around his waist. Necessity dictated that she press against him, but her stiff posture shouted her discomfort. She even spoke as little as possible, guiding sometimes with a gesture instead of words.

Grant tried to not be disappointed by her silence, or by her obvious reluctance to touch him. After all, such enforced intimacy had to be hard on a woman who was wary of men.

Especially a man who'd just kissed her . . .

Four

Lynn was in sensory overload.

As the hour progressed, the sun burned off the cloud cover, leaving a dazzling blue sky, and crisp, cold air. Drops of water clung to leaf and bough, making the rugged hills look as if they were dressed in diamonds. The Texas landscape could be harsh, and sometimes forbidding, but washed in the sunshine and dew, it beckoned those brave enough to climb into the rugged terrain and discover its rustic beauty.

But it wasn't the weather or the countryside that held her enthralled. To be honest, the kiss hadn't taken her completely by surprise. She suspected he'd wanted to kiss her last night, but she'd short-circuited any hopes of that. This morning, he'd demonstrated massive patience, given her plenty of time to make sure she hadn't felt trapped.

And of all the feelings surging through her like an overwhelming tidal wave, intimidation had not been among them. She had felt precious, beautiful, desired, feminine . . . but trapped? Most certainly not.

Maybe that was why she'd let him kiss her. Her curiosity had been aroused, and the gentleness in his eyes had tempted her to see if she'd fall apart in fear if a man touched her again. She hadn't, she was proud to say. It had also made her realize just how much she enjoyed the feel of a man's strong, sensual lips against hers, and a pair of powerful arms touching her so tenderly, as though she were fragile enough to break.

Of course, she was a long, long way from sex. She rolled her eyes at herself. To even extrapolate that far was a bit extreme, no matter how glorious the morning. She wasn't in the realm of ready for physical intimacy . . . but that kiss sure had been nice.

As they rode in silence, she tried to deal with all the additional information being fed to her brain . . . such as just how nice his butt looked in those jeans, just how trim his waist was despite the fact that he had to be edging forty. No midlife spread for this guy. Just how warm he felt, how solid.

Lynn tried to remind herself that once Grant was out of sight, he would be out of mind, but was having trouble believing it. Even if she could successfully put Grant out of her thoughts, she'd still be left with these awakened feelings that she didn't know how to handle. He probably thought her a shrew for not talking to him, but she couldn't form words at the moment. Her brain stayed too busy chasing ideas in circles until she felt dizzy.

At least worrying had passed the time. Before she even realized it, they were in sight of the cleared land she euphemistically called her backyard. A grateful sigh escaped her. She needed some time to process all that had happened, and she could only do that alone. She certainly couldn't do it while snuggled against the very man who had caused the confusion in the first place.

Grant reined Trouble to a stop by the stables and swung his leg over the front of the saddle to dismount agilely. Lynn envied him the ease of movement because she knew her landing wouldn't be nearly so graceful.

Over an hour of riding with no stirrups for support had
left her legs numb.

It would have been insane to refuse Grant's help when
he held out his arms to her, yet she hesitated. Not from
fear, as she might have expected, but from anticipation.
And uncertainty.

Finally she pulled her leg over and reached out, grip-
ping his shoulders tightly as she slid to the ground. She
nearly gasped from the sensation of being pressed so
closely, even though she knew he held her so securely
to let her test her legs. For an instant, pure instinct overtook her and she wanted to melt against him, to hold
him as close as humanly possible and absorb his essence.

She managed to let go before she embarrassed herself,
and gave him a grateful, if shaky smile. Her gait was
stiff as she led Trouble to his stall, but at least she hadn't
fallen on her face. Or collapsed into him.

"Bring Safe Bet in and put him in the second stall,"
she said, automatically beginning the process of removing Trouble's tack. "We'll get him fed and brushed before you take him home."

She jerked to a stop when Grant stilled her hands with
his own. "Let me take care of the horses, Lynn. You go
inside and get warm."

She looked up at his quiet, gentle, but oh-so-
masculine face, and froze in place. For one moment, the
temptation to give in, to let someone take care of her,
nearly overwhelmed her. Then too many years and too
much determination interfered.

"No, thank you," she said firmly, moving his hand
away to reach for the girth strap. "You tend to Safe Bet,
and I'll take care of Trouble. Then we can both go inside
for something hot and filling before you leave."

Though obviously unhappy at her refusal, he gave her
a curt nod. The horses seemed none the worse for wear
and were soon contentedly munching oats, their coats
clean and shiny after their brushings. Jake roused him-

self when Grant and Lynn emerged from the barn, stretching languidly in the pool of sunshine he'd sprawled into, and trotted toward the house.

Lynn felt increasingly awkward as they neared the back patio, and struggled with her reluctance to allow Grant inside. No man had been in her house—except Jeremy and he didn't qualify as a man just yet—since Leonard's death. Her invitation had a monumental feel, something so much more than simple courtesy.

Once again, he seemed to read her mind.

"Listen, Lynn, I appreciate the hospitality and all, but I think I'll pull the trailer around and get Safe Bet loaded, then be on my way."

"Grant, I—"

He stopped her with a gentle finger against her lips. "Don't say anything. My guess is you've had just about as much as you can take for one twenty-four hour period."

Heat suffused her cheeks. "I can't just tell you to go away like a stray dog or something."

Grant laughed. "Why not? You did yesterday."

"That was different," she said, her blush deepening. Then she realized Grant had skillfully led the way around the side of the house as they argued, saving her from having to actually make good on her invitation. As they rounded the corner, the porch came into view.

"Lynn!"

The female voice threw her for a loop. As her vision panned the front yard, she saw Nan's truck, with its trademark magnetic sign on the door proclaiming NAN'S TREASURES, WINTERHAVEN, TEXAS, and Nan herself standing on the top step.

Then Lynn noticed a blanket-wrapped figure on the swing.

Grant noticed, too.

She held her breath, watching as Betsy stood, clutching the quilt around her and moved slowly toward her brother. A series of emotions passed over his face. He was clearly relieved that she was all right, then he seemed to remember what he'd been through since yesterday. But compassion overcame irritation, and forgiveness proved the most powerful of all.

Tears welled in Lynn's eyes as she saw the love shining from his eyes as Grant held out his arms, and Betsy ran down the steps into his embrace.

Nan quietly made her way past the siblings to put her arm around Lynn's shoulders. "I told you everything would be all right. And you couldn't have picked a more perfect quilt for Betsy."

Stepping back with a serene expression and a confident smile, Betsy seemed a more mature version of the girl who'd come there for help a short week ago.

"She's right, Lynn," Betsy said softly. "Your help and this quilt have changed my life." She turned to her brother. "I'm so sorry, Grant. So very sorry for everything I've put you through."

He hugged her close and placed a kiss on her forehead. "Are you all right?"

"I'm fine. Better than I've ever been. And I'm going to prove it to you."

Lynn tugged Nan toward the porch. "Come on. Let's give them a little privacy." Then she realized Nan was staring at her. "What? Have I grown a wart on my nose?"

Nan shook her head. "Something's different. Are you all right? I tried to get you on the walkie-talkies."

"I'm fine. Just a bit confused. What's going on?"

"I think I need to answer that," Betsy said, pulling Grant with her up the steps.

Lynn couldn't help but notice just how much the two Majors looked alike as they sat side by side on the swing. They were both dark-headed and blue-eyed, both had strong features, and Betsy was certainly as beautiful as Grant was handsome. She had on an expensive sweater set and slacks, and for an odd moment, Lynn struggled against a sense of awkwardness.

Betsy's attire wasn't the issue, of course. The naivete and innocence still residing in her eyes, things Lynn hadn't experienced in a very long time, had raised a flag, reminding her that she had been carefree once. And like Betsy, had been unaware of the gift of living unburdened by fear. Lynn suddenly felt old and frumpy compared to that youth and beauty, and wondered how she could have thought Grant found her appealing.

Lynn frowned. Where had that thought come from? She didn't care what Grant thought about her appearance. One little kiss did not mean she'd suddenly rush for the makeup counter and worry over every strand of hair.

"I didn't want to run anymore," Betsy said quietly, but with a conviction impossible to ignore.

Lynn appreciated the interruption to her whirring thoughts, and held her breath as Betsy begged Grant with her eyes for understanding, and patience.

"I really am sorry, Grant," Betsy continued. "I'm embarrassed to realize how much I've come to depend on your getting me out of the messes of my own making. It's time for me to grow up."

He seemed stunned, obviously unprepared for his sister's frank admission. "How . . . why . . ."

She gave him a whimsical smile. "It's the oddest thing. I got to the cabin and was really restless. Then I took out the quilt and wrapped up on the porch. I'd sit there for hours and hours, watching the creek and the animals that came to its banks. Then I'd go to bed and snuggle under two or three quilts. I've slept better lately than I have in my entire life. I can't explain it."

Nan grinned from ear to ear. "I can—"

"Nan! Not now."

"But—"

Lynn glared a warning at her friend, glad that Grant

was too busy staring at his sister to notice. Even to Lynn, Betsy seemed calmer, more together than the nervous girl who'd come asking for shelter.

Grant relaxed against the slats of the swing and loosed a sigh that bespoke of too many promises broken. "Well, I'm sure not going to argue."

Betsy put her hand on his arm. "I know you don't believe me, that you think I'm just going to get home and take off again, but I give you my word. I'll do whatever I must to prove to you that I've changed."

He placed his hand over hers. "I can't say I'm entirely ready to believe you yet, Betts, but I'm willing to try if you are. But you shouldn't be trying to prove anything to me right now. The person you need to worry about is you." He pulled her into his arms then and cradled her head against his shoulder, obviously savoring the knowledge that she was safe. After a moment he released her. "Let's get your things, Betts, and get going. Mom and Dad won't believe you're okay until they see you."

She let the quilt drop from around her shoulders with obvious reluctance, stroking the water-colored hues of the medallion design with gentle fingers.

Grant knew immediately how Betsy felt about leaving behind the quilt. He'd experienced the same sensation in the cave after he'd covered himself with one of Lynn's creations.

Maybe she'd let him buy it. "Lynn—"

"Keep the quilt, Betsy," Lynn said softly, her expression gentle.

"Really?" Betsy asked, delight making her eyes sparkle.

"Really."

Grant stifled a chuckle as Betsy nearly bowled Lynn over with an enthusiastic hug. It thrilled him to see Betsy light up with such innocence and joy, but it was the moment of unguarded happiness that swept over Lynn's face that truly touched him. He hadn't known her long, but he'd never seen her without tension marring her features. Seeing even this momentary peace made her beauty border on the exquisite.

He couldn't remember being so affected by a woman. Ever. He hadn't even felt this connected to the woman he'd been married to for six years, for heaven's sake! And, sadly, he'd never felt anything remotely this powerful in all the time he'd spent with Veronica.

Grant put a hand to his forehead to check for fever. Surely exhaustion, and maybe exposure, could be blamed for his intense reaction to Lynn. Yes, that was it. He was just weary. As soon as he got some sleep he'd be back to his normal, logical self, and then there'd be no more waxing poetic about a woman's beauty or mystical connections.

Then Lynn laughed, and the sound washed over his soul like the sunshine that had swept away the morning haze.

"You're welcome, Betsy. Enjoy it."

Even though her voice was warm and sincere, Grant heard a strain of wariness as well. Lynn had reached her tolerance level, just as he'd reached his. Before he got even more sentimental or maudlin, he forcefully reminded himself that he'd been manipulated and led around by the nose. More than anything, that helped him get his head on straight.

It would have been easy, now that Betts was safe and he could go home, to just pretend that everything was all right. But he'd never been the kind to pretend. Certainly not when he'd been lied to and purposefully deceived, not just by Lynn, but by her cohort Nan as well. No matter how well-intentioned their actions, Grant found his anger growing again.

Knowing he'd probably never see Lynn again, he had a few things to say before he left.

"Betts, go get your stuff together, okay? We need to head out."

She nodded and went inside, clutching the quilt close to her again. Nan followed, murmuring something about helping Betsy "pack," leaving Grant and Lynn by themselves.

He stood and took a step toward Lynn. "Would you mind talking to me for a minute?" He wondered if his expression revealed any of the mixture of exasperation, amusement, and anger roiling around inside him.

Lynn seemed wary, as if she'd been expecting his request, but agreed, and walked with him down the steps. He noticed she pretended an intense interest in Jake's examination of the SUV, but he had no intention of being diverted again.

"You were going to lead me on a merry chase, weren't you." It wasn't really a question, of course. "You sent Nan for Betsy, and while you were being so cooperative, you were actually helping her get away."

He refused to feel guilty as he watched her struggle. She'd made choices, obviously out of a determination he couldn't help but admire. That did not, however, exempt her from the consequences.

She lifted her chin. "Yes, I was. Safe Bet throwing a shoe was pure luck . . . for me anyway." She paused, studying her boot tip before meeting his eyes again. "I want you to know, though, that I had made up my mind on the way back to help you find Betsy. I never expected to find her waiting for us."

Grant's smile was small. "It *has* worked out rather conveniently."

He closed his eyes and took a deep breath. As he let it go, he released the residual anger he'd been holding. He'd surmised by her reaction that Lynn expected him to be livid, but he had never been the kind of man to hold a grudge. What was the old cliché about everything ending well?

"I wish I had time to find out more about you, Lynn Powell," he said honestly. "And I hope someday something—or someone—makes those shadows around your soul disappear."

He felt her withdraw, even though she hadn't moved a muscle. "That's kind of you to say," she said, looking away, "but I really don't require sympathy."

Pity hadn't been his intention, but her posture sent a clear message that any attempt by him to clear things up would only muddy the waters even more. With regret, he kept his tongue still as the silence stretched between them.

Betsy, followed by Nan, stepped onto the porch interrupting the awkward moment. Grant stepped aside as his sister ran down the porch steps and wrapped Lynn in a hug.

"You take care of yourself, you hear?" Lynn said when Betsy finally released her, a noticeable huskiness in her voice.

"I'll be fine now, thanks to you. Nan told me how upset you were about my leaving my diary. I'm sorry I was such a ditz."

Nan moved closer. "You aren't a ditz, honey. And everything happens for a reason, remember that. Don't worry about a thing."

"That's right," Lynn affirmed. "You worry about you, and getting healthy."

Grant put Betsy's things in the truck and helped her into the cab while Nan retreated to the porch. He cautiously approached Lynn where she stood near the back bumper, bathed in the brilliant sunshine. She shivered despite the warming rays, and for an instant, he had the image of lying on a rug before a fire, his heels resting on the hearth . . . with Lynn by his side. Even though the picture was enticing, he shook it away as absurd. He had a question to ask her, one he should have asked earlier, and it was now or never.

He wasn't usually the kind of man to pry, but there was something about Lynn that had taken a hold of his heart, and he had to know.

"I'll pull around and get Safe Bet," he finally said. "But there's one thing I have to ask you, something I brought up in the cave but you rather skillfully avoided. Why are you so willing to risk yourself for strangers?"

Lynn rested her hand against the cool metal of the tailgate. He stayed silent, hiding his impatience as she decided how to answer. She'd flat-out said she didn't trust him, and she had no real reason to do so now, but he hoped she'd be honest with him.

Unconsciously, her hand went to her collar. He wondered at the odd habit, but he'd already asked one question and he sensed that another question would be one too many. This one would have to remain a mystery.

She finally took a deep breath and squarely met his eyes. "Because I was a woman who needed help at one time. And I received it. It's my duty to give back. There is so much pain in this world, Grant, and I need to do what I can to ease some of it."

He'd already divined that someone had hurt her, and asked himself what he'd expected? For her to give him names and dates? And why did he want this information? He was stunned by his own answer: Because he wanted to be her avenger. Wanting to know who'd hurt her had tied his gut in a knot . . . because he hungered to hurt him back. He was not a violent man by nature, but he protected what was his and those he loved. This burning urge to hurt was totally foreign to him, as was his urge to wipe the bruises from her soul.

He didn't have that power, the power to restore a soul . . . but he wanted it with an almost physical ache.

He'd read that cold and lack of sleep could cause dementia, which was the only explanation he could come up with for his irrational thoughts. But irrational or not, he couldn't dismiss the desire to defend her, protect her.

"I can't say I understand, of course, because I've never been in your position. I won't insult you by saying that I have." He paused, wishing he had the right words to offer.

"You're right, you can't," she said without rancor. "And to be truthful, you wouldn't want to understand. You don't want to know the fear of wondering if your life is going to be snuffed out on the whim of a man everyone around you thinks is an icon of virtue. You don't want to know what it's like to have your face beaten, your body kicked, your bones broken, to be in so much pain you pray for death because you don't think you can endure the agony."

He had no doubt shock etched his features. He thought he'd been prepared to hear this, but the words pouring from her grabbed his heart in a viselike grip. The need to reach out to her was undeniable, but when he did, she stiffened and he reluctantly dropped his hand back to his side.

"You're right; I can't begin to empathize, but I damn sure wish I could return those experiences in kind to the man responsible," he said honestly, working to control the blinding fury surging through his veins.

She smiled, sadly. "I wished for vengeance once, but it nearly destroyed me. I appreciate your very male, very testosterone-driven urge, but it's not necessary. To be honest, I've had enough violence in my life."

"Why didn't you take him to court?"

Lynn laughed. She couldn't help it. "Oh, yes. The courts. It's so sweet that you believe in justice, Grant. But statistically, most abused women don't get justice. They get platitudes. And restraining orders aren't worth the paper they're written on."

"But—"

"Abusers get out of jail, Grant. And they come back for revenge."

He stared at her, realization dawning. "You went underground."

Lynn tilted her head. "That's not obvious to you? I thought Betsy's notebook—"

"—didn't talk about you except where to find you. I thought you were just . . . just . . ."

"Some bitter ballbreaker? A man-hater trying to cause trouble?"

Grant had to drop his eyes. He was embarrassed that he'd thought exactly those words.

"So you're hiding." Indignation joined the anger he tried to suppress, resentment that such a beautiful woman would be forced to make such a sad choice.

"Just because I've come to terms with what happened doesn't mean I'm stupid. You can never trust an abuser. If the person who hurt me found me again, I have no doubt he'd try to finish the job he started five years ago."

"Then you can be sure I will never let anyone know who you are and what you do here."

"Just get Betsy home, and get her back on course. That's all I need."

"Besides going inside and getting warm."

"Yes, sir," she said dryly, mocking his authoritarian tone.

Grant had the grace to flush.

Their eyes locked as a moment of what-might-have-beens passed between them . . . if they had met under different circumstances, in a different time and a different place. It was as if time became suspended, and their hearts said a sad good-bye to chances lost.

"Go," she said.

He nodded and moved to the driver-side door. He looked back at her, wishing there was . . . more. More time, more words. He had so many things to ask her. Instead, he opened the door and slid behind the wheel.

Betsy gave him a curious glance. "Lynn's a pretty

special person, I think," she said, stroking the quilt on her lap.

He watched the beautiful redhead as she climbed the porch steps. "I think you're absolutely right."

Starting the engine, he fought the oddest sense of sadness as he headed for the barn.

Lynn waited beside Nan until the trailer had disappeared around the back of the house before she collapsed into her favorite rocker.

"Hey, are you all right?" Nan asked, concern coloring her voice.

"I'm okay," Lynn said as she tried to gather the strength to go inside. "Just a bit worn out."

"Emotionally as well as physically, I'd guess." Nan took a seat on the swing. "This ended up well."

"Much better than I expected, certainly," Lynn said, fingering her collar absently.

Nan studied her sturdy hands. "You aren't going to leave, are you?"

Lynn considered the question, then shook her head. "I don't think so. I believe our secret is safe with them."

"I'm glad. Very glad. You have too much magic left to perform here."

Lynn rolled her eyes.

"Stop that," Nan scolded. "You can't tell me you don't know that your quilts touch people."

"Of course I know that. But it's not magic. It's only good, old-fashioned comfort."

Nan took a turn rolling her eyes. "Some day you'll believe, Lynn. Some day."

Shrugging, she turned her head to watch for Grant's truck. She knew she should go inside and take a well-deserved shower, but she needed to see him go. She felt a bit silly, but she couldn't let him leave without a wave good-bye. How had she become so connected to a man in twenty-four short hours? It seemed unbelievable, but the facts were there in her soul. Undeniable. Indelible.

She would miss him. The very thought astounded her. Maybe his obvious love and concern for Betsy had caused her abnormal reaction. Maybe his inherent kindness could be blamed. Maybe his confession that he wanted to defend her had made her brain mushy. Whatever the cause, she had felt closer to a complete stranger than she could ever remember feeling toward anyone. She'd thought she was broken; Grant renewed the dream that she might be fixable.

The SUV finally came around the corner, and the pain in her heart increased. Grant and Betsy rolled down their windows and waved, and Lynn waved back, hiding the longing already building in her heart.

Her eyes drank in the stark handsomeness of his face as he drove by, the pure masculine aura of his body. It made her wish for a chance to find out if she could be a woman again, with a man like him. The image of her body, slick with sweat after a session of hot, pounding sex, followed by hours of slow, delicious lovemaking, came as clearly as a photograph into her mind.

Just as Grant reached the driveway, a loud whoop-whoop overhead caught her stunned attention. It obviously caught Grant's as well for he braked to a stop and got out. He jogged over to join her on the porch, taking the steps two at a time.

Lynn watched, amazed, as a helicopter landed in the huge clearing in front of her house. She wanted to ask Grant what was going on, but couldn't with the noise of the rotors drowning out all other sound. She cast him a questioning glance when the gale died down.

"I'll take care of this," he told her, stalking toward the helicopter, his posture rigid. "I told him I didn't need his help."

She edged closer to the porch railing, but froze when she caught a fleeting glimpse of the man in the helicopter. Dread such as she'd prayed she'd never feel again attacked her, but her mind refused to work coherently, to figure out the threat.

With her nerves screaming, and her stomach about to turn inside out, Lynn waited. The sun glaring off the windshield made it difficult for her to see the pilot, yet she continued to watch, in horrified fascination, as the door swung open.

And the devil himself stepped out.

Five

Lynn barely registered Jake's deep, fierce growling, and only by instinct grabbed his collar before he vaulted off the porch. A cold wind sent a shiver up her spine, and skittered red-gold leaves across the lawn. Normally that sure sign of autumn lifted her heart, but not today. The bright sunshine dimmed, as though a cloud had passed overhead, but when she glanced up, not a speck marred the pristine blue sky.

Time became a tableau as everything went into slow motion. Nan moved in to flank Lynn's side. Betsy bailed out of the truck and raced for the porch as if instinct drove her into the shadows.

Before anyone could speak, the sound of a small engine filled the air. The low rumble came in sharp contrast to the recent cacophony of the helicopter, and Lynn nearly cried when Jeremy pulled his four-wheeler to a stop near the porch. Why now, of all times?

Grant acknowledged Jeremy with a nod as he passed, but didn't stop for an introduction. Jeremy vaulted from his seat with the agility of youth.

"Wow, cool helicopter! Who does it belong to?"

The harsh tension on his mother's face caught even

the animated teenager's attention. His smile faded and he looked around, confused.

"Mom, what's going on?"

"Not now, Jeremy," Nan said, her voice tight and brittle. "Please, just go into the house. I'll explain in a while."

"But—"

"Now, Jeremy," she said, brooking no further argument.

With an aggrieved sigh, Jeremy climbed the stairs. Silently, Lynn willed him to move faster into the inconspicuous shadows with Betsy, or inside the house itself. But she knew it didn't matter. Trey never missed a detail.

Light-headedness and the metallic taste of blood from where she'd bitten her lip reminded Lynn to breathe. And when she did, an incalculable flood of terror rose to steal away every moment of happiness she'd gathered and held in her heart like precious flowers.

How was it possible? How could Trey be here, on her very doorstep? For the first year after the attack, Leonard had kept track of Trey through connections and plain, old-fashioned logic. Trey was a hugely successful businessman in Texas. Thanks to the proliferation of computers, and Trey's own Web site that posted updates on his new business ventures, it hadn't been hard to monitor his activities. The second year, after she'd lost Leonard, Lynn had continued to keep tabs on Trey. The third year, she refused to let him rob any more time and energy away from her than he already had, so she'd given the computer to Jeremy and spent her time healing, not playing amateur detective.

Most important, she'd refused to let her fear of Trey leach all the life from her soul. She'd been confident that the last place on earth Trey would hang around was the scene of his crime. He had never spent much time in the area even before his trip down homicide lane, so

she certainly hadn't expected him to do so after he'd
dumped her body in the remotest corner of his property.
That was such basic, common sense she'd never questioned the conclusion. Besides, his company had never
developed anything this far west. All his projects were
in Austin, Dallas, and Houston, where the big money
resided.

So what was he doing back in the heart of the hill
country? Back where he'd attempted murder?

Trey jogged the few yards from the helicopter to
where Grant stood, and looked at the people gathered
above him. Trey's eyes met hers, cutting through her
like the slice of a knife, more cold than the Canadian
wind swirling through the trees.

A smile she'd prayed never to see again as long as
she lived edged the full, sensual mouth that had once
whispered loved words in her ears . . . and threats of
death.

Lynn took short, tiny breaths to control a violent nausea. She watched, horrified, as Trey inventoried the situation in a leisurely glance. His eyes panned Nan's
truck, then Nan, then Jeremy's tall, lank form. The acid
of despair burned in her throat. By their stalwart presence, the people she loved were in dire danger.

She would never forgive herself if anything happened
to them.

A voice in the back of her head screamed, "Run!
Hide!" But her feet seemed glued to the floor. She knew
she was practically crushing her friend's hand, but from
the moment Nan slipped her fingers into Lynn's cold
grasp, she'd held on for dear life . . . and tried to pray.

Controlling Jake demanded the rest of her strength.

With deliberate coolness, Trey directed his attention
to Grant. "Did you have any luck?"

Grant's tall, lean body was taut with anger, giving his
posture a military bearing. He looked like a general

about to dress down a soldier. "Yes, I did. But I also asked you not to come unless I called."

"Hey, buddy, don't thank me." Trey chuckled, giving Grant a light punch to the shoulder. "I'm glad to help. After all, we've got a business venture to get off the ground. Anything I could do to keep down delays is always a bonus."

Clearly, gratitude was the last thing on Grant's mind, but either Trey was being his usual, calculating self, or he was unbelievably obtuse. Knowing him, Lynn was sure the former was the case. Trey never did anything out of altruism.

Then her brain replayed what he'd said. A business venture? Grant and Trey were business partners?

God above! She'd been pouring her heart out to a man in bed with evil incarnate. She'd fed him, let him use one of her quilts, been concerned about him. She'd had a fantasy, no matter how fleeting, of resting in his strong arms.

She'd let him kiss her!

Lynn stumbled back into a chair, hugging Jake close to her with both her arms. Jake's growl deepened, his fangs bared wickedly, and she fought the temptation to let him go and do as his instincts commanded. Instead, she held him tightly, needing him against her more than life itself.

"That's him, isn't it?" Nan whispered, placing her hand on Lynn's shoulder.

She nodded woodenly, feeling Jeremy's sharp curiosity emanating from behind her. She knew he was puzzled by their strange behavior, but there was nothing she could do about that. How could she explain absolute evil to a young man who was still so very innocent?

With Jake before her and Nan on her left, Lynn searched for some measure of reassurance, only to find an aching certainty that her life had been irrevocably changed in the proverbial, clichéd blink of an eye. The warm world she'd created was crumbling like a sand castle at high tide.

She fixated on the fact that her friends were in jeopardy, and terror held her in thrall. She should never, never have asked Nan to help her. Lynn berated herself that if she'd just figured out a way to take care of things by herself, Nan would be safe at the shop and Jeremy would be explaining why he was back early from his trip to Houston.

Lynn was appalled that her instincts had been so horribly wrong. Again. For the first time in five years, she'd let her guard down, and the results were devastating. Hell had come for another visit.

With calculated timing, Trey cast her a long look. Then he slowly turned away. "Well, I seem to be intruding. I'll just head on home, since you've got everything under control."

Grant gave one sharp nod, and turned back toward the porch. Either he had not seen Trey's outstretched hand, or chose to forego a final handshake. Lynn didn't particularly care either way, but it was one of those details her mind seized on at the expense of other things ... such as oxygen.

Trey took his time returning to the helicopter and climbing into the pilot's seat. After he put on ear protectors, the engine wound up. After what seemed an eternity to Lynn, he finally took off. She would have sworn she could feel Trey's eyes boring into her, even though the distance and the sunshine reflecting off the windshield made that impossible. She finally let Jake go, and he bounded into the yard, barking ferociously at the retreating bird.

Grant searched Lynn's face, clearly puzzled by her reaction. "What in the hell is going on, Lynn? You're white as a sheet."

She pulled her shoulders back, fighting to hold herself together. She'd collapse as soon as he was gone, but for now, she shrugged and presented him with her best poker face.

"You look scared to death," he pressed.

"I can't see how that matters. You've done what you came to do. Please, just go."

Betsy came out from behind the ficus tree, her quilt clutched around her with white-knuckled fingers. "Grant, please take me home."

Lynn could see he was torn between the plea in his sister's voice and his curiosity. She made no attempt to alleviate his dilemma, though. All she cared about was getting them the hell away from her, off her land. Land that had revived her, nurtured her, and fed her, given her peace and years of comfort.

Land she was about to abandon.

The bitter reality that she was about to lose everything she'd worked so hard for brought a welcome, sustaining surge of anger. It infuriated her to accept that she had no choice but to leave. Trey knew she was alive, and she doubted she had much time to make her escape. That he had given no hint of recognition to anyone but her was hardly surprising, not when he undoubtedly had plans to come back and succeed where he'd once failed.

Lynn stood and gathered her courage. "Good luck, Betsy. Have a good life."

With surprising strength, Betsy turned to her brother. "Grant, could you please get the truck started? I'd like to say good-bye in private."

Astonishment crossed Grant's features, followed by a fierce frown, but with a tip of his hat to Lynn and Nan, he returned to his SUV.

Betsy threw herself into Lynn's arms. "I'm so sorry. I've done something awful, haven't I?"

Lynn gave the girl a reassuring pat on the back. "It's all right," she lied, unwilling to traumatize Betsy with the truth, or make the girl feel guilty about things that couldn't be changed now.

With anguished tears in her eyes, Betsy shook her head. "No, it's not. He's going to hurt you."

The premonition in her voice made Lynn shiver. "Listen to me, Betsy. There's one thing I can promise you. I'll never be hurt again. Not by the man in the helicopter, not by anyone."

Betsy tried to smile, but it came out weak. "You're being too kind to me, considering the damage I've done. I'll leave, but I'll never forget you, Lynn, or what you did for me. I'm going to be all right now."

Lynn pulled a smile of her own from the depths of her reserves. "Then this was all meant to be. Don't fret. I'll be okay." She paused. "But, Betsy, please listen to me. I must ask you not to talk about this to Grant."

"But—"

"Please, please promise me you'll do this."

"Well, okay," Betsy said with obvious reluctance. "But be careful, Lynn. That man . . . scared me."

"Go," she said gently, giving Betsy a push.

Betsy had just made it back to the car when Grant's door opened and he came up the stairs again. Grinding her teeth together to hide her frustration, she waited, wondering if he was ever going to leave so she could get on with the urgent business at hand.

"Lynn, I just wanted to apologize before I left. I didn't know V. T. was going to show up here."

"I'm not sure what you want me to say, Grant."

He shrugged awkwardly. "I guess I'm not sure, either. I just wanted you to know that I'm sorry. And if there's anything I can do to help rectify this situation—"

"There's not. But your offer is appreciated."

He stared at the floor for a moment, then back at her, as if he were reluctant to leave, but there was no way she was going to encourage him to stay. In fact, she hoped her signal was loud and clear that the conversation had ended.

Finally, he gave her a curt nod and left. This time she

didn't move until the trailer lights had rounded the bed in the drive and disappeared from sight.

"Lynn?"

Jeremy's voice was frightened, but he was trying so hard to be adult, to be a man, that she felt like laughing and crying at the same time.

"Your mom'll explain things to you, sweetie. I just can't right now."

He accepted her gentle rebuff and stepped back. Nan moved forward at the same time.

"I've got a lot to do," Lynn said, scouring the front of her property with hungry eyes, trying to memorize every tree, every bush, every hanging plant on the eaves. She would never see this place again, and even though she hadn't moved a foot yet, she already felt the loss deep in her heart.

Pulling herself together, she turned and faced Jeremy and Nan. "Okay, troops, I need you. I'm so sorry to involve you both—"

"If you say another word about that I'm going to be very upset with you," Nan scolded, her eyes misting with tears. "And you don't want me to get cranky."

Lynn managed a weak laugh at Nan's silly threat, and forced herself not to cry, especially with Jeremy watching so intently. With a hand on the boy's shoulder, she met his innocent brown eyes. No matter how often he combed his wavy blond hair, it was perennially mussed, and she gave in to the urge to brush a lock of bangs off his forehead. She was going to miss his gentle aw-shucks grin more than she could imagine. He'd been a great help to her, and a sweet friend.

"Jeremy, I need you to take care of Sassy. She's about to foal so I have to leave her. I'll send your mom Sassy's papers as soon as I can so she can transfer the title into your name."

"Lynn, where are you goi—"

"Don't ask questions. Just listen. Please go get Hot

Shot from your place. I don't need a saddle, but I do want your saddlebags. Bring the horse and the bags back here, and if you will, saddle Trouble for me and have him waiting out back. Would you do this for me?"

"I'll do anything for you, Lynn," he said, hurrying to his four-wheeler. He started the engine and looked up mournfully. His heart was in his eyes and for a second, Lynn wasn't sure she could bear one more tear in her soul. He drove away, his shoulders drooping. Lynn had never pretended Jeremy was hers, but if she'd ever had a son, she would have wanted him to be just like the young man about to disappear around the curve.

Lynn found a chuckle somewhere in the midst of her pain. "I'm gonna miss that boy," she confided to Nan. "He gave my ego a real boost."

"He's got a major crush on you, you know."

She nodded. "I know. And I hate hurting his feelings."

"Are you kidding?" Nan asked, following Lynn into the house. "You've been wonderful! Kind and patient, but never crushing his ego. As his mother, I appreciate that more than you know."

They wrapped their arms around each other and held on.

"Oh, Nan, what am I going to do without you?"

"You're going to be fine. And maybe, someday, you can come back here. We'll pick up like you never left."

Tears rolled slowly down Lynn's face as she backed away and turned to the tiny second bedroom. She couldn't talk as she looked at her desk on one side of the room, and her quilting center on the other. Her throat was too tight and her heart too hurt. With determination, she wiped her face and opened a drawer in her rolltop, searching until she found the folded papers she'd put away years before.

"Here's my power of attorney, Nan. You can keep the place or sell it if you need to when tax time comes around."

"I will not," Nan said hotly. "I'll take care of this for you, so you'll always have a home."

"Nan, we can't be sentimental. You do what you have to do. Don't let this property be a burden. Sell it and put the money in Jeremy's college fund. Or expand the store. Do something so that I know I'm paying you back for all you've done for me."

Nan's face was intractable. "We will not discuss this. Let's get you packed." She went to retrieve the satchels they had just stuffed the day before, and took it upon herself to re-pack them with more food and water.

With Nan taking care of her provisions, Lynn became a whirlwind, pulling money and jewelry from hidden stashes, folding warm clothes and finding her extra boots. She took survival supplies from the storage cabinet, pausing when she pulled out a pack of heavy-duty thermal underwear designed especially for wilderness camping, and remembered as if it had been yesterday when she'd sent in the order. She'd prayed she'd never have to use them, or any of the other supplies she'd collected over the years, but it seemed her prayers hadn't been granted.

She added blankets made of a reflective material that seemed impossibly thin to the pile. She picked up her survival knife next and pulled it from its sheath. The wicked-looking blade had a handle with formed finger-holes for maximum grip, and an edge that would slice through anything short of stone or steel.

Compound bow. Arrows. Retractable fishing rod. Waterproof first aid kit. The rest of her water purification tablets.

As the pile grew, so did the ache in her heart. Leonard had taught her how to use it all. How to survive. But at what cost? When would she be able to stop surviving and start living?

She pulled her shoulders up from their slump, and sniffed back a fresh wave of tears. They were a weakness she couldn't afford. She forced herself to focus as she checked the expiration dates on the antibiotics and pain medicines in their protective cases.

Lynn barely noted when Jeremy returned, but was grateful when Nan went with him to the stables to prepare the horses.

She needed the silence.

As she continued to work, the room began to swim and Lynn sat down, clutching the arms of her chair as a wave of dizziness overcame her. She reached instinctively for the comfort of her needle, and the instant her fingers found the tiny piece of metal, light flashed before her eyes, as another vision overtook her . . .

. . . A young woman sat on the front seat of a Conestoga wagon and Lynn knew somehow this dark-haired girl was a newlywed. She didn't look old enough to be dating, much less the wife of the strapping young man with a huge grin on his face who moved forward to take her in his arms, swinging her around in a circle.

As the man moved off, an elderly woman came into the picture, holding out a small box and notebook.

"This is all I have to give you, Charlotte, my child. You must never give up your dreams."

Charlotte took the box and hugged the woman tightly. "Of course I won't, Granny Mae! I'm about to embark on a grand adventure, and when we get to Colorado, I'm going to start having babies. Dozens of them!"

Mae touched the girl's cheek, a pale smile gracing the old woman's face, but didn't respond.

Putting her hand over the weathered one, Charlotte smiled as tears formed in her eyes. "You were so good to me. You couldn't have loved me more if you'd been my real granny. I wish you'd change your mind and come with us."

Looking off into the distance, Mae shook her head.

"Well, you take care of yourself, Gran. You hear? I'll write you. I promise."

Mae accepted a kiss and walked away, her shoulders slumped.

The scene shifted. The once white canvases that had covered the wagons were now black. Wood frames smoldered. Bodies lay everywhere.

Charlotte rocked back and forth on her knees beside the burly young man. An arrow protruded from his chest.

In quick succession, more images came. Of a funeral. Of a passing of seasons. Of Charlotte, now a woman, running a boardinghouse full of tired miners, passing her evenings with a needle in her hand and a quilt on her lap. Men tried to court her, but each time she sent them away, and went to her lonely room to pick up a tintype of the handsome young man . . .

The last thing Lynn saw was the needle—*her* needle— being placed in a case and packed into a trunk.

Gasping for breath, Lynn sat bolt upright, her eyes clearing. The increasing number of these flashes disturbed her deeply, and she wished she knew what was causing them. Now, though, was certainly not the time for her mind to go wandering down fantasy trails.

"Lynn? Are you all right?"

She forced a smile as Nan and Jeremy pushed into the room, worried expressions on both their faces. "I'm okay. Just a bit light-headed. I need to get something to eat."

"We have the horses ready."

Lynn stood and pulled Nan and Jeremy close. "Thanks for all your help."

They didn't talk much as Lynn forced herself to eat a meal of hot leftovers and a protein drink. She topped off her Thermos with strong tea, and carefully tightened down the lid.

Jake whined softly from his place by her feet. She
knelt down and hugged him. "You can't go this time,
boy."

He barked sharply, as if arguing.

"I'm sorry. It'll be cold, rough going and your old
bones just aren't up to it."

He barked again, pressing closer to swipe his tongue
over her chin.

With her heart breaking, she reached for the leash on
the counter and clipped it on his collar. She could barely
see as she handed Nan the lead.

"Please go," she said, hardy able to speak.

Nan gave her a tear-filled hug. "You take care of
yourself. And get me a message as soon as you can."

"I will."

Mother and son walked away, and Lynn tried to close
her ears to Jake's heart-rending whine.

When they were gone, she looked out over the horizon and felt her stomach tighten. For a moment, she felt
a sense of déjà vu. A mere twenty-four hours ago she'd
been on Trouble, ready to set out into the hill country.
Grant had been there, his broad-shouldered form sitting
confidently in his own saddle, bundled against the coming storm.

This time the weather was with her . . .

. . . and she was completely alone.

The sun was still high when Grant returned Safe Bet to
his stable and unhitched the trailer. He pulled to a stop
in front of the house, and asked Betsy to wait in the
truck while he spoke to Murdock. She agreed readily,
surprising Grant when she said with vehemence that she
never wanted to see *that man* again.

Only an overburdened sense of courtesy had him stopping at the house at all. He was royally ticked off at
Murdock for interfering, and he couldn't stop thinking
about how upset Lynn had been. Not that he could blame

her. He'd given her his word that no one would know what had happened, and then Murdock had made his grand entrance.

Stepping on the boards the carpenter had placed on the veranda to protect his work in progress, Grant proceeded to the door. The housekeeper let him in and asked him to wait in the office.

Murdock came in, holding a pistol case and looking harried. He stopped short, in obvious surprise. "Grant! I'm sorry, I don't have time to discuss the house right now."

Grant eyed the gun case, an uneasy feeling settling in his stomach. "Going hunting?"

After a distracted glance at his hands, Murdock seemed to collect himself. In a flash, the harried expression disappeared and in its place came a jovial smile. "Good joke, there. No, just getting ready to clean it, then I've got to head to Austin for a meeting. But you're not here to talk about my gun collection. Your sister is all right?"

"She's fine. I just wanted to let you know I've taken Safe Bet to the stable. He threw a shoe but he's fine."

"Good, good. Glad I could help."

Grant held his tongue. He certainly hadn't offered thanks. "Well, I'll be going. Betsy's waiting in the truck."

"Listen, Grant," Murdock said, escorting him to the front door. "Are you sure I can't talk you into coming with me to dinner this evening? I think I mentioned yesterday that I'm meeting with the bankers I want to finance our project."

"I haven't committed—"

"I know, I know. And I don't want to push, you know that. I was just hoping you'd changed your mind."

Grant decided that Murdock had missed his calling. He should own a string of used car lots that would no doubt have vehicles with heavyweight oil in the engines and odometers rolled back. Not trying to push . . . like hell.

"Nope, no change of mind."

"Well, I'll be back later tonight and have a few things to take care of first thing tomorrow. I'll give you a call and catch you up to speed."

If Grant had any doubts about his decision, they were now gone. Hell would freeze over before he'd do business with Murdock again. The house had neared completion, and once the final punch-out was done, Grant had no intention of speaking to the man again, much less developing a subdivision with him. His gut was redlining in warning, and he would trust his instincts.

Grant got in the SUV and slammed the door. He was good and ready for this day to be over.

Time for life to get back to normal.

Lynn checked Trouble's cinch one last time and gave him a solid pat on the neck. "I'm sorry to do this to you, boy. You deserve a good rest but I'm afraid I just can't give that to you right now."

Glad that no one was around to see, Lynn pulled her box from her pocket and checked the needle one last time. Normally she carried the needle in her collar, but she would take no chances with her most treasured possession as she set out on such an arduous journey. It would stay deep in her pocket, in the case, where it couldn't accidentally slip out. Assured the little piece of metal rested comfortably in its velvet nest, she replaced the lid and—

"Hello, Elizabeth."

Lynn whirled in panic at the sound of that dreadful voice. Her hand went immediately to her belt and she surreptitiously pulled her nun-chaku from her waistband, hiding it between her arm and her side.

"Trey." She managed to sound surprisingly normal.

"I almost waited until tomorrow morning to come

visit, but I was on my way to Austin and something told me I should stop by here first. It looks like I arrived just in time."

"Time for what? To kill me . . . again."

"Liz, Liz . . . There's no need for such histrionics."

Histrionics? She looked at the tall man standing before her, still fit and handsome, the model of civility to the untrained eye, and wondered if someone was going to call out, "Cut. Stop camera." Surely this was either a movie, or a bad dream.

Trey took a step toward her and she backed up quickly.

"Don't come near me, Trey."

"But, Liz—"

"My name is Lynn now."

"That's absurd. I married Elizabeth Dian—"

"Get out of here, Trey. Leave me alone."

"I can't leave you alone, Liz. We're husband and wife. And now that I know you're all right—"

"We've been divorced for years. You left me for dead—"

"No judge can undo our vows, Liz. You know that."

He smiled, and it chilled her.

"I went back, Liz. To find you. But I had to assume you'd been . . . abducted."

Lynn stared at him, gaping. "Abducted? *You* abducted—"

"We needed to talk, and you weren't being cooperative. If you hadn't made me so angry, things could have turned out so much better than they did."

She was speechless. She looked around wildly, wondering what to do. How could she get away . . . ?

"You need to come home with me. I love you. I've always loved you." And with that, he calmly pulled a gun and pointed it at her. "It's time to get things back to normal. Once we've had a chance to talk, I know you'll calm down and any . . . unpleasantness . . . will be forgotten."

She stood motionless, forcing her fear away, becoming cool and logical. Although it was her worst nightmare, she had to get closer to him. She couldn't outrun a bullet, and her only hope was to catch him off guard and disarm him.

Did she have enough training? She'd practiced her martial arts religiously, just as she'd promised Leonard she would, but now that the moment was upon her, could she do it?

Her cool resolve became cold certainty. She'd do whatever it took. She'd never go willingly into this man's clutches ever again.

It took every ounce of skill she had to force a smile. "Of course, Trey. We'll talk." She nodded as she spoke.

"Excellent!" he said, giving her a bright grin.

The gun never wavered.

"My car is a bit far away, I'm afraid," he said apologetically. "I wanted to surprise you so I hid it further down the road."

Lynn was sure there was some logic to this conversation in Trey's warped mind, but knew it was useless to debate with a stalker.

"Of course," she said, reinforcing her flagging smile. She took a tentative step toward him, keeping her chucks between her and Trouble. She prayed the sweat forming on her palms would not make the weapon slip. She tightened her grip until her fingers tingled.

Another step and another prayer brought her almost within range.

"I should probably put the horses up, don't you think?" she asked in the most reasonable tone she could manage, trying to sound unsure and needing his advice.

"They'll be fine. I'll send one of the boys over to take care of them."

Damn! She wanted to get her hands in that pack and

on her throwing stars. If she could get back in the barn, there were any number of items she could use as a weapon. She doubted Trey would consider a garden spade a deadly implement, but she could turn it into one if need be.

"Okay," she said reasonably. "Just let me get some things from my pack—"

"No, Liz. We need to go. I'll have your things brought over."

She took two deep, silent breaths. She had no choice now.

With every appearance of confidence, she took another step closer. Then another.

She waited until he glanced away.

With lightning speed, she spun the free end of the nun-chaku and let it fly against Trey's wrist. He cried out in pain as the gun dropped to the ground.

His face was filled with betrayal and rage.

Spinning, she swept his feet from under him, and reached for the gun as he went down with a grunt.

"Lying bitch!" he spat, grabbing her leg to take her down with him.

Her fingers brushed the gun, but he pulled her toward him with a hard jerk. She tried to surge forward, but his grip was too strong.

Reassessing, she turned over, and let the chucks fly again, this time aiming true for the side of his head.

The sound of solid wood connecting against his skull was sickening.

As was the sound of his head thudding against the ground.

She scrambled up and grabbed the gun, whirling toward him. She was shaking so badly she dropped her chucks and used both hands to steady the revolver.

Then she realized his eyes were closed. She stared, wondering if she'd killed him before she saw blood slowly dripping down his temple. He was still alive.

Blood didn't bead unless there was a pulse.

For a moment she couldn't think. Didn't know what to do.

She held the gun, her finger shaking against the trigger.

So much pain. So much fear. And it would never end. Never. She'd never really been free. She'd just deluded herself into believing she could have something resembling a normal life.

Anger coursed through her, filling every cranny not already occupied by fear. She'd spent five years learning how to breathe again, and in one instant, he'd stolen her peace. Again. No one should have the right to do that to another human being.

She steadied her aim, taking a deep breath.

It would only take—

No!

She jerked her hands down to her sides.

She wouldn't. She couldn't.

If she gave in to the voice in her head urging her to finish him off then she would be no different than Trey. She knew she couldn't live with that, could never forgive herself, if she became a murderer.

She stared at him, horrified at just how far she'd nearly let this demon drive her.

It took a moment, but she found her center again. She took slow, deep breaths and considered what to do. There was no telling how long he'd be unconscious so she needed to act fast. She wasn't strong enough to move him, but with every muscle straining, she turned him over. With a length of rope from her saddlebag, and a lot of grunting, she had his hands and feet tied.

She retrieved the gun she'd placed on the ground and raced toward the barn. Without another moment's hesitation, she wrenched open the lid of the barrel she kept for used motor oil and threw the gun in. The heavy metal made a dull thunk as it hit the bottom.

Replacing the lid, she raced back to Trouble and threw herself into the saddle. She grabbed the reins of the pack horse and kicked them into action.

She couldn't help but look back. He lay as she'd tied him. Unmoving.

As she kicked Trouble into a run, she wondered if she'd made a mistake in letting Trey live . . .

Six

Grant tapped his fingers on the steering wheel as he drove. Surprisingly, he and Betsy had hardly spoken since they had started the drive back to their parents' house. But their silence was comfortable . . . a stark change from the last time they had made this type of drive. Yet, the closer they drew to home, the more agitated Betsy became.

As for himself, he kept fighting the need to turn the car around and check on Lynn one last time. He couldn't seem to shake the sensation that something was wrong.

That was silly. Of course something was wrong. He'd brought a stranger to her property, and he couldn't blame her for being mad. After all, he'd assured her that no one would know about what had happened and then Murdock had set a helicopter down on her lawn. He'd put her operation in jeopardy, and she had every right to be angry.

Several times he'd been on the verge of bringing up his concern with Betsy, but each time he'd vetoed the urge before he could get a word out. Betsy had enough on her mind without him adding unfounded worries. No sense burdening her with his guilt.

Besides, their parents were waiting for them to arrive,

anxious to see that Betsy was indeed okay. If he turned around, he'd only delay the inevitable and for Betsy's sake, they needed to get it over with. The anticipation of their parents' displeasure had to be as nerve-wracking for her as the actuality.

As he pulled into the driveway of the palatial home he'd built them on the shores of Lake Travis Grant looked at his father standing with his mother in the doorway and realized exactly what he'd look like in about thirty years . . . if he was lucky. He'd still be trim, his hair would be a distinguished silver, and his mind would still be sharp and keen. He might even be a United States District Judge. His mother was still beautiful and healthy, fighting her age every step of the way, and wore her mantle as a society matron proudly.

As to be expected, the elder Majors waited until everyone assembled inside before launching into Betsy. Those of breeding did not air their linen on the front lawn . . .

"Young lady, do you know how much stress you've caused your mother—"

"And your brother, let's not forget. I can't believe you've put us all through this again—"

Grant had always been in on the tag-team effort to get Betsy to open her eyes, but this time, he defended her.

"Whoa, Dad! Mom! Listen a minute."

They stopped and turned to Grant, their surprise evident. Grant wasn't cooperating with the expected replay of an old scene, and for the first time, he realized how pointless their harangues had been. Betsy had changed when she'd been ready to, and all their griping had only made things worse.

"Betsy's had a . . . well, revelatory experience. I think things are going to be different this time."

"Well, I should certainly hope so. My nerves have been stretched beyond—"

"Mom," Grant said gently, "Let it go. Give Betts a chance to show you that she's changed. She's promised me she'll go see the doctor tomorrow, if you want her to. Whatever it takes to show you—all of us—that she's serious."

Betsy smiled her thanks and placed a kiss on Grant's cheek. With the wind taken out of their sails, there was nothing left to do but prepare for a civilized dinner in the formal dining room. Grant had to smile at the pretentiousness of it all, but his parents had a right to their own foibles. He might be just as happy with dinner on a TV tray with the game on, but this was their home and he respected their wishes for proper attire and formal settings.

After helping Betts get her things to her room, they went their separate ways to freshen up and rest until dinnertime. When they reconvened in the dining room, the mood was restored to a tolerable, if not comfortable, level.

As Betsy told her story over the course of the meal, sounding confident and almost serene, Grant's pride in her grew, as well as his certainty that a dramatic shift had occurred. Her new maturity made her seem, paradoxically, both older and younger at the same time.

The excellent wine served with the scaloppine di pollo relaxed Grant and made him realize just how weary he was. It had been a hell of a couple of days, and the tension had finally caught up with him. He hadn't gone to bed early in a decade, but it suddenly seemed the right decision. The drive to his home on the north side of Austin was decidedly uninviting, and he certainly didn't want to face the mountain of paperwork waiting on his desk. With a quick word to the housekeeper, he knew his bed here at his parents' house would be ready before the tiramisu was finished.

After coffee had been served, he gave wishes for a restful sleep to his parents, a kiss to Betsy's forehead, and then headed for the room that was kept prepared for his infrequent stays. He attributed his decision to stay also to the desire to be near Betsy, in case she needed a little additional moral support.

Grant shut the door behind him and looked around the room that had been done by the most expensive decorator this side of New York. As he'd expected, a fire had been lit, and the bed turned down. The decor certainly didn't reflect his style, but then, he didn't live here. The heavy brocades and dark woods may be considered masculine, but he preferred light woods and cool tones, but he decorated for comfort, not ratings among the social elite.

Grant used the phone to check his messages, and listened dispassionately to a long, terse message from Veronica cataloging every date he'd missed or rescheduled, and ending with a rather cold pronouncement that maybe they should reconsider their standing. Grant had news for Veronica if she thought her little guilt trip had done anything more than sign the death warrant to their relationship. He had no use for manipulative people.

He wondered if he should introduce Murdock to Veronica . . .

He picked up the newspaper he'd swiped from his father's study on the way upstairs and settled on the chaise lounge to catch up on current affairs. He'd just gotten to the sports section when a knock sounded at his door.

"Grant?"

"Come on in, Betts. What's up?"

Betsy scraped her fingers through her freshly washed hair and tugged at the belt to her robe. "I gave my word," she whispered mournfully, staring at the window.

Dread filled Grant. He'd been anticipating something all evening, but he hadn't been able to identify the nagging sense of impending trouble. Now it was pounding on him like a sledgehammer wielded by a demolition crew. It was about Lynn, he was sure of it.

Grant stood and put an encouraging hand on her shoulder. "Betts, please." It made sense that her dilemma somehow involved Lynn.

"She's in trouble, Grant. I just know it."

"Trouble? How?"

"From the guy in the helicopter. She was scared of him. Really scared—I could see it in her eyes."

"She knows Murdock?"

"I'm sure of it. She wouldn't tell me anything, but it was clear that something was wrong. She seemed to be barely breathing."

Grant scrubbed his jaw. He had sensed fear in Lynn, but he'd assumed it was just her reaction to a strange man on her property, just as she'd been afraid of him at first. It hadn't occurred to him that she could possibly have known Murdock personally.

"Please, Grant. I know you think I'm a ditz, but we owe her. *I* owe her. Please say you'll check on Lynn."

Grant took his sister's hand. "I promise. First thing in the morning I'll drive back out and make sure everything's okay."

Betsy relaxed and rested her head against his chest for a minute.

"Thanks, big brother. For everything."

"Yeah, yeah," he said, giving her a little push. "Go to bed, brat."

With a giggle he was delighted to hear, she left for her own room.

His smile faded into a frown as the door shut quietly behind Betts. He considered heading right back out, but forced himself to stay put. With all he'd put Lynn through, it would only add insult to injury if he scared her witless in the middle of the night.

Worry joined him in the bed, and the sleep Grant had been sure was moments away didn't come.

• • •

It was dark when he stirred, the grass cold against his face.

He realized he was tied when he tried to use his arms.

With slow deliberation, he tested the restraints. It took time, but he eventually slipped his arms from under his legs. It took much longer to slip the knots, but he was a patient man.

He stretched as he stood, putting a hand to the sticky mess on his forehead. Stepping cautiously, he headed toward the house. Best to clean up before he made his next move. Maybe she had some milk to ease his aching stomach. It was the least she owed him after this little fiasco.

He didn't hurry.

There was no need.

He'd find her.

Grant ended up rising before the sun. Sleep had eluded him for most of the night, his mind too occupied with thoughts of Lynn to let him rest. How did she know Murdock? If they were acquainted, as Betsy seemed so sure, why hadn't they said anything to each other when they had all be standing on Lynn's lawn?

He knew that Murdock had been involved in a nasty divorce. He'd volunteered the information over a couple of beers when they'd begun tossing around the idea of the subdivision. Come to think of it, the man tended to volunteer a lot of information about himself, and Grant had thought that strange from day one. He wasn't the kind of person to offer personal information, so he assumed others wouldn't either. Now that Grant thought about it, it was as though Murdock were trying too hard. Just one more clue confirming his instinct that Murdock wasn't trustworthy.

So, again, how did Lynn know the man? Old lovers? The thought made Grant grimace. Still, if Murdock were an old lover, could he have been the one—

Grant shook his head. While he had decided he would not be doing business with the guy, he didn't want to believe Murdock was capable of the violence that had hurt Lynn so badly. Surely, Grant reasoned, he would have recognized that kind of evil in a person, sensed something so very wrong.

His conscience prickled as he considered Betsy's desperate plea. She'd been truly frightened. Had she seen something that he hadn't?

With a grunt, he kicked off the blankets and got out of bed. A quick shower restored his energy, and he wrote a note to his parents explaining his sudden exit. He told himself he was going to feel stupid when he showed up at Lynn's and everything was all right, but he climbed into the SUV anyway, and headed toward Winterhaven. The morning sun crept above the horizon behind him and there was a definite nip in the air.

As he drove, Grant tried to convince himself that Betsy had misread the situation. Undoubtedly, Lynn would be quite displeased to see him, especially after Murdock's appearance yesterday, but at least Grant's conscience would be cleared once he established that Lynn was all right. Then he could get to work and get his life back on track.

Tension tightened his neck as he pulled up to Lynn's house. No Jake barking. No lights on. No movement whatsoever.

He shrugged, thinking maybe Lynn was a late riser. Or a very early one.

Grant found himself oddly reluctant to get out, but he thrust his misgivings aside. He went to the door and knocked, checking the expanse of the front yard while he waited. When he received no response, he headed around the back only to find the same stillness there.

As he continued forward, he kicked something in the grass. He bent down and picked up a small box wet with the morning dew. Opening the lid, he saw a tiny needle and he had a flash of the very first moment he'd seen Lynn, the needle catching the sunlight, a quilt on her lap. With a shrug, he put the box in his shirt pocket and headed for the barn.

It was completely empty. He would have assumed she'd gone for a ride on Trouble except for the fact that the pregnant mare was neither in the stable, nor in the pasture.

The hairs on the back of his neck were standing straight up as he ran to the house, skidding to a stop when he saw the patio door.

It had been kicked in.

He stared at the savaged portal, not wanting to believe his eyes as he studied the splintered jamb. Thinking of the gun he had under his front seat, Grant regretted not bringing it with him. He almost went back to get it, but decided against it. If Lynn was in trouble, he wasn't wasting one precious second.

Swinging the door open silently, he listened expectantly, but no sound came from the interior. Piles of debris littered the floor where a hutch had been knocked over, and glass and shattered stoneware crunched under his boot as he stepped inside. He winced, but kept going, afraid that at any moment he would find something that would haunt him forever. The image of Lynn lying somewhere, hurt, burned behind his eyes.

The place was a wreck. Furniture was upended, and at first he thought the place had been ransacked. Then he realized it was as if an animal had gone berserk, destroying things out of pure, senseless violence.

He figured he should have been relieved when he found no one in the house, but he wasn't. Sprinting out of the house to his truck, Grant drove like a demon into Winterhaven. Shops opened early in a tourist town, so it was no surprise that the morning sun also brought COME IN signs aplenty.

Which explained why his gut took another twist when

he arrived at Nan's Treasures and saw that the windows
were dark. The instant he parked, Grant jumped out to
test the door, grunting in frustration when he found it
locked. He stared into the street, realizing he had no idea
where Nan lived.

His next stop would have to be the sheriff's office, to
report Lynn's disappearance and the damage to her
house, but he doubted the deputy who took the report
would help him find Nan. Grant was well aware he was
an outsider in a small town, and would probably be
treated with courteous distrust.

Feeling equally foolish and frustrated, he looked into
the shop windows one last time. Cozy lamps, obviously
left on as night-lights, allowed him to see a bit of the
interior. He was about to leave when something caught
his attention. Shielding his eyes, he pressed his face
closer to the paned glass and noted quilts and dolls and
knickknacks galore.

He had just about given up when he realized the boot
on the floor by the counter was attached to a leg. It was
no prop.

Without hesitation, Grant grabbed a flashlight from
his truck and hurried back to knock out a pane of glass.
He reached in and felt impatiently for the locks, finally
managing to free a dead bolt and a chain by touch. Shoving the door open, he raced around the counter.

Nan lay on her side, her face bruised and smeared
with blood from a cut lip, a quilt clutched in her hands.

Falling to his knees, Grant gently touched her shoulder. His first instinct was to pull her into his lap, but he
had the presence of mind to consider that she may have
an injured neck. He could paralyze her for life if he
moved her. He gave a quick glance to the counter, snarl-
ing when he saw the phone had been pulled completely
out of the wall.

He patted his pocket and cursed when he pulled out
the needle box instead of the cell phone. He tossed it on

the counter and patted again. He hissed in frustration. He'd left the phone in the truck.

"Nan? Nan, can you hear me?"

She groaned, her eyes fluttering open. She tried to turn her head toward his voice, but Grant placed a gentle hand against her cheek to prevent her. He didn't want her to hurt herself. "Grant," she managed in a croaking voice.

"Are you all right? Can you move?"

"Hurt," she whispered, her eyes squeezing shut.

"I know," he soothed gently, giving her shoulder the lightest of rubs. "I'm going to get you to the hospital."

"Trey," Nan said, trying to open her eyes again.

"You want a tray?"

"No," she said, her forehead creased in frustration. "Trey. Going after Lynn."

As if he were there again, Grant saw Murdock's study in his mind's eye, and the housekeeper coming in. "Mr. Trey?" she'd said, her voice thick with a Spanish accent. Then he remembered the embossed name on the letterhead: Vernon Tremaine Murdock, III.

Trey.

"Nan, are you saying V. T. Murdock is Trey?"

She nodded, barely, and swallowed. "Lynn's ex."

"Nan, Murdock's ex-wife was named Elizabeth, not Ly—"

Grant sat back on his heels and closed his eyes against his own stupidity. Lynn had been abused. She ran an underground railroad. The last thing in the world she would have used was her real name. He recalled again the fear in Lynn's face when she'd seen Murdock. It had been no normal fear of men: it had been abject terror hidden behind bravado. Dear God, Betsy was right.

"Nan, did Murdock do this to you?"

She nodded, just another small movement of her head. She licked her lips. "Came in for Lynn." A tear slid down her swollen cheek. "Jeremy," she croaked.

"Jeremy's the boy who came on the four-wheeler yesterday?" Grant asked. "Your son?" he surmised.

"Yes," she whispered. "Should be okay. At the . . .
ag . . . farm."

Grant frowned. "Nan, I'm sorry, I don't understand."

She struggled to sit up.

"Nan, stay down. You're hurt."

"Have to . . . get . . . to Jeremy."

"You said the ag farm." He had a vague memory from
high school of the Four H club having its own land
where they kept the animals they raised for show.

She nodded. "Call the Sheriff. Ted. He knows Jeremy."

She wouldn't be pacified until he helped her sit up
and lean against the counter. He took a moment to flip
some switches and with the better lighting, he saw that
she was badly bruised, but didn't appear to be bleeding.
Of course, he couldn't see internal injuries, and knew he
had to get her to medical help.

He hurried out the door and flagged down the first
person he saw on the boardwalk. "Call the sheriff and
an ambulance. A woman's been hurt in here."

The man raced into a shop and Grant returned to
Nan's side.

"Nan, what about Lynn. Where is she?"

"Ran. Yesterday."

"She's alone?"

It stunned him how powerfully the image came of
Lynn, solitary, on horseback came to him. And how vi-
olently he reacted to the thought of her being hunted,
isolated. Vulnerable.

"Nan, I can help her. Tell me where she's gone."

"Can't. Gave my word."

Grant pounded a fist into his thigh in frustration. First
Betts, now Nan. "Nan, listen to me. If the damage I saw
at Lynn's place, and on your face, is any indication of
Murdock's intention, she's needs help. She can't face
him by herself."

Nan's struggle played out on her bruised face. "He's crazy," she whispered.

"No," Grant said fiercely. "That's too easy an excuse for him. He knows exactly what he's doing." Grant took Nan's hand. "Let me help."

She studied him out of the eye not swollen shut. "You're partners with him."

"No, I'm not. I was considering doing a joint venture to develop a subdivision, but from the beginning I had reservations. Now I know why. Please, Nan. Trust me."

She swallowed again. "I don't . . . think . . . you'll find her, but I'll draw a map." She appeared a bit more alert as she cleared her throat. "Lynn's heading for the piney woods. East."

"Thank you, Nan. You won't regret this."

A car came to a gravel-grinding stop outside and in seconds, the room swarmed with people. A tall man in a tan uniform raced over and knelt on Nan's other side, eying Grant suspiciously.

She gave a lopsided smile. "Ted. How'd you get here . . . so fast?"

"Magic," he said with a gentleness belying the blazing anger in his face as he took in her injuries. "I was just over on the highway headed for the courthouse when I heard the call on the radio."

"Lucky me," she whispered with a tiny chuckle.

"Hey," he teased, gently brushing her hair back from her forehead, "who says there's never a cop around when you need one?"

She smiled at his weak joke. "Ted, Jeremy's at the ag farm. Please. Get him."

He immediately reached for the radio attached to his belt. He gave the order for Jeremy to be picked up and taken to the station, and that he be guarded until Ted himself arrived.

A tear slipped down Nan's face.

"Hey, now," Ted said, "none of that. Jeremy's going

to be fine. But you need to tell me what's going on."

Grant answered. "A man named V. T. Murdock did this. He also broke into Lynn Powell's place."

"Who are you?" Ted asked suspiciously, his face hard.

"Ted," Nan said, "this is Grant Major." She took several shallow breaths and wrapped her arm around her bruised ribs. "He's a . . . friend."

Grant sent her a grateful smile. All it would have taken was one word, and he had no doubt he'd be cooling his heels in a jail cell.

"What happened?" Ted asked, still obviously leery of Grant, but more obviously concerned about Nan.

"Lynn's—"

"Murdock is Lynn Powell's ex-husband," Grant interrupted so Nan could save her strength. "He's going to try to kill her."

"And just how do you know this?"

Grant forced down his frustration. "It's a long story and I'm sure Nan can give you all the details. I'm going to go find Lynn and help her."

"Just a minute," Ted said. "You're not going anywhere until I have some details."

"Ted," Nan croaked, her strength obviously weakening, "please let him go. Lynn's in trouble." She looked at Grant. "I told that bastard that she was headed west, to the Davis Mountains. I hope I bought her some time."

"Me, too. You did good, Nan. I'll find her. I have to." Grant met the sheriff's eyes. "I need a horse."

Ted's brow furrowed. "A horse? Why?"

As quickly as he could, Grant explained that Lynn was heading to the piney woods to hide, and had gone on horseback. If he was to find her, he had to follow where a truck couldn't go.

"Ted, please. Just let Grant get to Lynn while you go after Murdock."

When the lawman finally gave a grudging nod, Grant released the breath he'd been holding.

"Hurry, Grant," she begged.

A deputy arrived and received instructions from Ted to take Grant to the county's stable. Grant placed a gentle kiss on Nan's brow, despite the glower he received from the sheriff. Ted promised to protect Nan and Jeremy, and Grant had no doubts the man meant to do exactly that. It was clear the man had more than a professional concern about Nan, and that helped relieve the guilt pounding in Grant's skull. None of this would be happening if he hadn't led Murdock straight to Lynn's doorstep.

"Grant, wait!" He had been about to leave when Nan's voice sent him whirling back around. She held out the quilt she'd been clutching against her. "Take this. It'll protect you."

"What—"

"Don't argue with her," the sheriff said unexpectedly. "When she gets started about these quilts, she won't give up."

Trying to hide his confusion, Grant took the blanket and left again. He didn't deserve such kindness from Nan. He'd brought suffering to her, and to Lynn, and it was clawing at him like a mad grizzly bear. He wanted to wait until medical help arrived to make sure she was going to be okay, but he had to pacify himself with the knowledge that Nan was in good hands.

Lynn was not.

Lynn awoke with a start. She'd overslept? Good God, how could she have overslept at a time like this? Admittedly, the cave was dark, and she'd kept a cold camp, but now the sun was bright outside.

She was only a couple of hours east of Winterhaven. Stopping so soon had felt foolish, but Trouble needed the rest and the last thing she could afford was for him to go lame. Or for him to trip in the dark. So she'd risked camping at her last provisioned cave before heading to the dense pine forest where Leonard had a tiny cabin. No one knew where the cabin was, not even Nan. She knew the direction Lynn was headed, but not her final destination. Nan didn't even know the cabin existed.

It would take her days to get there, but she knew that no one, not even Trey, would be able find her once she made it to her destination and disappeared under a canopy of pine.

With panic-induced speed, she packed the few items she'd taken out last night and hurried to the horses. There hadn't been room for them in the cave, but thankfully, the weather had held. It had been cold, but they'd been fine in their heavy winter coats.

Sweat beaded her forehead by the time she saddled Trouble, and tied the packs on Hot Shot. The sun was much too high for her comfort, fueling her frustration. Her hands were shaking in fear.

When she heard a horse trotting up behind her, she didn't stop to think. She threw herself into the saddle and kicked Trouble into a run. Bless his valiant heart, Trouble responded to the touch of her heels against his flank as though struck by lightning.

Branches whipped at her face as she coaxed Trouble to go as fast as he could on the rough terrain. Her pursuer was determined, though, and she could hear the horse behind her as if it were a demon breathing down her neck.

"Lynn," she heard a male voice shout. "It's Grant! Hold up!"

She risked a quick glance behind her and saw that it was indeed Grant, but fear had her in a stranglehold. She urged Trouble up a hill.

Tears formed in her eyes, and she silently cursed the fates that had allowed her plan to go awry so quickly. She put her hand on her survival knife, determined that if she went, she would do some damage first—

"Lynn!" Grant shouted again. "Nan's been hurt."

Nothing could have stopped her.

Except that.

After a few more yards, she reluctantly reined Trouble in, patting his neck. "Thanks for trying, boy."

Trouble tossed his nose up as if he understood, and she let him have slack to drop his head as he recovered.

Grant reined in next to her, and Lynn felt a stab of guilt when she looked at his lathered horse. The poor animal's sides were heaving like bellows as it tried to catch its breath. Grant had obviously ridden hard and fast to catch her.

"What's wrong with Nan?" she asked suspiciously, keeping her hand on her knife. She felt an odd sense of guilt for doubting him, and couldn't explain an almost dizzying urge to trust him. She forced herself to stay suspicious; her life was at stake here.

"Murdock got to her, trying to find you."

Lynn covered her mouth as a horrified, "No!" came from her tightened throat.

"I should have killed him while I had the chance," she said, her face hardening with resolve. She had to get back to town, to check on Nan. She started to turn Trouble when Grant grabbed her bridle.

"What?" he asked, not letting go when she glared at him.

"He caught me as I was leaving. We scuffled and I knocked him out." She shook her head, reliving the scene of yesterday, not seeing the man before her. "I had his gun in my hands."

She looked down at her fingers. "Why?" she whispered, more to herself than to Grant. "Why couldn't I do it?"

Grant's hand came into her field of vision as he covered her wrist with his warm touch. "Are you seriously asking why you couldn't shoot Murdock? Even I can figure out that you're not made for cold-blooded murder. Of course you couldn't do it."

She cocked her head a bit to the left. "Don't be too sure you know me," she said wryly. "Everyone has a breaking point. I just should have found mine sooner. If I had had more guts then Nan wouldn't have been hurt."

"Lynn, that's nuts. This is not your fault."

She didn't listen to him. Nothing could convince her of what she knew in her heart. She just wished she'd had better instincts yesterday. She had been absolutely positive he'd come straight after her. It wasn't as if she'd had time to cover her trail. There was no reason for him to go after Nan, but that was her first mistake—assigning reason to Trey. And her second mistake was assuming.

Grant misread her silence.

"She's gonna be okay, Lynn. You can't go back there."

"Jeremy—"

"Is fine. He was out at the school farm and the sheriff picked him up. I have the distinct impression that the sheriff is going to take personal responsibility for their safety."

Grant let go of her bridle and gave her time to absorb the information.

"He's coming after you, you know."

She didn't pretend to misunderstand. "What do you think I'm doing out here? Just going for a casual nature hike?" She turned Trouble and headed back to retrieve Hot Shot. Hopefully he hadn't gotten spooked and would be placidly waiting.

Grant followed suit, though he didn't kick his mount into a trot. He caught up with her easily enough as she rounded up the pack horse.

When she saw him, she frowned fiercely. "Leave me alone."

"I can't do that. We need to talk."

"We have nothing to say to each other. Now go away before you slow me down any further."

"I'm not going away," he insisted, urging his mount next to hers. "You're in danger."

Lynn's laugh was more a snort of disgust than merriment. "Really?" she asked with mock surprise. "And what makes you think I need either your revelations or your company?"

"Lynn, stop. Just for a minute."

She reined up and faced him. "What can you possibly have to say to me that's worth my precious time? I've got to get away and you're slowing me down."

"I may have also saved your friend's life. Can that cover five minutes?"

Guilt made her face flush. "Don't use my friends against me. That's low."

"I'll do whatever it takes to get you to listen. Please, Lynn."

"Five minutes," she said, glancing at her watch. "And I'm not kidding."

"If you keep going, he's going to find you. He's got a helicopter and can cover a heck of a lot more ground than you can. Nan directed him toward the west, but it won't take him long to figure out he's been duped and then he'll start a search in this direction."

"Who says he won't keep heading west?"

"It's just logical, Lynn. Please. Let me help you."

She couldn't help laughing. There it was again, that testosterone-driven earnestness. "I appreciate your offer, Grant, but you can't help me. No one can. I have to help myself."

"That's nuts! Murdock is going to find you. If you'll just listen to me, maybe I can help more than you know. I can hide you, if that's what you want. Or I can help you fight him."

"Fight him? Oh, sure," she said with derision. "I'll

just get a restraining order and then everything will be
hunky-dunky."

"Well, at least it's a place to start," he said defen-
sively. "It's the place to begin to reclaim your life so
you don't have to run away. Lynn, my father's a U.S.
judge. He'll help you."

"Grant, Trey tried to kill me," she said, enunciating
each word. "No court in the world can stop a stalker.
Politicians make pretty laws to grab votes, but they have
no teeth. Law enforcement is hamstringed. It all equals
the same thing: victims have no one looking out for
them."

"But—"

"I have no proof, Grant." She closed her eyes and
prayed for patience. "The only man who saw me at the
bottom of a ravine about ten miles from here is dead.
And he wasn't a witness to the crime. All he could have
testified to was the condition my body was in. It's my
word against Trey's, and you can be sure he's got an
alibi." She smiled sadly. "One of us is a pillar of the
community. The other is a woman who's changed her
name and been a recluse for the past five years. Who do
you think a jury will believe?"

She rubbed the heels of her hands against her forehead. "Actually, Grant, forget a trial. No district attorney
in America would take the case to a grand jury for an
indictment in the first place."

"But—"

"This is ridiculous to even discuss!" she said, cutting
her hand through the air between them. "Just go home,
Grant. Forget you ever met me and pray Trey forgets
you as well."

She wasn't sure what she expected. She knew Grant
was the kind of man not easily dissuaded, still, the vehemence in his expression took her aback.

"I'm not leaving you out here."

"Then you're really dooming me. I don't need your

help. I don't need your protection. I need you to go away."

"No."

"Fine. Do what you want. But your horse is exhausted and I can't slow down for you."

"We'll make do."

Tears came to her eyes, stunning her. Maybe it was the stress, maybe the fear, but in that instant the image of him paying the same price Nan had, or worse, made her want to cry out in anguish. She had enough guilt over Nan.

"You can't do that!"

"I can. I will. I'm not leaving."

"You," she said through clenched teeth, "are the most stubborn, aggravating, infuriating man I've ever met."

"Guilty as charged."

"How do I know you're not working for Trey? How do I know you're not part of his trap?"

Lynn had never seen fury manifest itself in a man's eyes before. Grant was red-faced with anger at the accusations in her questions.

"I have never," he said in a vehement whisper, "hurt a woman in my life. I didn't know what kind of monster Murdock is, and I sure didn't know you two had a connection or I would never have even considered doing business with him."

She wouldn't apologize. She couldn't. Her life was in jeopardy. She wasn't going to waver even for a second. "Kinda twists the short hairs to realize you've been duped by him, doesn't it?"

"We can talk about that later."

Lynn grunted and turned back in her saddle to set Trouble in motion. She was done talking. They were wasting daylight arguing and she didn't have the luxury of debate. If he could keep up with her, then so be it.

• • •

Travelling with a packhorse definitely slowed her down, which meant, of course, that Grant was able to stay within sight distance. She tried to keep her mind off of him, which wasn't easy despite the fact that she was getting a headache from straining to hear the sound of rotors cutting the air above her.

Part of her needed to believe she'd get away. But the realistic part knew it was only a matter of time. Trey would find her. But when he did, she would go down fighting.

Another piece of her was intensely curious as to how Trey and Grant had gotten together and just what exactly their business was. It had to do with development of real estate since that's what Trey did, and Grant was a builder. She was smart enough to put two and two together and get that answer. But her natural curiosity wanted the details . . . a curiosity she'd choke on before she'd indulge.

Because that would mean she cared . . .

Clearly, though, it was better to concentrate on those questions than examine her reaction to his announcement that he wasn't leaving. She'd been self-sufficient for five years. She didn't need him. She didn't need anyone.

Then why was her heart a little lighter, her shoulders a little less weighted, with him steadfastly following behind her? And why did her pulse quicken when he looked at her with those deep blue eyes?

Settling her hat firmly on her head, she decided she was sure she didn't know. And didn't care.

Besides, in a few days her odd attraction to him wouldn't matter anyway. She'd either be dead, or she'd find a way to disappear whether Grant liked it or not. Either way, she'd never see him again.

Seven

Grant shifted in the saddle and swallowed a curse. Nothing, short of getting off this horse, would relieve the numbness in his butt.

He patted the bay's neck in silent apology. The mare had been amazing, giving her all whenever he asked. She was very responsive, and a beautiful mount, but no horse was comfortable after eight hours.

He looked at the beautiful backside in front of him—Lynn's, not Trouble's—and forced his eyes to focus elsewhere. It was bad enough his backside was asleep without adding further discomfort. Instead, he thought about how she'd steadfastly refused to acknowledge him for the first several hours on the trail.

When they'd stopped for a break, she'd given him a wide berth, and he'd respected her need for distance. The silence had provided a welcome opportunity to collect his thoughts. It seemed he hadn't had a moment of real downtime since he'd met Lynn, and this was the first time he had had to ponder just why this prickly woman intrigued him so.

Quite possibly it was because he'd never known a woman with so much internal strength. It wasn't that he didn't know any strong women, but that he'd never

known anyone, male or female, who'd endured what
Lynn had. He felt a sense of shame that he had turned
a blind eye to the issue of domestic violence. Like most
people, since it hadn't impacted his family, the idea was
abstract despite the coverage from the media.

Her ordeal was one that either broke a person completely, or made them stronger. It was clear to him which
category Lynn belonged in. She had prevailed against
overwhelming odds, and he was deeply impressed.

Yet, no matter how much he admired her, no matter
how much martial arts training she had, Grant's stomach
sickened at the thought of her going one-on-one against
Murdock. She'd gotten away from him once, but could
her luck hold out a second time? Murdock outweighed
her by a hundred pounds, and was driven by the urge to
hurt . . . or kill.

Lynn was convinced she could handle herself, and he
believed in her. But he also believed he was better qualified for the job. He knew his opinion was politically
incorrect in the extreme, but then, he'd never pretended
to be P.C. He was southern born and bred, and a real
man protected those weaker than himself. Lynn was
tough, he had no doubt. She was talented, he knew for
a fact. But when push came to shove, he wanted to be
the one facing Murdock's fists, not Lynn. She'd already
been there once, and Grant would be damned if she'd
ever feel that pain again. Not if he had breath in his
body and could prevent it.

Whether she wanted a rusty knight errant or not, he
had already donned the armor, and nothing and no one
could make him abdicate his role until Lynn was safe
and secure. Truly safe, once and for all.

Eight hours and seven minutes later, Lynn had to give
Grant credit. He was tenacious.

Which only deepened her aggravation. She didn't
want to think about him. She didn't want to admit she

wasn't completely opposed to his company. And she sure as hell didn't want to admit that seeing his face, so open and concerned, had made her heart do a little jump and her insides go squiggly.

She wondered if the stress of these past few days had sent her completely around the bend. How the merest thought of attraction had even entered her brain was a mystery beyond comprehension. She was running for her very life, and yet her pulse did the Snoopy dance whenever Grant was near? She was obviously certifiable and needed to make an appointment to be fitted for a straightjacket.

Shoving her thoughts aside, Lynn used the fading sunlight to check her compass and her watch. They'd travelled with only the most necessary breaks, yet they weren't nearly far enough along for her comfort. Reluctantly, when she came across a ravine that would shelter the horses from the wind, and had enough space for the two of them to roll out their sleeping bags, she stopped to give the horses a much-deserved rest.

"Let's make camp," she said, her neck tight with tension.

She'd found a small creek and decided to take advantage of the natural water source for the horses before moving on. At least the descending darkness gave her hope that Trey would have to go to ground as well.

Grant nodded, and without waiting for instructions, began to unsaddle his horse. She glared at him when he started to help with Hot Shot, but he backed off without arguing. His frown mocked her stubbornness, but she wasn't ready to be reasonable just yet.

Lynn hadn't tethered Trouble because he was whistle trained, and so he took the opportunity to enjoy his freedom by promptly rolling in a pile of nearby leaves to get the saddle creases out of his coat. Lynn laughed, enjoying Trouble's antics. If only her biggest worry was an itchy back.

Hot Shot hadn't carried the burden that Trouble had and thus contented himself with a few good shakes and shudders to work out the kinks. As she and Grant gathered grass for the animals, Lynn marveled at their resiliency. Seemingly unfazed by the long trip, the horses were soon munching contentedly on the winter grass.

It didn't take long to set up a cold camp. They pulled two logs close together for seats, but neither of them was inclined to sit just yet, not after eight endless hours in the saddle.

"I think I'm going for a walk," Lynn said. "If I can walk at all," she finished, muttering.

"What, no roll in the leaves?" Grant asked with a tip of his head in Trouble's direction.

"As tempting as that sounds," she said with a chuckle, "I think I'll settle for a good, old-fashioned stroll."

"Would you care for some company?" he asked, his voice a study in casual unconcern.

Lynn knew better. "Sure," she said, pulling a flashlight out of her pack. It was a little late now to be aloof.

The moon was bright, allowing them to navigate the edge of the streambed with little assistance. With the weather turning cool, the night was unusually quiet. A few brave crickets trilled out to prospective mates, but all in all, it was still.

"Living in the country, I'm used to it being peaceful, but this much quiet is a bit unnerving."

Grant nodded as he stretched his arms over his head. "I haven't been in the woods in years, so it feels really strange to me. I like it, though." He paused. "I just wish I was here under different circumstances."

Lynn stopped and picked up a small twig to distract herself from watching Grant's graceful movements. A man that tall, that broad, shouldn't be that elegant, she decided. But once again Grant wasn't cooperating.

"Protein bar?" she asked, reaching into her jacket

pocket not because she was especially hungry, but because she needed the distraction.

"Thanks, but I brought some food with me . . . dehydrated packs and such. I grabbed as much as I could at the hunting store at the edge of town while I waited to make sure Nan was going to be all right. I don't want to be a burden on your supplies, Lynn."

"I appreciate that, but have one on me for now."

She was sure he hadn't intended to make her feel bad, but his reminder that her friend was hurt brought a fresh, sharp stab of sorrow.

He seemed to read her mind. "She's all right, Lynn. She's pretty bruised up, but she's going to be fine."

Lynn wished she felt relieved, but she didn't. If anything, she felt more guilty than ever.

Finishing her meager dinner, she folded the wrapper and put it in her pocket. She thought about the pouches of water stashed in her saddlebag, but what she really wanted was a giant mug of hot tea. She could pull out the little single-burner propane heater/stove, but she didn't want to risk the light it would give off, even for a few minutes. She could survive a couple of days on high-energy rations and water. It wasn't the most exciting cuisine, but it would keep her body healthy.

She pushed away from the tree she had been leaning against and walked slowly toward the campsite, Grant at her side. Having Grant there felt right. He didn't need to fill the stillness with words. He was content to simply walk with her. And that deeply touched her.

She hadn't imagined herself with a man again for a long time, and she thought she had prepared herself for loneliness. But Grant's quiet presence made her realize she'd deluded herself into thinking she had accepted a life without companionship. A lump formed in her throat when she realized that Grant was exactly the kind of man she'd always dreamed of—strong, intelligent, caring, protective. The lump thickened with the knowledge that she could never have him.

Yes, she found him physically attractive. It would be foolish to deny something so obvious. But she also found him emotionally attractive, and that was a thousand times more dangerous. Despite her best intentions, she had opened up to him almost from the beginning. That was a sure sign he was a significant threat to her equilibrium.

And if she knew one thing, she had to keep all her faculties about her. She was on the run for her very life, and now had his life in the balance as well. She didn't have time to be drawn off-center . . . no matter how sexy the magnet.

They wound their way back and Lynn patted Trouble's neck as they passed the animals. She paused by her supplies and picked up a quilt, needing the comfort more than the warmth.

Her heart gave a little blip when Grant stopped by his own saddle and carried over a Mariner's Compass that she'd recently placed in Nan's shop. A compass . . . how appropriate.

"I just finished that quilt," she volleyed, not really sure what information she was looking for.

"Nan insisted I bring it with me, not that I needed much encouragement."

"That's sweet to say."

"It's the truth. I have a good bedroll, but I remember sleeping on the hard ground two nights ago, and yet not getting stiff at all. But I had to unkink about every muscle in my body this morning after sleeping on a very nice mattress."

Her brow furrowed in confusion.

"I think Nan's right. I think there's something special about your quilts and I'm willing to take the chance tonight."

She felt heat flushing her face and was grateful there

wasn't enough light for him to see the blush staining her cheeks. "That's silly, Grant. As I've told Nan a thousand times, they're just blankets."

He draped a corner of his quilt over his leg. Moonlight bathed the fabric in luminous beams filtering through the trees. The white background seemed to take on an ethereal glow, and even in the darkness the rich colors of the intricate pattern made their mark.

"Just blankets," he repeated softly, running his fingers along the rows of amazingly tiny stitches.

She cleared her throat. It was bad enough she had to argue about this with Nan. She didn't feel like hashing it out with Grant.

"Whose horse did you borrow this time?" she asked to change the subject.

"The sheriff's. When Nan told him the story, he was concerned about you. He's going after Murdock, but he's not hopeful of finding him."

"I can't say I'm surprised. I'm amazed Ted lent you his horse, though."

"Nan was rather influential in his decision."

Lynn smiled. "Well, it could have something to do with the fact that Ted has a crush on her."

Grant returned a grin. "I thought he seemed inordinately concerned. It was pretty clear he was more than professionally interested."

"I'm hoping she'll open up to him. After her divorce, Nan put her heart under lock and key and I'm betting Ted's the guy to take it out again. He's a great guy—" She stopped short at the amazed expression on Grant's face and chuckled. "Hey, just because I have issues doesn't mean that I think every man on the planet is bad."

"Then I hope he gets the chance to show her how to love again." He looked out over the moon-dappled trees. "Just like I hope you get the chance, too."

The sincerity in his voice nearly bowled her over. But

one thing was for certain, she wasn't ready to discuss her heart, particularly with a man who had her immensely confused.

"That's a subject I'd rather not get into right now."

"I understand. I'm sorry if I made you uncomfortable."

She gave him a small smile to let him know she accepted his apology.

"Let's change the subject," he offered. "Why don't you tell me about your family."

"I don't have much to tell. My parents died in a car wreck just before my divorce was finalized, and I don't have any siblings. I was never close to my extended relatives. I have an aunt on my mother's side who lives in Florida and two uncles on my father's side, one on each coast."

"Don't you think they were worried about you when you disappeared?"

"Possibly, but it's just as likely that they think I went on with my life. In a way, I'm grateful I don't have any really close relatives, because it made disappearing easier. I didn't have anyone calling for searches or anything like that."

"Don't you ever wonder, though, about what happened to your old life? Didn't anyone notice an abandoned apartment, unpaid rent, bills, etcetera?"

"Actually, I'm pretty sure I know exactly what happened. Leonard called my apartment manager and was told that I'd cleared out my things. When pressed, the manager said my neighbors saw me, but I didn't stop to talk. Of course 'I' was wearing a ball cap and sunglasses, but no one thought anything strange. The manager was given a P.O. box to forward any mail to."

"That's a rather elaborate scenario. What about your job? Did you work?"

"Trey is nothing if not methodical. I have every confidence in the world that he paid off any bills that came in. No collectors looking for me, don't you know." She shrugged. "As for my job, I was working as an administrative assistant for a huge computer firm, so it's not as though I was noticeable. I didn't dare call and make inquiries, though. I'm assuming he gave them some song and dance about why I suddenly quit, but I'll probably never know the answer to that one."

"Unbelievable." He shook his head in amazement.

"Hmmm, come to think of it, now that I'm technically no longer 'dead,' I should find a way to get to a branch of the bank that has my settlement money. Unless Trey found a way to get to it, I should have a tidy sum just collecting interest."

"That's good to know. That you have something to fall back on."

She shrugged, but doubted the action came off as nonchalant as she hoped. "If I live long enough, anyway."

"Hey, don't say that," he said sharply, a frown marring his forehead.

"Why? Because it disturbs you? You'd better accept right now that if you insist on staying with me, you could just as likely end up dead, too. We are not talking about a man who will listen to reason."

Grant leaned forward and rested his elbows on his knees. "I do believe you. When I took his horse back, Murdock said he was going to Austin, but he obviously planned on coming straight after you. It's pretty scary to think that he can compartmentalize all this." Grant acted as if he were reading a sheet of paper. "Dinner, seven-thirty. Plan murder, nine to nine-forty-five."

"And it's pretty scary to realize that he actually believes he'll get away with it and be able return to his life as if nothing has happened," she added softly.

"How could you have married someone like him?"

They were both surprised by his blurted question.

Lynn tried to contain her cynicism. Even Nan had asked that question, not realizing her insensitivity. "Do you think he manifested these behaviors right out of the box? When Trey and I first met, he was dashing and personable. Yes, he was arrogant, but that was a facet of him that I used to like."

"But he changed, obviously."

"He took a severe blow to the head on a job site, but I don't know for sure if that's the cause. It wasn't a sudden shift. Over the next two years, he became possessive. There were other subtle changes, too. Then the day came that he slapped me."

Grant's fingers fisted against his thigh. "I'd like to return the favor," he muttered.

Lynn cocked her head. "What is it with men?" she asked, knowing the question was rhetorical. "The answer to violence is not violence."

"You're telling me you didn't want revenge? And that you don't want it now, after everything he's put you through?"

"Of course I did! But I also refused to let my anger rule my life. Retaliation was not going to make my pain go away, or ease the situation."

"I understand that," he said, "but for most men, the thought of a woman being hit is untenable. I realize that I may be stepping on feminist toes here, but I take protecting what is mine seriously. I will protect my family, and especially my sister, with my life. And if I'm ever lucky enough to fall in love again, I'll protect my wife just as fiercely. If that makes me a Neanderthal, then so be it. But I refuse to apologize for it."

Lynn's smile was warm even as she shook her head. "Don't you get it, Grant? That kind of sentiment isn't offensive. It could be, of course, if you acted like an overbearing jerk, but I know that's not what you're saying."

"I'm glad you see that."

"It does beg the question, though, of why you're feeling so protective of me. We have no relation. I'm not even a distant friend. So why in the world are you risking your life?"

"Because it's my fault you're out here."

Lynn cut the air with her hand. "Nope, that doesn't wash. I've thought a lot about this, and it's pure coincidence that you happened to be doing business with Trey. Betsy may have been the catalyst, but it's not anyone's fault."

"You can choose to believe that, but I consider myself responsible." His expression was intractable.

"It's obvious we aren't going to agree here so I think we should drop it," Lynn said tersely, a frown of her own revealing her frustration. "Have I mentioned that you're—"

"—stubborn? Yes, but then, it appears you could give even me a few lessons. Does it diminish your strength to have someone care about you?"

"Care about me? You don't even know me!" She couldn't sit still any longer. With no other excuse for movement, she rummaged in her bags for water packets. She handed him one and stepped away, not really sure what to do with herself.

It was a sensation she despised, this awkwardness, this sense of displacement. Having to accept that her hard-won sense of inner peace was an illusion, and a fragile one at that, was disconcerting. She struggled with resentment. Not at Grant, of course. He hadn't done anything more than bring the truth to light.

"I know enough," he said with quiet sincerity.

"Really? You think you know me after the short time we've spent together? It's just an illusion created by the intensity of the situation."

He shook his head. "I don't agree—"

"We're not agreeing on much of anything, are we?" she interrupted pointedly. "You have appointed yourself my protector, no matter how I feel about it, and now *you're* trying to tell *me* how the situation will work out."

She stopped abruptly and covered her face with her hands. After a moment, she dropped them, and took a deep breath.

"Grant, I honestly appreciate what you're trying to do, but you have to listen to me. I can tell you a lot about assumptions, about drawing conclusions too quickly. After all, I thought I knew Trey."

She laughed, but the sound contained little amusement.

"Then came the physical abuse. The first time I was so stunned, and he was so contrite. I convinced myself the whole thing was some kind of cosmic anomaly, blamed the stress of his job. I even believed him when he said it would never happen again. But of course, it did. The man I'd fallen in love with beat the hell out of me."

"You didn't stick around, though. You got out before he . . ."

Her smile wasn't unkind. "Killed me? So tell me again, how do you know someone after a few days? I knew Trey for years."

"I'm not a psychologist, Lynn. I don't understand the vagaries of the human mind. But I do know I can't spend every day of my life suspicious of the people around me. There has to be some baseline of trust in the human spirit, even if there are those who don't obey the rules."

Lynn stared at the bright face of the moon, and tried to come up with a suitable response. She'd avoided this very question for years by remaining in her seclusion. Life had seemed easier when she didn't have to deal with people, Nan and Jeremy notwithstanding.

"You're being rational, of course," she said. "And if reason were the rule, then Trey would have accepted the divorce and let me go. Needless to say, that isn't what happened."

"What did happen, if I may ask?"

"The second time he hit me, I drove straight to an attorney's office and filed for divorce. The whole thing went smoothly. Too smoothly. Now I realize Trey had been planning to come after me all along. A generous settlement was a great cover."

Grant gave her sideways smile. "Logical, in a twisted sort of way."

Lynn still had enough humor to laugh at the black humor. "Yeah, you're right. Anyway, I'd grown complacent and after the final divorce hearing, Trey asked if he could take me out for a drink, to say good-bye. I was so arrogantly sure that I'd shown him how tough I was that I said okay. A drink in a public place? What would happen?"

Grant grimaced. "I can see what's coming next."

She returned to her seat and pulled her quilt around her. "Have you ever heard of the drug Rohypnol? Well, when I woke up, I was being dragged across rough pasture about ten miles from the cabin where Betsy was. And when he realized I was awake, the beating began in earnest."

Grant started to reach out across the space between them, then reluctantly pulled his hand away. "Lynn, I'm sorry. I shouldn't have asked."

She took a shaky breath and shrugged. "It's okay. You're risking your life by following me so you deserve to know the whole story. I was foggy from the drugs, and I'd never taken a self-defense course in my life so I was a living punching bag. It was November, and an unseasonable cold front had the temperature in the thirties."

The wind picked up, as if in reminder of that night. She shivered but continued.

"When he pushed me down a thirty-foot ravine, I'm sure he had every confidence that if the beating didn't kill me, the fall would. And if the fall failed to do the job, the weather would. And if the weather failed, there's always feral animals willing to finish off a wounded prey."

Grant watched Lynn's face as she spoke, and wondered if she had any idea how hard it was for him to hear her talk. Everything in him, every ethic, every moré, every lesson learned from the time he was born made him want to take her in his arms and hold her close, shield her from the pain she was reliving. And then go punish the man who'd hurt her.

He knew she was skittish, but even if it had meant hard time at Leavenworth, he couldn't stop himself from reaching out to touch her arm.

"I'm so sorry," he whispered, thrilled that she didn't withdraw.

"Thank you," she said, her voice barely audible.

Lynn looked at the horses, the saddlebags, the pile of items that now accounted the sum total of her possessions. There was an emptiness at her side, where Jake's furry, reassuring body belonged. She shivered as the wind moaned through the trees, and suddenly it was too much.

A tear formed, despite her best efforts to blink it back, and slid down her cheek without permission.

And another followed. She ducked her face to hide her mortifying display, but a tiny sob escaped.

"Hey," he said, softly. Gently. He moved to crouch beside her and put a hand on hers. "It's all right," he whispered.

"No," she said, her voice barely a whisper. "It's not all right. It will never be all right."

He stood and pulled her to him. She wished she were stronger, braver, able to refuse the comfort of his arms. But she wasn't. She was cold, she was exhausted, she was empty. And for just five minutes she needed to not be alone.

She didn't argue when he slipped off her hat, his own

following quickly behind. Bathed in moonlight, he looked down at her face and her eyes drifted shut under the intensity of his concern. She could feel his eyes tracing her nose, her cheeks, her chin.

A kiss was inevitable.

She met his descending mouth with hungry demand. She knew she surprised him, for she'd surprised herself, but she didn't care that she was acting out of character.

She didn't care about the cold, either. She let her quilt drop and slipped her arms around him. He wrapped his quilt around them both, never taking his mouth from hers. He enfolded her in warmth, slanting her head so that nothing hindered his exploration.

Their kiss was a melding of mouths, a mating of lips and tongues in a dance that had a rhythm of its own. It started out wild and hungry and urgent, and somehow settled into a meeting, an invitation, a hello of souls.

She slipped one hand from the cocoon created by the blanket. Reaching up, she touched his stubble-rough jaw. Her fingers traced his strong, masculine ear and smoothed back his silky black hair. He captured her hand and carried her palm to his chest, pressing so that she could have no doubts about the mad beating of his heart.

Magic.

She didn't believe in magic. That was Nan's department. But this man, this moment were nothing less than mystical. Never had she felt so safe, so cherished.

Grant planted soft kisses on her cheeks, her chin, under her left ear, then her right. She tilted her head, inviting his attention. He'd worked one hand under her shirt and the feel of his strong fingers splayed against the bare skin of her back made her shiver . . . and not from the cold.

Traces of his crisp cologne tickled her nose when she buried her face against his shoulder. She couldn't remember ever feeling this comforted, this complete . . .

and from something as simple as an embrace.

"Lynn, I—"

She lifted her head and placed her finger against his lips. "Shhh. Don't say anything. Just kiss me again."

He acquiesced with relish, pulling her even closer and claiming her mouth with a passion that made her gasp with delight. She reveled in the moment, grateful that her mind was filled with nothing but the sensations overwhelming her.

She'd been so sure that she could never enjoy anything like this again, never feel anything but terror with a man this close, but she'd been wrong. Thank heaven she'd been wrong. She reveled in everything about this moment, from the touch of his hands to the taste of his tongue, from the smell of his body warm and intimate against hers to the sound of his ragged breathing in her ear.

Then a branch snapped.

And reality kicked her in the gut as she jerked out of Grant's arms and spun around, passion turning to terror in the space of a heartbeat.

The horses whinnied in alarm, but instead of the demon she expected, she saw a raccoon that had slipped from its branch and was scurrying away with wounded dignity.

She hung her head, trying to calm her racing heart. She heard Grant pick up her quilt and shake it out, but she couldn't move as he stepped up behind her and draped the soft fabric over her shoulders. When he put his hands on her arms, she stepped away.

"Lynn—"

"Please don't apologize."

"I wasn't. I was going to ask if you're okay."

Raising her head, she turned to meet his eyes. "No, I'm not okay. You've just proved how very, very dangerous you are."

"What?!" Shock colored Grant's features, obviously taken aback by her statement.

She made a vague gesture with her hand. "You distract me at every turn. If that raccoon had been Trey, I'd be dead right now. If I hadn't been playing kissy-face with you, I'd be armed. I'd be ready."

"Lynn—"

"No, there's nothing to talk about. I'm going to get some rest. I'm leaving at first light, and you're going back."

"Like hell—"

"This conversation is over."

True to her word, she didn't speak again as she began to set out a perimeter alarm. The invisible nylon string with bells attached was crude, but effective. If Trey came skulking through, she'd have a moment's notice to take up arms and defend herself.

But as she settled down, she admitted her perimeter defenses were useless against Grant.

He'd already snuck past.

Eight

"I don't understand why you have to do this tonight," Ted said, unable to hide his displeasure as he unlocked the door and ushered Nan inside her store. "You should be in bed."

Yeah, your bed, she thought, then blushed at the illicit image. Ted hadn't pushed at all in that direction, but he certainly was being pushy about protecting her. *If you'd let me go to my own home, I wouldn't be in such a turmoil.*

"Because," Nan responded with a dark look that quelled any further argument, "if I don't do this now, I might not be able to face it tomorrow. The old fall-off-the-horse-get-right-back-on thing."

Nan hurried around the room and lit every lamp to dispel the shadows. In some ways, she wondered if she'd made the right decision as she looked around the shambles of her store. Seeing her precious treasures thrown like so much trash to the floor hurt her soul as much as Trey's fist had hurt her body.

Ted stood by the door, his arms crossed over his broad chest, but she ignored his worried impatience. She had no doubt that if he were facing some similar dilemma, nothing and no one would keep him from facing his fears. Since she was a woman, she apparently was supposed to meekly acquiesce to his wishes. Well, she had news for him.

She had to admit he did look kinda cute standing there, even if he *was* glowering. His uniform was still sharply pressed, though heaven only knew how after the day they'd had. With his usual Southern charm, he'd taken off his hat the moment he'd entered the building and she decided she liked him with or without the brown Stetson. He looked dark and sexy with it on, but with the light playing on his blond hair he looked younger and less stern.

Jeremy was safe at Ted's with a deputy staying by his side until they returned. When she'd called from the hospital, the deputy had told her Jeremy had fallen asleep on the couch, exhausted no doubt from the tension of the day.

Nan picked up a floppy-eared bunny made of muslin and calico, and perched it back on the shelf where it belonged. Someone had already righted a table that had been knocked over and she took a moment to rearrange the items that had been haphazardly placed on the surface.

She drifted over to the shelves of bean-bag animals and adjusted a placement or two, knowing good and well she was avoiding the main counter. She had to face this demon, which was why she'd demanded they stop by before going to Ted's house in the first place, but she had to do it at her own pace.

She wasn't as brave as Lynn. She couldn't just stand up to her fears, chin thrust out, shoulders back ready to take them on. Instead, she continued to meander, picking up the knickknacks and flummery that had been thrown to the floor in the skirmish.

Shivering, she paused at the lotions and soap display, squirting some raspberry-scented hand cream into her palm. The scent was certainly more soothing than the

antiseptic smell from the hospital clinging to her skin
and clothes.

She rubbed her hands together, remembering how
she'd tried to empathize with Lynn as she'd told her
story, but Nan's divorce had never involved violence.
For the first time, she had a tiny inkling of what her
friend had felt, and her admiration for Lynn increased a
hundredfold. Jeremy's father had been cold and cruel
toward the end, but his weapon had been words, making
her feel worthless.

She put a hand to her long, sandy-blond hair tied back
in a braid, and then to her puffy cheek. She'd never felt
more mousy in her life, or less desirable.

She risked a glance at Ted and wondered when he
would realize she wasn't anything special. Soon he'd
move on to one of the pretty girls who always buzzed
around him at the fire station dances. It was inevitable,
which was why she hadn't agreed to anything more serious than a few lunches, and one early dinner. Still, it
was flattering that he kept asking.

Her life was just fine, she told herself. She had her
shop and she had Jeremy. The shop kept her too busy
for romance anyway, she decided, running her fingers
along the shelf of ceramic and crystal treasures shaped
in everything from the sublime to the ridiculous.

Finally she had no choice but to turn around and look.

The blood drained from her face as she stared at
the floor where she'd lain, barely conscious, in more
pain than she'd ever conceived possible. She sensed,
though, that the violation of her innocence had been far
worse than any damage done to the store. Never again
could she naively believe her world was safe.

But her true cry of distress came when she spied a
small box on the counter. She hurried forward and
opened the lid, hoping against hope . . .

"Oh, no," she whispered, anguished.

"Nan?" Ted said, hurrying forward. "What's the matter?"

"It's the needle," she said, her words barely audible.

"Pardon?"

She cleared her throat. "It's Lynn's needle."

"And . . ." he prompted, a quizzical look on his face.

"And it's disastrous," she choked out, tears spilling down her cheeks.

Ted took Nan's shoulders and turned her to face him. "Nan, we're going back to the hospital. I think you're having a reaction to the medicine."

She pulled out of his arms, shaking her head, and made her way to one of the wooden rockers she kept strategically placed around the room.

"Lynn's out there, without any protection."

"Grant—"

"*If* Grant finds her, then they're both in danger."

Ted knelt on one knee beside Nan and grasped her shaking hands in his. "Nan, you're being—"

"Silly? Yes, I know that's what you all think, but I know this needle is special." She caught the skeptical look he was trying to hide. "It is," she said insistently.

"Okay, honey," he said soothingly.

Nan wondered if he was even aware of his endearment.

"I don't know what I should do," she said, staring into the velvet-lined box. She touched the little needle, not at all surprised to find it warm against her fingertip.

"Have faith," she heard a voice say.

"Faith?" she asked, looking at Ted.

"What?" he responded, staring at her as if he were truly becoming concerned. "Come on, Nan," he said gently, helping her to her feet. "Let's get you home."

She looked at him quizzically. "I thought I was going to your house tonight."

An endearing blush stained his cheeks. "That's what I meant," he said gruffly.

A warmth spread through her, surprising her. She looked at Ted with new eyes, despite the fact that one was still quite swollen.

Putting the top back on the box, she tucked it safely into her pocket as she turned off most of the lamps and locked the store. Then she walked beside Ted to his car.

Grant was up long before the sun . . . again. He sat on a tree stump and watched Lynn sleep. Or rather, he watched the darkness where she'd placed her sleeping bag. The moonlight had long disappeared and the almost total darkness had been disconcerting at first. Then he'd considered that it was as much a friend as foe. It would be damned difficult to find the campsite in the first place, and a flashlight beam would be as visible as a beacon, giving him warning if anyone approached. He would leave his off until Lynn awoke and turned hers on, signaling it was time to break camp.

Their conversation played over and over in his mind, all serving to make him determined to stay with her. To protect her.

But she didn't want protecting, she'd said.

Well, too bad. Did she think he could slink away like some yellow coward? Go back to his home, his job, as if he'd never met her? Didn't she know what kind of menace she was facing?

The more he thought about it, the more insulted he became. Maybe they hadn't known each other long, but the events they'd been through so far certainly should count for something. They certainly did in his mind.

Besides, every time he touched her he wanted her as he'd never wanted a woman before. She made his blood pound as if he were running a marathon. She made his skin tingle and his hands ache to touch her. The passion lurking in her eyes made him lose track of reality, and her body called to him with a melody that he felt within his very bones.

If that didn't prove she was in his system well and good, then nothing did. Grant considered himself a practical man, and he'd never been one to sit transfixed and think about a woman. To recall every nuance of her face. To remember every second of her lips against his, her body pressed close in a cocoon of warmth.

He hardened painfully at the memory, and stifled a moan. The last thing she needed was sexual advances, but with nothing but darkness to distract him, all he could think about was losing himself in her.

He didn't know much about psychology, but he had to assume by her response to his kiss yesterday that she had reached some level of recovery after her trauma. She'd responded to his kiss as a woman responds to a man, and he was damn sure that hadn't been fear in her dreamy expression. If it weren't for that stupid raccoon . . .

That gave him hope.

Hope? Of what?

Running pell-mell on horseback was hardly conducive to romance. Once it was all over, she'd want to put her life back together without any memories of the painful past.

He certainly qualified as part of the painful portion since he had set these events into motion. Just what did he have to offer her anyway? A big bank account wouldn't entice a woman like Lynn. After what she'd been through, she deserved to be cherished.

He wasn't sure he had enough in him anymore to give Lynn what she needed.

The old tag-line fit so well: been there, done that.

Got the divorce. And lost half his assets.

He had no desire to go through that again, thank you very much. It wasn't losing the money; he could handle that. It was losing part of himself again that scared him.

"If you're going to sit there and fidget, we might as well get ready to go."

Her voice startled him. An intense wave of guilt made him distinctly uncomfortable. "I'm sorry I woke you."

"You didn't." She clicked on a flashlight and set it on the ground beside her. "Sheer exhaustion granted me a nice nap, but I've been lying here for hours trying to figure out how to make you go away."

Grant doubted the illumination from the beam reached his face, but he raised an eyebrow in her direction anyway. "Thank you for that lovely compliment."

She stood and stretched, obviously unaware of the intriguing picture her silhouette made as her lithe body bent and twisted to ease her tight muscles.

"Don't be offended. I'm just trying to save your life."

He frowned, fiercely, and wished she could see him. "Lynn, you'd better get it through that incredibly stubborn, incredibly beautiful red head of yours: I'm not leaving."

She started at his words, then she sighed. "You are—"

"Infuriating, I know. I think we've covered that ground."

"Well, you are," she said, shaking out her quilt and folding it neatly.

Grant moved closer to her and started packing his own gear.

There was a faint lift to the sky off to the east, just a promise of dawn. The darkness didn't seem to hamper her, though, as she had her sleeping bag rolled and tied in no time. She grabbed her flashlight and headed toward the horses.

Grant enjoyed watching her. Even in the shadows, she had a grace and economy of movement that was a feast to his eyes. He didn't study people much, but he decided he could spend hours just watching Lynn.

And kissing her.

That would definitely be an acceptable way to pass the time as far as he was concerned. He could think of even more desirable ways to make the hours fly by, but instead he concentrated on his own bedding. Better to keep those thoughts at bay for now.

Snapping on his light, he began saddling his horse and getting his things arranged. He knew better than to try and saddle Trouble for her. She had independence down to an art and would not take kindly to being treated as helpless.

Good heavens, if there was one thing he didn't consider her, it was helpless.

"You know," he said thoughtfully, tightening the girth strap, "there's something I haven't asked yet."

"What's that?"

"Why you're doing this by horseback."

"You mean, why didn't I pile into a car and head for the highway?"

He nodded, then realized she probably couldn't see him. "Exactly."

"First and foremost because I don't own a vehicle or have a valid driver's license. And secondly, I figured it was easier to spot a car on the highway than a horse in the woods."

"Isn't that rather—"

"Alarmist? Extremist? I'd prefer to think of it as logical."

"I sense you have more method behind your madness than you're letting on."

She merely shrugged.

He stopped in his tracks, staring at her as realization dawned. "You *know* he's going to find you. Us. In fact, you're planning on it."

She gave an aggrieved sigh. "Haven't I said that all along? Didn't I tell you to go away so he wouldn't hurt you? He'll probably find us by tomorrow."

"Then, why?" He gestured to the horses, the provisions.

"Because while I needed to believe the fantasy that I'd get away, my gut knew all along that I'd have to see him face-to-face again. But this time, by God, I'm meeting him on my terms, in a place where I at least have a chance of surviving. Most especially, where no one else can get hurt."

She stared into the trees, an unexpected calm settling around her. "I'm going to end this once and for all. One way or the other."

"Lynn—"

"If I survive, then I'm going to head into the wilds and disappear."

He gave a distressed sound. "What do I have to do to make you listen? I can help you."

Lynn reached up and caressed his cheek. "There's nothing you can do. This is my fight, and I'll see it through."

Her steadfast resolve robbed him of a response. Nothing he could say would sway her, and it twisted his gut into a knot. Even though her plan had a certain merit, it still left him out of the equation, made him a bystander.

Murdock was the one pushing the issue, leading Lynn to believe she had no options. Still, Grant was impressed with her determination. Forcing Murdock to play out the conclusion on her terms, and minimizing the risk to others, spoke volumes about the depth of this woman's character.

Which did nothing to ease his dilemma.

He didn't want to lose her.

When Lynn set Trouble into motion, Grant automatically followed behind. He had to come up with a plan.

And fast.

With typical perversity, the weather had turned downright hot, forcing them to shed coats and long sleeves as the morning hours progressed. Grant was amazed at Lynn's new calm, and he was both stunned and pleased when she guided Trouble next to him on a particularly long stretch of open country. The thorny mesquite thickets seemed to be less frequent, and patches of prickly pear were giving way to kinder ground.

Grant had had to swallow a groan when Lynn stripped down to a cotton tank and applied sunscreen. He'd watched hungrily as she rubbed in the creamy lotion, his own palms itching to assist her.

It certainly didn't help his dilemma that her beautiful breasts were molded by the ribbed fabric, forcing his imagination into overdrive. He was fixated on the juncture where her shoulders met her elegant neck, and could almost feel the warmth of her skin against his mouth. He'd trail fire down her collarbone, to the hollow of her cleavage, bury his face—

"We've talked a lot about me," she finally said as the horses plodded along. "Too much so. It's your turn on the grill."

Hell, he'd been on the grill for half an hour now . . .

He shook himself out of his sexual trance and raised an eyebrow. "Why the sudden interest?"

She shrugged. "I guess I'm tired of just having my own thoughts for company."

"So I'm merely a distraction?" he asked, feeling miffed.

"Maybe a bit. Is that all right?"

He took a deep breath and then exhaled slowly, accepting her answer. As much as he did not want to talk about himself it would be a good way to get his mind off his groin.

"You really want to know that I was born in McAllen, moved to Austin when I was fifteen, went to the University of Texas for both undergrad and law school—"

"You're a lawyer?" she asked, obviously amazed.

"Is that so hard to believe?"

"I . . . I guess I wasn't expecting that. You're a builder, aren't you?"

"Yep. I passed the bar and got my license, but never hung up a shingle."

She chuckled. "Interesting choice of phrase, considering your profession."

He returned a laugh. "Freudian slip, obviously."

"So why bedrooms instead of courtrooms?"

He bit his tongue to keep from jumping on the entendre. There was certainly one bedroom he'd like to—

"Um," he cleared his throat, "probably because I was too busy trying to fulfill everyone's expectations but my own."

"Kinda like you were pressuring Betsy?"

Grant cut her a glance. "Touché."

She gave him an apologetic smile. "I wasn't trying for a shot. Honestly. That one kinda slipped out."

"It's all right. Especially since you're correct. I'd just never thought about it like that."

"It's hard, when you want the best for someone, to let them make their choices, even if you think they're making mistakes."

He acknowledged her point with a nod. "In my case, I actually enjoyed law school, but I had this nagging frustration that something was missing. I couldn't put my finger on it until I went to work for a general contractor the summer after my second year. I did everything from the lowliest grunt work to apprentice carpenter and electrician."

She tilted her head and pursed her lips. "You don't seem like the gopher type to me."

He was willing to laugh at himself. "I think we all do things when we're young we can't imagine doing now."

"Naivete can be a wonderful thing."

"True. Once I'd seen a set of blueprints and started asking questions, the end of the story was inevitable."

"Did you go back to school?" she asked, sounding truly interested.

"No, I learned the old-fashioned way. I apprenticed to the builder I'd been working for. He taught me more than any professor could."

"Oh, I understand that," she said fervently. "I had a mentor who was so much more than just a teacher. He saved my life."

"I'm guessing here he taught you how to use nun-chaku and a survival knife."

She nodded somberly. "Leonard and Jake found me in that gully. He taught me everything I know about taking care of myself."

"I wish I could thank him."

She cut him an odd look.

"So, how did you and Murdock meet?" Grant asked to get her all-too assessing eyes off his face. As he expected, she looked away.

"At a conservation benefit in Dallas."

Grant gave the puzzled glance this time. "Murdock?"

"Um hmm. He was trying to make points with the city council, showing them how committed he was to the environment so they'd approve his latest development."

Grant snorted. "Money talks."

"It certainly does."

"The development was approved?"

"Without a hitch."

"Figures."

She nodded, then paused. "But I'm not exactly being fair to Trey. Believe it or not, he was fairly honest back then."

He couldn't hide his skepticism.

"Oh, don't get me wrong," she assured him, adding a chuckle, "personal success was always a top priority with Trey. He just wasn't obsessed . . . yet. He may have charmed the pants off the city council, but he'd also designed an award-winning plan that was environmentally friendly."

Grant encouraged her with his attentive silence.

"That's one of the things that attracted me to him. He

was so passionate, so charismatic. Things didn't start changing until several years later."

"After the accident."

She gave her head a little shake. "The irony is, if he'd been wearing a hard hat, things might have been different."

"You think the blow . . ."

"I don't know, maybe. I did a lot of research about head injuries, but I couldn't get his doctor to listen because nothing appeared to be wrong. Trey was already showing one face to me and another to his doctor and the professional world."

"That's scary."

She stared off at the horizon, then shook herself and gave him a stern look. "Hey, you turned the table on me again. No fair."

Grant hid his unrepentant grin by turning his horse toward an inviting creek winking through the trees. "Let's take a breather."

To his surprise, Lynn agreed without an argument. He could only assume she was as sticky, and ready for a break, as he was. For the first time, Lynn was the one following, and Grant decided, macho or not, he liked being in the lead. It wasn't in his nature to be second.

They stopped near the bank, both groaning as they dismounted. A shared glance turned into a shared laugh.

Lynn assessed the water with hungry eyes. She could have knocked him over with a feather when she said, "I'm going to take a bath."

He was hard before she'd finished the sentence.

"Um—"

"I know, it's ridiculous to take the time—"

"Actually, that's not what I was thinking—"

"But who knows how long this warm weather will hold? The horses need a break, so I'm going to take advantage of the rest stop to get rid of some of this grit."

He reached up and held on to the saddle horn for dear

life, resting his forehead against the saddle as she rummaged in her supplies and came up with a bar of soap and a change of clothes. He stood transfixed as she walked deliberately toward a weeping willow and disappeared behind the canopy of leaves.

"You hide the horses under the willow . . . and stay there yourself. You can go next." She obviously expected him to be a gentleman and stay by the horses, the willow fronds providing both cover for the horses, and privacy for her . . . if he stayed put.

Honor had nothing to do with his remaining in place after moving the horses into the shade. The fact that he was straining his jeans near to bursting did. He wasn't moving until he got himself under control.

Then he heard a splash, and she screeched.

Instantly imagining Lynn facing a snake, a wild bear or Murdock himself, Grant tore around the horses and plunged through the canopy of leaves.

And stopped dead in his tracks.

Lynn was standing waist deep in the water, her hair slicked back. Her arms covered her breasts, and her hands trembled against her throat.

"Lynn—"

"It's f-f-f-reeezing. I'm s-s-s-orry I s-s-screamed."

"You scared the wits out of me, woman."

"I'm s-s-s-orry. Go away n-n-now."

"After the scare you just gave me you're going to make me leave?" he asked, taking a teasing step closer. "Besides, you need someone to wash your back and I know just the volunteer."

"Grant, that's n-n-not funny."

He took off his shoes and socks. "I wasn't trying to be funny. I think you're idea of a bath is terrific."

She whirled around, gliding deeper into the water, and he was certain he'd never seen anything more beautiful than a wet redhead with her skin goose-pimpled from the cold.

Then she utterly surprised him. She turned back around and sent a splash of water over his toes.

"Hurry up," she invited.

"Why the change of heart?"

She shrugged. "I just decided to be impulsive. I think I deserve to be a little impetuous, all things considered. Once you get used to it, the water feels great. Come on, don't be chicken."

Chicken? Rooster maybe. And a damned randy one at that.

"Turn around," he said as he unbuttoned his shirt, not at all opposed to her change of heart but still feeling a bit modest.

She giggled. "You're kidding."

He paused with his hand on his belt buckle. "I'm entirely serious."

With a provocative look, she swam away. He kept his eye on her as he stripped and hurried to the water's edge. Even with her warning, the shock of cold as he jumped in took his breath away.

It also helped his embarrassing dilemma . . .

She was right, though. After the initial blast, the water felt good on his heated skin.

He dunked his head and when he came up, Lynn sent the soap over to him with a splash.

"Thanks," he said, putting the clean-smelling bar to work. He was as grateful as she for the opportunity to get rid of some sweat and grime. He just wished he had a razor.

All too soon, though, it was impossible to ignore her naked beauty. His temporary reprieve was over. He closed his eyes, grateful for the cover of the water, and wondered how he was going to convince her to get out first.

When he opened them again, his entire being focused

on the woman standing directly in front of him, only inches away.

With her hair slicked back and her skin pink from the cold, she was absolutely beautiful. Water danced on her shoulders. Provocative droplets slid down her cleavage. He couldn't look away.

She took the soap from his white-knuckled grip and threw it over to the bank. He stood rock-still as she used her hands to pour water over his chest and smoothed away the last of the bubbles.

"Lynn—" he choked out.

"Shhh."

She took her time with her ablutions, making him wonder if it was possible to spontaneously combust while standing in the middle of a near-freezing creek.

"Lynn—" he tried again.

"Shhh. Just let me enjoy this moment, however brief."

How could a man say no to a request like that? How could any man deny this beautiful vixen anything?

He couldn't remember feeling this transfixed. Not even in the most callow moments of his youth could he recall being spellbound. But Lynn had certainly bewitched him, leaving him powerless under her touch.

When he could stand it no longer, he pulled her to him, making no effort to hide the effect she had on him as he wrapped his arms around her. There was nothing between them but a few drops of water.

He kissed her hungrily, heatedly, showing her with his mouth and his hands just what kind of fire she'd ignited inside him. She returned his kiss without reserve, her hands exploring his chest, his back, his hips.

He groaned as she squeezed his behind and pressed herself closer, gliding her feminine softness against him.

Time. Place. Danger. None of that mattered.

Nothing mattered but her tongue against his, her breasts against his chest, her legs wrapped around him, cradling him.

He backed her toward the bank. His whole body burned with the need to lay her down on the grass and bury himself inside her. Her breath was as ragged as his, the noises deep in her throat driving him wild.

He set her on her feet as they reached the bank, letting her go only for the merest second to spread their clothes on the ground to protect her skin. Hungrily, desperately, he followed her down to reclaim her mouth—

Just as the sound of rotors cut through the air.

Nine

The world exploded into madness.

The horses went into a frenzy, breaking their tethers and racing away, manes flying, from the monster in the sky.

The fury from the blades whipped away the hanging willow fronds, revealing Lynn and Grant madly scrambling into their jeans and shirts. She cursed that they no longer had even the illusion of protection as they jammed bare feet into boots and ran for the thicker tangle of trees a few yards away.

Yards that felt like miles with a helicopter flying in a tight circle above them. Lynn searched for anything to use as a weapon, noting that Grant was doing the same. With the horses gone, their only pitiful retaliation was a good-sized rock in each hand. Hardly comforting when their Goliath was encased in aluminum and Plexiglas, and out of reach.

The first shot rang out. Lynn found herself flattened on the ground, Grant covering her with his body. The breath whooshed from her lungs and she lost precious time gasping for air. She gave him a hard shove with her elbow and scrambled to her feet.

"Damn it, Grant," she yelled hoarsely as she headed

for the relative cover of some dense oak trees. "Get over here!"

He joined her in the vee of a triplet of trees, the branches whipping wildly as the helicopter moved round and round like a shark moving in for first blood.

She was amazed at her clearheadedness. She wouldn't say she was calm, but as she watched the sky, she felt . . . fatalistic. There was something about anticipating an event for years that made even the extreme seem . . . anticlimactic. Of course, the other posible answer could be that she had fallen headfirst into shock.

She didn't move when Grant placed his hand on her shoulder. His attempt to comfort her, reassure her, was kind, but she was too detached to appreciate his efforts. Besides, she was too busy castigating herself.

Twice now she'd let her hormones distract her. The first time should have been a warning, but she hadn't listened. For a moment she wanted to blame Grant for distracting her, but she knew that was a lie. She'd issued the invitation to join her in the water, and she had touched first. She'd gone willingly into his arms. Of her own volition, she had lost herself in their kiss. She had eagerly given herself to him. Now she was paying the ultimate price for those moments of joy. Worse, Grant would pay as well.

As she tried to shake herself out of her self-recrimination and formulate a plan, the helicopter bobbled overhead and a succession of bullets thunked too close for comfort into the rough bark of the oak trees.

Lynn ducked, trying to grab her hair and control it as it stung her face. "Lucky shot," she said under her breath. Not that she needed to be quiet with the cacophony created by the blades.

She had the childish urge to hurl her rocks at the windshield, no matter how useless the gesture.

The copter bobbled again as Trey tried to fly and

shoot at the same time. Lynn and Grant stayed low. Bullets continued to fly over their heads.

As the oak branches shifted and swayed, she watched, horrified, as the blades chopped into the top of a tree. The body of the bird swung wildly as Trey swerved left, then right as he obviously fought for control. The helicopter listed toward the water, hovering for a moment as though he'd recover. Then, with a violent twist, the 'copter nose-dived into the creek.

The rotors churned giant chunks of mud and water before grinding to a halt. The scream of tearing metal assaulted her ears, providing a macabre score to the moment. She couldn't take her eyes away as the blades bent and the body of the copter landed nose-in, crumpling as though a giant hand had destroyed a toy in a fit of pique.

Even though she'd seen it with her own eyes, it was hard to believe what she'd just witnessed. In the unnerving silence that followed, Lynn looked at Grant. She waited, expectantly, but as seconds stretched into a minute, the silence remained.

"Will it explode?" she asked, as she began to move cautiously from the cover of the trees. She wrinkled her nose against the smell of leaking fuel.

"I have no idea," he answered as he stepped beside her.

"At least it's in water."

He gave her an odd look, nodding slowly. "I . . . guess so."

She was transfixed by the wreckage. "That way, if it does catch fire, maybe it won't burn down the whole area."

"Lynn, are you all right?"

She barely noticed he'd taken her shoulders into his hands until he gave her a gentle shake.

He grimaced. "I mean, in the general context of the moment. I know things aren't all right."

"I think I'm okay," she said, frowning. "I can't seem to focus my thoughts."

"It's called shock. Now listen to me. You're going to see if you can get the horses. I'm going to check out the helicopter."

His words snapped her out of her daze, catapulting her into an adrenaline rush. "Are you crazy?" she screeched, wrenching out of his arms. "We've got to get out of here."

She marched away, arms swinging. The emotions roiling inside her were overwhelming: hatred, anger, fear, confusion. But as she considered what she was doing, her strident steps came to a gradual stop. Her shoulders sagged. Her head bowed. Finally, she turned around and stared again at the wreckage half-buried in the water.

Then she looked at Grant. Even with the distance between them, she saw compassion, an understanding of her conflict in his beautiful, gentle eyes. She walked back to his side.

"We have to see if he's dead," she whispered brokenly.

"I know," he answered, putting a comforting hand on her arm. "Not for his sake, but for yours."

Shaking her head slowly, she said, "I won't be what he is. If he's not dead, I won't leave him trapped to die like a wounded animal."

"The bastard doesn't deserve your concern."

She gave him an arch look. "Didn't you just agree with me that we had to do this?"

"Yes, because if we don't, guilt will keep you his captive forever." Grant dropped his hands from her shoulders. "But he still doesn't deserve your sympathy."

"I . . . I can't honestly say it's compassion. But . . . I have to know. One way or the other."

Grant took her arm to stop her as she moved toward the water. "We've agreed we'll check the wreckage, but we're doing it my way."

She tore her eyes from the stream. "What?"

"He could be conscious, but trapped. And he has a gun. So I'm going first, to check things out. You're staying here."

"I will not—"

"Lynn," he said evenly, "for once you are going to take the orders instead of giving them. Don't think I won't tie you to that tree if I have to."

She was taken aback by the fierce conviction in his voice, and the earnest intensity in his eyes. Though it grated, she accepted his ground rules with a grudging nod.

Grant grabbed a stout stick and approached the downed bird with due caution. She put a hand to her nose as the smell of fuel and oil reached a nauseating level.

As he waded into the creek, Lynn watched carefully from the bank for smoke, or sparks, or any indication that flames were present. She might not leave Trey trapped, but neither was she willing to risk Grant's life in an inferno.

She held her breath as he reached the canopy and took a quick glance inside. He dropped back down, crouching to make himself as small a target as possible. He waited a moment, then slowly looked in again.

He signaled for her to come over. She rushed to his side and saw why he'd let her approach. Trey was unconscious, his body thrown like a rag doll across the cockpit, one arm twisted cruelly behind him. Blood smeared one side of his face.

With no small effort, Grant jacked open the door and Trey's head and torso fell free. His legs were trapped by the wreckage. Grant took the brunt of the body's weight while Lynn stretched out her hand to check for a pulse.

She froze, her fingers inches from his neck. With the

moment upon her, she was petrified, unable to touch this personification of evil.

"Lynn," Grant prompted with a grunt as he held the majority of Trey's weight.

Pulling herself out of her trance, she placed her fingertips against his throat for a moment, then jerked way, wiping her hand on her blue jeans. Lynn met Grant's eyes and nodded.

"He's alive."

Grant's mumble in response could have meant anything from disappointment to resignation.

There was nothing left to do but attempt to extricate the body from the wreckage. As she hurried to the other side of the cockpit to see if she could free Trey's legs, Lynn gave a prayer of thanks for both Grant's presence and his strength. It took everything she had to wrench open the passenger-side door and find a position from which she could maneuver Trey's legs from under the mangled instrument panel. With a grunt, she tore the fabric of his pants from where it had been caught by torn metal. As each second passed, she prayed nothing would spark the fuel spreading in an oily ribbon over the surface of the creek.

By the time they hauled Trey over to the bank, Lynn and Grant were both panting raggedly from exertion.

When she got her breath back, she hurried to the area where they'd shed their clothes and returned with Grant's T-shirt. She tore it in two with a vicious yank, and made a pad to press against Trey's forehead.

As she stared at her hands, one cradling Trey's head, the other pressing the makeshift bandage against the wound, she could feel Grant's frustration coming in waves. She struggled for the words to make him understand why she was nursing the man who'd just tried to kill them. Easing Trey's head to the ground, she finished tearing the shirt into strips.

After she used the strips to secure the pad, she rested

her palms against her thighs. "Grant, I know this makes no sense, but even after all he's done, I can't treat him like an animal. I thought I could be ruthless. I wanted to be, but I was wrong."

He took her chin in his hand and lifted her head until she looked at him. "I could have told you that," he said gently, a smile warring with his agitation. "But I should confess that once we got him out of that helicopter, I came this close to throwing you over my shoulder and hauling you out of here, willing or not."

"But you didn't," she challenged. "Throw me over your shoulder, that is."

"Only because I would have robbed you of the one thing you need right now. Peace of mind. If I could come up with a way to get you out of here but still manage that, I'd leave this bastard in a heartbeat."

Lynn's breath came fast, but it was no longer from the exertion. She felt the heat of his eyes on her and an almost palpable sense that he wanted to pull her into his arms. As a fission of awareness shimmied up her spine, she wasn't so sure she'd object.

Such a feeling should have been impossible, considering the circumstances, but the fact remained that she was looking at a man who made her pulse race and her heart flutter. With very little effort.

"You stay with Trey," she said, pushing to her feet and breaking the intensity of the moment. "I'll see if I can make Trouble come to me."

Grant surged to his full height and took her shoulders in his hands. "I don't want you to go alone, but I know it's the only way."

She nodded and stepped out of his grip. "Trouble wouldn't respond to you and I don't want Trey to wake up and start this crap all over again."

He watched her head toward the willow tree again with a decidedly reluctant face.

She took the time to gather her extra set of clothes

and the underwear and socks she hadn't had time to put
on, redressing behind the curtain of fronds. She returned
Grant's shorts, socks and hat to him, then jogged off in
the direction the horses had run. She called for Trouble,
whistling as loudly as she could.

It took a good twenty minutes to find the gelding.
When he finally trotted toward her, she praised him pro-
fusely, patting his neck with a grateful hand as she struggled with her frustration that she was taking too much
time. She needed to get back to Grant, but she could
hardly blame Trouble for being frightened. The thought
of a helicopter spooking the horses had never entered
her mind.

She checked on Grant again, then went in search of
Hot Shot. She found him grazing some distance away,
seemingly unfazed by his recent scare, her supplies apparently intact. After giving the search another good
half-hour, she finally gave up on Grant's mount.

"Maybe we'll get lucky," she said to Grant as she
returned to the crash site, "and come upon him later."

He nodded noncommittally.

With the temperature beginning to drop, their first priority was changing into dry clothes. Lynn kept her back
turned as they dressed, not only out of modesty, but
because she didn't trust herself not to devour Grant with
her eyes.

"We're going to have to get Trey in the saddle, and
tie him on," she said, setting her hat on her head. "I've
never tried that, but I'm guessing it only looks easy in
the movies."

"No doubt," Grant said dryly.

After stripping Trey's wet clothes off, they wrapped
him in a quilt.Then it took a concerted effort on both
their parts to get him on Trouble. Trey muttered as they
jostled him, and Lynn gave a grateful sigh when he
didn't awaken. Lynn tucked her quilt more securely
around him, hoping it would keep him from going into
shock.

After consulting her maps, Lynn determined they should head south.

"If I'm right about our location," she mused, "we should intersect a county road in a few hours, but unless someone comes along and stops to help, we'll never reach the town I think is about ten miles away before dark."

"Well, we'll just have to make do, I guess," Grant said, tugging his hat down on his head.

"We could always ride double on Hot Shot," she suggested reluctantly.

"But then we'd have to leave the gear. What if we get stuck out in the open again tonight?"

They watched each other as they considered the options. Lynn spoke first. "I say we take the gear. Better to walk and have protection from the elements than to be stranded with no food, no water, and no blankets."

"I can't believe we're doing this," Grant muttered as they began walking. "I know it's the right thing, but it still sucks."

Lynn didn't respond. The effects of the day were taking their toll, and she was on the verge of collapsing into massive hysteria. It would take all her energy to get through the night without dissolving into a puddle of tears.

She also had to face the fact that her plan had not worked. She was no closer to being free from Trey than when this all began. Forcing back the urge to cry, she decided that if Trey lived, she was changing her plans.

Next time, she'd try the highway. She'd borrow Nan's truck and drive as far and as fast as she could, then hop a plane for somewhere. Anywhere. Australia, maybe.

A little voice suggested that Trey should be locked up for what he'd done to Nan, if nothing else. Then she wouldn't have to abandon her home right away. And maybe she'd have some time with Grant—

No! That was the kind of thinking that would doom her. She had to stay hard, stay focused. There was no other way.

She ignored the stab of distress that shot through her at the thought of never seeing Grant again . . .

When he began slipping off the saddle . . . again . . . Grant pushed Murdock back into position with a grunt. He had already strained his shoulder, and having to baby-sit a felon only made his resentment climb through the roof. What he really wanted to do was push the bastard off the other side. He wished he'd just grabbed Lynn's hand the moment the helicopter had crashed and run as far and fast as possible. But he hadn't, and now he was stuck trying to save this worthless piece of trash.

He decided he wasn't as noble as Lynn. His desire for revenge increased as the hours marched on, and he despised feeling helpless as she became more wan and withdrawn. He felt he could only react to what was happening, and that was antithetical to his nature.

He cursed the sun's early demise beyond the horizon. If it were summer, they'd have at least two more hours of daylight. Instead, they were soon travelling by flashlight down a pitch-black road. He had bullied her onto Hot Shot, but without a saddle, she'd had to ride bareback. When Lynn got down to walk for a while to relieve her numb backside, she stumbled and fell painfully onto her hands and knees. Grant had had enough.

"That's it." he said as he helped her to her feet. "We're stopping."

"But Trey—"

"To bloody hell with the man. You're getting some rest."

Even though they were both exhausted, they settled Murdock on Grant's sleeping bag, and took care of the horses before they even thought about their own needs.

"Lynn, just sit down. I'll get a fire going."

"I can do it," she insisted, swaying on her feet as she wrestled with the saddlebags at her feet.

Anger gave him a surge of strength. Taking her shoulders into his hands, he gave her a gentle push toward a large rock.

"Sit," he ordered sternly. "I mean it, Lynn."

She looked for a moment as though she was going to argue, then her shoulders sagged and she sank to the stone seat.

Grant took her silence as acceptance, and worked fast to get some water boiling. Lynn needed something hot and filling, then she needed to sleep.

He frowned when he saw she had stepped over to check on Murdock. Jealousy, anger and fear roared through him before he could tamp them down.

He knew she had to face her demon; better that she do it now when he was unconscious.

Grant rolled out her sleeping bag and moved to Lynn's side. Helping her to her feet, he led her over and made her stretch out her legs.

"Wait!" she said, bolting back upright. "I need my needle."

"Your needle? What in the world made you think of that now?"

"I don't know. I can't explain why, but all of a sudden I just need it. It's in one of the saddlebags. In a little box."

In the blink of an eye, he remembered the box he'd kicked while walking through Lynn's yard, and then tossing it on Nan's counter.

"Um, Lynn, I don't think—"

"I have to have it, Grant. I have to. It's my . . . I don't know . . . good luck charm."

He settled beside her and took her hand. "Lynn, it's not here. Nan has it."

"Huh? How is that possible? I—"

"You must have dropped it somehow when you were leaving. I found it, and took it with me when I checked on Nan. I didn't think to bring it with me."

Her face crumpled and tears streamed down her cheeks. Then she began to sob uncontrollably. He pressed her against his chest, trying to comfort her, but nothing seemed to console her heart-wrenching agony.

"I'm so sorry," he whispered again.

He understood that she was releasing more than her pain over the loss of her needle, but it still nearly tore out his soul to hear her in such pain.

The tears, though, achieved a purpose. She fell into an exhausted sleep, still hiccoughing wetly even as she rolled instinctually onto her side.

He set a packet of sports drink and straw near her. He wanted to be ready to help her drink as soon as she awakened. He'd fix her some stew later as well, but for the moment, she needed the oblivion of slumber more than she needed food. Covering her with his quilt, he planned on fixing himself something to eat . . . as soon as he was done with Murdock.

A glance at Lynn confirmed she was out like a light. Without hesitating, Grant took a length of rope and tied Murdock's wrists together. Then he drove a stout stick into the ground, pounding it with a rock with all his strength. Once Murdock's ankles were tied together, and then to the post, Grant felt a small measure better. As a final precaution, he found Lynn's perimeter wire and attached the bells to the ankle bindings.

He'd bet money Murdock had a broken rib or three, and combined with his head injuries, it was unlikely he could have escaped, but Grant was not going to take any chances.

Grant reluctantly replaced the quilt Lynn had insisted on wrapping Murdock in, which meant he couldn't see the man's hands. The quilt was necessary, though, since Lynn's prediction of shock seemed to be coming true.

Murdock's skin was clammy and his pulse elevated. Grant wasn't sure what else to do but keep the man warm, so he stoked the fire and tucked the blanket in tightly.

Murdock's eyes popped open, making Grant jerk back in alarm.

"I'll get her," he whispered feverishly.

From his glassy look, Grant wasn't sure if Murdock even knew where he was or who he was talking to.

Grant leaned closer. "Over my dead body, you son of a bitch. You've scared her for the last time."

Murdock's eyes were closed before Grant finished his vow. Swearing, he settled into position and set Lynn's compound bow within reach. He wished he had his horse, or more specifically, the gun in his saddlebag, but he'd have to make do. He had Lynn's survival knife a hand's breadth away on his other side. He considered hauling out her nun-chaku, then felt silly because he didn't know how to wield them. He supposed it wasn't entirely unreasonable to want an arsenal at his disposal to protect Lynn as she rested.

Grant kept the fire going, watching Lynn's face in the flickering light. When she mumbled in her sleep, he hurried over and settled beside her, resting his back against the rock so he could soothe her when she became restless. Smoothing back her beautiful hair was equally calming to him, and he relished the feel of the silken strands under his fingertips.

"You are so beautiful," he whispered in the darkness. "And so strong. You awe me."

She turned toward his whispered voice, but didn't awaken.

"What am I going to do with you, Lynn?" he asked her, stroking a finger down her soft cheek. "What am I going to do with *me*?"

She didn't have an answer for him, any more than he had an answer for himself.

He didn't realize he'd dozed until a touch on his shoulder had him jerking upright.

"I'm sorry," he said automatically. "I didn't mean to fall asleep."

She looked only marginally rested, and her eyes had a haunted air.

"It's my turn to take watch. You rest, Grant."

"No, I'll stay up with you."

"Lie down," she ordered, using the same tone he'd taken with her earlier.

With a small smile, he obeyed, noting as his eyes drifted shut that she didn't sit until she'd found her nunchaku and set them next to her bow. He would have liked to somehow tease a smile from her, but he fell instead headlong into oblivion.

Lynn rubbed her eyes and stretched, trying to energize her sluggish senses. It was only midnight, but it felt like the wee hours of the morning already. She checked on Trey, noting that he had been tied up. Checking Trey's eyes with a flashlight, she was fairly certain he had a concussion on top of his other injuries. His pupil's were still unevenly dilated, and his skin was clammy.

She moved away and stoked the fire, careful not to look into the inviting flames. If she gave in to the urge to watch the mesmerizing flicker, she'd be half-blinded if she needed to look away into the darkness.

As if drawn by a force she could not resist, she returned to Trey's side and squatted on her heels. Wrapping her arms around her knees, she forced herself to stare at Trey instead. It was time to face her demon.

She hated him.

She hated him for what he'd done to her. She hated him for what he'd become. She hated him for his part in what *she'd* become. Even though she was a stronger person now, she would never forgive him for turning her world inside out, for making her afraid. For hurting her beyond description.

He had made her doubt herself, blame herself, for things that were not in her control. It had taken years to accept that she was not responsible for being beaten. There were no excuses, no justifications, for his actions. She would, however, accept her part in the demise of the marriage. Before he had become violent, they were already more housemates than lovers because she would not be a trophy wife or a convenience.

She had just begun to explore what she wanted out of life, to figure out her own career and dreams, and their lives had gone in separate directions. Except for the occasions where she'd agreed to play hostess, they had rarely spent time together. The harder he'd tried to control her, the more she'd pulled away. And the angrier he'd grown.

As she watched him, and let her thoughts flow, it surprised her to find she was still angry with him for changing. Or more accurately, she was mad that he *hadn't* changed. A marriage, like any relationship, had to grow and Trey had wanted an everlasting honeymoon. He hadn't seen that the constant giddiness could evolve into a closeness that would have made the romance deeper, more intense. Instead, he'd wanted constant, hot spontaneity.

And he'd lied to her about babies. She'd wanted at least three or four. Being an only child, she'd dreamed of having a house full of children to love and raise. She'd seen them in her mind, imagined their names, their personalities. Only to have Trey strip that very primal dream from her.

She wiped a tear of regret from her cheek, then rewrapped her arm around her legs. She'd wondered more times than she could count if things could have been different. If she'd made better choices. If Trey had gotten help . . .

As she stared, Trey suddenly jerked his head toward her.

She gasped and fell backward, crab-crawling with desperate speed to her bow. Her hands trembled as she scrambled to her feet and notched an arrow. She drew it back, aiming straight for his heart.

She held her aim until her arms were in agony waiting for him to move. His eyes fluttered open, but then fell shut again. He laid still but she stayed as she was, gasping for air, until she had no choice but to relax her stance.

When she accepted that he was still unconscious, she pulled the arrow off of the bow and put it on the ground beside her.

Burying her face in her arms, she sobbed silently, rocking back and forth as she struggled to be quiet. She battled against the sense of despair that this was never going to end. That she would be afraid for the rest of her life.

With effort, she found a measure of calm. Watching Grant helped remind her that she thought she would never feel desire again, and he'd proved her wrong. She thought she'd never want to be in a relationship again, and he'd shown her how much she did. But just as strongly, this day showed her that dreams didn't always come true.

And it hurt. More than she could bear, she feared.

She took a deep breath and decided she needed to focus on one moment at a time. For now she was obligated to a course of action, but once she was free of the burden lying unconscious on the other side of the fire, she would make new plans.

"Hey," said Grant softly, startling her out of her thoughts. "Come here."

She looked over to see him holding the quilt up in blatant invitation. She only hesitated for a second. Taking the bow and arrow and chucks with her, she moved to the pallet and slid down beside him.

Right now she needed the comfort of human contact more than she needed to be independent.

She settled on her side, closing her eyes for a moment. Pure bliss flowed through her when he fitted his comforting warmth against her back. Curling her arm under her head, she resumed her watch with her fear at bay.

For the moment.

Nan swept the final pan of debris into the trash can and gave Lynn's living room an approving nod. Hampered by sore ribs and aching muscles, she had moved slowly, but she had finally finished cleaning up the place. Jeremy had been a tireless help, but she suspected her darling son thought his mother had popped a rivet. Had a screw loose. Lost a few bricks from her wheelbarrow.

Men, she thought as she glanced at Jeremy, now asleep on the couch, and Ted who stood glowering by the fireplace. She noted that he'd been glowering at her a lot in the last twenty-four hours. She assumed it was because she wouldn't agree to stay behind locked doors every minute of the day. She hadn't been foolish though. She had agreed to a deputy staying close by, and had promised to stay at Ted's house until the situation was resolved.

She appreciated his concern, but instinct had told her if she gave in to her fear and tried to hide, it would be a long time before she felt safe again. More important, she had Jeremy to worry about. If she crawled into bed and pulled the covers over her head, she'd most likely traumatize a child who was already scared, and trying not to show it. For her son's sake, she would forge ahead as if she wasn't terrified to the soles of her boots.

"Nan, it's midnight. Let's go, honey."

"Honey, huh?"

His blush made her smile. She'd never been able to

kid around with her ex-husband but she was enjoying teasing the strong, quiet lawman. It was rather fun.

"Nan," he said warningly.

"Thank you for fixing the doorjamb," she said to throw him off-kilter.

"You're welcome. It's not truly fixed, but at least the door will shut." He gave her a pointed glance. "Now, let's go."

Nan sobered. "I don't want Lynn coming home to find her place a wreck. It's bad enough that so many things were broken, but it would devastate her to find the place trashed."

"And now it's not. My deputy said you worked like a fiend all afternoon."

The deputy would know because he'd been assigned to keep a close eye on her and Jeremy while Ted had tried to locate Trey. They'd had quite a row over the fact that no one had physically gone to search. The detectives had tried calling his secretary and his business associates but no one had seen him. He hadn't filed a flight plan with any of the nearby airports, but then, no one had really expected him to. Ted had been just as frustrated that Nan's injuries had not been sufficient to justify an all-out manhunt, but no matter how he felt on a personal level about the situation, he was still the sheriff.

Logically, she accepted Ted's explanation. She understood that there was no proof that Trey had vandalized Lynn's house, nor had he made any threats that could be corroborated by a witness. Still, Nan had argued until she was blue in the face that there had to be *something* Ted could do. He finally made some calls, and a personal friend was going to take him out in a private helicopter to search for Lynn and Grant at first light. That was the best he could do.

She'd hugged him, then, surprising them both.

And then he'd kissed her.

Oh, man, had he kissed her. Her lips tingled from the mere memory.

Pausing by the couch where her son was sleeping, she brushed a lock of Jeremy's hair away from his face. She struggled with what he would think if something grew between her and Ted.

With a sigh, she straightened. "Okay, let's go."

Ted half-carried Jeremy to the car. He curled on his side in the backseat, hardly opening his eyes.

Nan and Ted shared a smile.

"The resiliency of youth," she said with a loving look at her son in the dim glow from the car's dome. Then they were plunged into darkness as Ted shut his door and the light clicked off.

Ted drove with his trademark caution to his house, and once again hooked an arm around Jeremy's waist to help him inside to the spare bedroom. In no time the teenager was under the blankets sound asleep.

It wasn't until Ted had pulled the door shut, and they were effectively alone, that Nan felt nervous. Jeremy's presence in the room with them at Lynn's had been an easy barrier between her and the sexy sheriff. Of course, knowing that her darling son had once slept through tornado sirens took away the illusion of a chaperon, but Ted didn't know that.

But did she really need one?

Did she really want one?

"Ted, do you have any tea?" she asked casually as she straightened the plaques and awards adorning his mantel.

He gave her a look that said he knew she was uncomfortable, but he obviously didn't realize what being in his house was doing to her.

"Would you like herbal?"

"Perfect," she said, forcing a smile.

Anything that would delay going to his bed. Being the gentleman he was, he'd insisted she take the master bedroom. He'd slept on the couch last night, but for all his courtesy, she'd tossed and turned. She'd wondered if he was getting any sleep on a sofa that didn't accommodate his long frame.

Then all she could think about was him lying there, in a pair of pajamas still creased from the package. Which had then made her consider what he normally wore to bed. Which of course made her wonder if he wore anything at all. Then she'd begin to imagine what his body looked like with nothing on but a tan.

And on it had gone until she'd finally fallen asleep. Which led to dreams of Ted clad only in his brown Stetson.

"Nan," he drawled, holding out a cup of steaming tea.

She jerked out of her reverie, turning away so he couldn't see the furious blush staining her neck and cheeks. Tonight wasn't going to be much more restful than last, she was sure.

When she had herself under control, she turned back and accepted the mug, joining him by the fireplace.

"Thank you for coming with me to Lynn's."

He arched a brow at her as if to ask where else he'd be.

She cleared her throat. "Anyway, when you go out with your pilot friend tomorrow, please take this." She set her cup on the coffee table and took the needle and case from her pocket.

"Why would I need that?"

"It's for Lynn. If you find her."

She tried to hide the distress in her voice, but Ted was too observant. Setting his own cup on the hearth, he took her in his arms and tucked her head under his chin. His hands gently stroked her back, more soothing than she would have dreamed possible.

"She's going to be all right, Nan. I'll find her."

She hesitated only a second before wrapping her arms around his back, hugging him tightly. Closing her eyes, she enjoyed the sensation of being held, smiling when she felt him rub his cheek against her hair.

So much for mister tough guy, she thought, not at all opposed to experiencing this softer side of the stoic sheriff.

Maybe, Nan wished hopefully as they stood in the peaceful silence, *he'll try to kiss me again.*

She certainly wouldn't object.

Once again the lanky lawman seemed to read her mind for he tipped her chin with his knuckles . . .

. . . and lowered his mouth to hers.

Ten

Grant awoke with a start. He jerked upright, his heart pounding. Was that a shot?

He released a breath when he realized the fire must have popped. Lynn was looking at him curiously, Murdock was still passed out, and the night was quiet.

Scrubbing his face with his hand and feeling foolish, Grant pulled his sleeve back to check his watch. Four o'clock in the morning. As he rubbed the sleep from his eyes, he tried to calculate how much he'd pay right now for a full, uninterrupted night's sleep . . . preferably with Lynn by his side.

"Well," he said, moving to sit on the rock next to Lynn, "why don't we change places?"

"I'm fine," she said, inching away from him.

He frowned. She was clearly uncomfortable. It was equally clear that now wasn't a good time to ask her about it. Then again, she jumped up and moved toward her saddlebags, not giving him the chance to ask, if he had been so inclined.

"If you're rested, let's get going. We can follow the road in the dark."

"I think you should take another nap first. I slept too long, and for that I apologize."

She paused in her rummaging. "I'd rather get going."

"Not until you've eaten."

He handed her the packet of sports drink he'd set out earlier, watching her sternly until she finished the entire contents. After that, he quickly prepared a ration of stew and shared it with her.

Then, and only then, did he give in, even though he was in no hurry to manhandle Murdock back onto Trouble's back. Grant was no weakling, but it was damned hard hauling around one hundred and eighty pounds of dead weight, especially when he despised touching the man.

However he was also anxious to get Murdock into the hands of law enforcement at the earliest opportunity. Of course, if he roused long enough to give Grant a fight, that would be just fine, too. He wouldn't mind saving Lynn more sleepless nights, and saving the taxpayers the cost of a long trial . . .

By the time Murdock was situated on Trouble again, Grant vowed the man wasn't getting off that horse until he was thrown onto a gurney.

Despite Lynn's bravado, her clear exhaustion dictated a slow pace. She was back in stubborn mode, refusing to get on Hot Shot no matter how he asked or bullied.

"For Pete's sake, Lynn, just get on the damn horse."

"I'm not getting on the damn horse. If you think Hot Shot needs a rider, you get on."

Grinding his teeth, he aborted the useless argument. He could tell she was using all her concentration putting one foot in front of the other. Her focus also effectively put him out of her mind, he assumed, and wondered why she needed to distance herself from him again.

Despite the circumstances, or maybe because of them, he thought they'd become closer, and not merely in context. She'd let him comfort her over the loss of the needle, so why was she isolating herself now?

The sky was barely embracing the sun when the chopping sound of helicopter blades reached them from a distance. Grant and Lynn looked at each other in a panic, and with desperate strength, grabbed the halters of the horses.

Trouble tried to toss his head, not fully frightened but aware that something was wrong.

"Oh, please, oh please," Lynn said under her breath, making soothing noises to Hot Shot.

They watched as the copter made its way toward them, but to their immense relief, the pilot set the craft down a good distance away.

"Must be a horseman at the stick," Grant offered, feeling incredibly grateful.

Then reality set in and Lynn let go of Hot Shot to get her weapons from the saddlebag. She gave Grant the bow without hesitation. She had a set of wicked-looking metal disks in one hand, and her nun-chaku in the other.

The spotlight blinded then, but after a moment, a figure came jogging toward them. Grant tensed, unsure if the man was friend or foe. They were sitting ducks . . . or standing ducks as it were.

Grant didn't like the feeling.

"Lynn?" the figure called out. "Is that you?"

Lynn's shoulders slumped in relief. "Ted!" she called back. "Yes, I'm here."

The sheriff joined them a few seconds later, raising an eyebrow at Murdock's body on the horse.

"Very long story, Ted," she said. "I'm so glad you're here. How's Nan?"

"Nan's fine. Jeremy's fine. Are you all right?" Ted jerked his head in Trouble's direction. "Is that—"

"We're fine. Yes, that's Trey," Lynn confirmed.

"Is he—"

"Alive. Not necessarily well, though. He's been unconscious since this afternoon. He crashed his helicopter while trying to shoot us. I'm no doctor, but I'm pretty sure he has a concussion, perhaps internal bleeding."

Grant noted a distinct tightening in Ted's jaw. He didn't look happy in the least.

"Lynn, there's not enough room in the helicopter to take everyone. It's just a small, private job."

"I understand," she said, sighing wearily.

Grant understood as well. He didn't like it, but he knew what had to be done. "Get that bastard to a hospital. Lynn and I will ride to the nearest town and find transportation back to Winterhaven."

Ted eyed Grant, and then nodded his acceptance.

"I'll radio in and have a deputy meet you in Shamrock. It's only about five more miles down the road."

Great, thought Grant. *Two more hours on horseback. At least they could both ride and cut the time down. When this was over, he'd never get on a horse again—*

"Ted," Lynn said, breaking into Grant's thoughts, an obvious reluctance in her voice. "We lost the horse you let Grant use. I'm so sorry—it bolted when Murdock showed up in his helicopter. You didn't happen to see it as you came in?"

He shook his head. "No, but I'll get the word out to the owners around here. We'll do another search by air if Beast doesn't show up soon."

"Beast?" Lynn said, breaking into the first smile Grant had seen in far too long.

Ted actually blushed. "My witch of an ex-wife hated him, and the feeling was mutual. She called him Beast and I kept the name cause it ticked her off."

Grant and Lynn both chuckled.

Then Grant sobered. "Ted, there's a gun in that saddlebag. It's mine. I have a conceal-and-carry permit, but I'm concerned about someone finding it before you do."

Ted nodded. "In that case, I'll get extra help on it. Thanks for letting me know."

"Well," Lynn said, blowing out a huff of air, "let's get going. You'll find Trey's helicopter in the creek due west of here. There's a grove of oak trees and a huge

weeping willow beside the water, but I'm sure the
wreckage will be easy to spot."

"Especially from the air," Ted agreed. "I'm going to
take Murdock to the hospital in Winterhaven. It's the
nearest decent trauma unit, which is just fine with me
since I want this son of a . . . dog . . . where I'm in control of security."

Lynn put a hand on Ted's arm. "Thank you."

He patted her hand awkwardly.

"Ted, will you have room to take my saddlebags?
They're so bulky and Grant's got to ride Hot Shot bareback."

"We'll make room." He turned to Grant. "Would you
help—wait. Lynn, Nan said to give you this the second
I saw you."

He reached into his pocket and held out a small box.
With a cry of pure joy, Lynn snatched it away, yanking
off the cover to look inside.

"Oh, thank you!"

She threw her arms around his neck and hugged him.
Then she stepped back to look into the box, touching
the needle almost reverently.

Grant itched with jealousy that she'd thrown herself
so easily into the sheriff's arms when she'd been distant
from him.

Lynn turned her back, obviously overcome with relief.
He wanted so badly to join her, but her posture didn't
invite such a gesture.

He didn't have time to dwell on it. With the rotors
now still, Ted was leading Trouble over to the copter
where the pilot waited. Grant jogged after him and after
brief introductions and handshakes, the three men got
Murdock situated.

Grant found it exceedingly odd that Murdock now
held the edges of the quilt together over his chest in a
white-knuckled grip, even though his hands were still
tied. He didn't recall seeing that before now.

He warned Ted to be careful in case Murdock was faking his unconsciousness. Grant relayed the incident by the fire where Murdock had opened his eyes. He hadn't seemed aware of his surroundings, but Grant didn't want any chances taken.

At Ted's direction, the pilot went back to his seat and stayed with his gun drawn, watching Murdock while the sheriff walked Grant back to Lynn's side.

"If my deputy isn't there when you arrive, y'all wait at the Roadside Cafe, hear? He'll pick you up and bring a trailer for the horses."

"Great. We'll be there," Lynn said.

Grant wanted to say he was checking Lynn into the first hotel they came to, then wondered if Shamrock even had a hotel. Somehow he doubted Lynn would be willing to comply, even though his intentions were purely honorable. A hot shower, a hot meal, and a clean bed. Those were his priorities at the moment.

Ted left reluctantly, but he was no more reluctant than Lynn and Grant as they looked at the horses.

"Come on," Grant said, interlocking his fingers and bending low so that he could give Lynn a boost into the saddle. "It's almost over.

Their eyes met as his words slowed. They both wanted nothing more than for this to be over.

Right?

Lynn broke contact first, settling herself in the saddle and taking up the reins. Grant pulled himself onto Hot Shot. Neither of them spoke until they reached the cafe in the center of Main Street two hours later.

They got more than a few curious glances as they took a seat in a much-used booth. To say they were disheveled would be kind, even in a cowboy town.

"Coffee," Grant said before the waitress even reached the table, "And tea—"

"Coffee," Lynn contradicted.

The waitress shrugged and turned on her heel, heading for the kitchen.

"I thought you didn't like coffee."

"I'm not crazy about it, but tea's not going to cut it right now."

He wanted to talk with her again, but she slipped out of the booth before he could find the right words.

"I'm going to wash my hands. I'll be back."

Grant looked at his own dirty fingers and decided to do the same. Not unexpectedly, the booth was empty when he returned, his hands smelling of the ubiquitous pink liquid favored by gas stations and tiny restaurants. He couldn't complain though. The chemicals had certainly taken care of the grime. Probably a layer of skin, too.

He'd never paid all that much attention to his hair, but with his hat off, it was pretty scary. He chose to forego custom and put his Stetson back on, and planned on keeping it there.

The coffee arrived. Grant took a huge sip, scalded his tongue . . . and didn't care.

Lynn returned shortly thereafter and concentrated on her coffee. She was a bit more delicate with her cup, which saved her a blistered tongue Grant was sure.

Frustrated by Lynn's silence, he was about to strike up a conversation again when the bell over the door jingled. Growling in frustration, Grant took a healthy swig of coffee as a khaki-clad officer walked over to them.

"Miss Powell?" the young man asked, removing his cowboy hat, "I'm Deputy Nelson. Sheriff Carlisle sent me?"

"Thank you for coming so quickly," Lynn said, holding out her hand. "This is Mr. Major."

They exchanged handshakes with the deputy and slipped out of the booth. Grant tugged his wallet from his back pocket and dropped a five on the table without waiting for a check, certain it would more than cover the cost of their coffee.

Trouble and Hot Shot were retrieved from the alley and went into the trailer without a protest. Lynn and Grant both gave groans of relief as they sank into the soft seats of the tan Suburban bearing the county logo.

"You folks okay?" Nelson asked, starting the engine.

"Just tired," Grant said, keeping his eyes closed in the backseat.

"Get comfortable then, and I'll have you home in no time."

Grant's eyes popped open and he looked at Lynn. She sat forward in the front seat so he couldn't gauge her reaction to the deputy's words.

He wondered if home was a place she wanted to be. As hard as she'd been trying to get away, she was back at square one and he guessed she had little to no reserves of strength left.

Regardless of either of their desires, they were in Winterhaven with surprising speed. It probably only felt fast after their snail-paced travel, but Grant was still caught offguard.

"Deputy," Lynn said politely, "please stop by Nan's Treasures."

Nelson nodded and pulled the truck into the alley so the trailer wouldn't block the road. Lynn jumped out at the sight of her friend on the porch. Grant followed more slowly, watching with a twinge of envy as the two women hugged fiercely.

Grant shook his head to clear his mind and motioned to the deputy. "Why don't you take the horses on to Miss Powell's barn? If you'll put them in the stable, I'll bring Miss Powell home and groom them when I get there."

"I'm afraid I can't do that, sir. I'm not supposed to leave her alone."

"She won't be alone. I'll be with her."

"That's not—"

"What," Lynn interrupted as she returned to the Suburban, "are you two arguing about?"

"Ma'am, I've been ordered to stay with you until
Sheriff Carlisle says otherwise."

The deputy nodded politely toward Nan when she
joined them, but returned his attention immediately to
Lynn.

Lynn actually smiled. Grant had expected her to be
furious.

"I appreciate that, Deputy, but you can tell Ted I'm
just fine. He's taking care of the one thing that has me
worried, so I'll head home and clean up, but I can do it
by myself."

"I can't—"

"Not a chance in hell," Grant interrupted, lowly and
fiercely. "Until Murdock is behind bars, you are not
staying alone."

Now Lynn was furious.

"Just who appointed you my guardian? I have had
enough. I've had more than enough. You and every
other male on this planet are going to leave me be."

Grant crossed his arms over his chest. "You have one
of two choices. Him, or me."

"I've already chosen neither."

"Then I'll bunk on the front porch, and Deputy Nelson can take the back patio."

She looked for a moment as if she'd explode, then
the vinegar seemed to drain from her. "I'm being unreasonable," she said, as if to herself.

She lifted her head and gave him an apologetic smile.
"I . . . uh . . . feel a bit silly. Of course Ted wants someone with me. I'm just not used to having people involved
in my affairs."

Grant's frown faded. "Why don't we get you home
so you can get some rest. We can argue more later, if
you'd like."

She smiled at his weak joke, then turned to Nelson. "Deputy, call Ted and tell him I said I wanted Grant to stay."

"But, ma'am—"

"Call, Deputy. I insist."

Nelson turned with almost military precision and went back to the driver's seat. When he returned a few moments later, he simply tipped his hat. "I'll take your horse over now, ma'am. Miss Heatherfield, do you want me to take yours to your house?"

Grant had forgotten Nan's presence until she said, "No need for the extra trip. Just put Hot Shot in Lynn's other stall. I'll have my son get him later."

The deputy tipped his hat and took his leave.

Putting a hand on Nan's arm, Lynn urged, "Come over after you close the shop."

"Give me a few minutes to clear out these customers, and I'll be right behind you. Jake will be so excited you're home."

"I can't wait to see him," she said, her eyes bright.

Nan hesitated. "Lynn, you need to be prepared. Trey destroyed some of your things inside the house. I've cleaned up, but just be ready, okay?"

Closing her eyes, she nodded. "Thank you, Nan. I—"

"Just go get cleaned up. I'll see you in a few."

Grant couldn't get a handle on why he felt awkward as Nan walked away. He'd been alone with Lynn almost from the moment they'd met. Yet as he keyed the remote access buttons on the door of his SUV, and took the spare key from its hiding place, he felt like a teenager out on his first date. And nothing about this situation was remotely reminiscent of a date!

Shaking his head, he started the engine and headed for her place, feeling as though they'd come full circle.

And he was no closer to figuring out what was in his heart.

• • •

Lynn let the scalding water pound her neck. She'd
washed her hair three times and used a half a bottle of
shower gel on her skin but was still reluctant to end her
shower. Finally she turned off the taps. Grant deserved
some warm water and if she stayed any longer, the hot
water tank would be bone dry.

She'd tried to bully him into taking a shower first and
he'd given her such a look she'd backed down almost
instantly. He didn't say anything, but it was as clear as
if he'd shouted it that a gentleman didn't take a shower
before a lady. Her little house only had one bathroom,
so there was no compromise of simultaneous bathing.

Instead, he'd stomped out to the barn to take care of
the horses, saying once they were both clean, they were
going to eat something and then collapse for a few
hours.

The man certainly was bossy . . .

She'd called out to him through the back door as soon
as she was dressed, telling him she'd put an old pair of
Leonard's jeans and a flannel shirt on the bed for him.
Leonard's jeans would be a little big around the waist,
but he'd been almost as tall as Grant so hopefully he
wouldn't feel too foolish.

Before he'd headed for the bathroom, he informed her
that he'd left the saddlebags in the barn. They could wait
until tomorrow to be unpacked. The horses were fed and
brushed, and seemed happy to be in their stalls.

After offering her sincere thanks, she headed for the
kitchen to rummage for something to fix. Pancakes were
the fastest, easiest thing she could think of, and luckily,
the milk in the refrigerator was still fresh. It wouldn't
take but a minute to whip up some mix and heat the
griddle.

Nan came in while she was beating minuscule lumps
out of the batter. Lynn pointed to the table with her
whisk.

"Sit. Prepare to be awed by my culinary skill."

Then she dropped to her knees to hug a rapturous Jake, letting him cover her chin with sloppy kisses as his tail wagged so hard he could hardly stay still. He whined in glee as she scratched him from nose to tail and back again.

"I missed you, boy," she said, stating the obvious. Jake clearly returned the sentiment. "You're such a good dog."

She gave him her undivided attention until she felt he was satisfied with his greeting, then she sent him to his blanket while she went back to work.

Nan tilted her head to the side as Lynn thoroughly washed her hands and ran a wet paper towel over her chin. When she picked up her whisk again, Nan said, "You're awfully cheery after what you've been through. What gives?"

"I think there's some psychological term for it, but I'll call it Scarlet O'Hara syndrome. I'm not thinking about anything until tomorrow." Lynn slowed her stirring, and then looked at her friend. "The truth of the matter is, I'm sick and tired of being scared. I know it's just an illusion, but for the next few hours, I'm going to pretend that my life bears some minuscule resemblance to normal."

"Count me in on the charade then, honey. You deserve it. Oh, before I forget, a rancher found Beast and they recovered all of Grant's possessions in the saddlebags."

"He'll be glad to hear it." Putting the bowl and utensils next to the stove, Lynn sat down and cupped her chin in her palm, elbow on the table. "Thank you for cleaning up the house, and for warning me. It was a bit devastating, I admit, but I'm okay now."

"Jeremy was a big help. So was Ted."

"Ted again, huh? Do tell."

Nan blushed prettily. "He's hardly left my side. Only

his immense sense of duty sent him after you and Grant. I think every deputy in this county is on some kind of rotating watch around me and Jeremy."

"I can't say I mind that," Lynn said, her gaze dropping to the table. "I'm so sorry, Nan. I can't—"

"You can stop that right now. You didn't do anything. You didn't cause anything. You are my friend and I don't blame you, so just zip it, missy."

Lynn's laugh was watery. "I don't think I deserve you."

"You're right," Nan said, nodding with mock seriousness. "I think I'll use your guilt to con at least six or eight quilts out of you."

"Sold!" Lynn said, slapping her palm on the table.

The kettle whistled and she busied her hands making giant, steaming mugs of fragrant tea.

"How's Jeremy?" Lynn asked, spooning sugar into her cup.

"He's shaken up, understandably, but physically he's fine. I didn't make him go to school today and he's been nearly glued to my side in the store."

Lynn blew over the rim and took a careful sip. "Where is he now?"

"Helping Ted. Well, 'helping' may be a rather extreme term, but Ted has been terrific about letting him hang around. I can't think of a safer place for him, so I'm delighted."

"Nan," Lynn said, scratching nervously at a speck on the table, "what are you going to do?"

"What do you mean?"

"I mean when Trey is loose again. He might want revenge against you for helping me."

Nan inhaled sharply. "He's going to prison, of course."

"Honey, you can't be that naive. He's got tons of money. As soon as he's conscious, he'll get a fancy lawyer and be out on bail in no time."

Nan slowly nodded in agreement. "You're right—I didn't even think about that. I'll talk to Ted and see what he thinks."

Lynn's eyebrows rose alarmingly close to her hairline. "You'll talk to Ted? As in consulting him? Wow, something pretty amazing has happened around here."

A dreamy expression came over Nan's face. "He's so cute, Lynn. Especially when he's being protective and gets exasperated with me. He's not much of a talker, and the more perturbed he gets, the less he speaks. And when he gets really perturbed, he kisses me."

Lynn cut her a sideways look. "So let me guess. You've become an expert at rattling a certain sheriff's chain, so to speak."

Nan giggled. "So to speak. Jeremy and I have been staying at his house, at his insistence. And even though having Jeremy close by is a deterrent to certain . . . um . . . activities, I think things have been developing nicely."

Her smile faded suddenly, and Lynn leaned closer, concerned. "What's the matter?"

"I'm just wondering what the heck I'm doing, talking like that. Flirting with him has been fun, but I'm just kidding myself about how he feels."

"Excuse me?" Confusion marred Lynn's forehead. "A few seconds ago you were extolling his virtues."

"Oh, don't you see? He's not really interested in me. He's just doing his job and things got a little . . . out of hand. It'll all blow over when things are back to normal."

"I think I'm going to wring your neck," Lynn said, pouring another cup of tea and putting the pot on the cozy with a little more force than necessary. "It sounds like he's crazy about you."

"I seriously doubt that," Nan said, shredding a napkin nervously. "Besides, I have to think long term. I have Jeremy to consider. And you know the gossip about Ted vowing to never marry again after his divorce."

"Oh, please," Lynn said, taking what was left of the napkin from Nan's busy fingers. She pushed the fresh cup of tea closer. "I've told you a thousand times not to listen to gossip. You've got to take the chance, Nan. Ted is a wonderful man, and he's obviously flat-out crazy about you. Don't throw that away."

She sat back in her chair and pinned Lynn with a look. "And isn't that a bit of the pot calling the kettle black? When are you going to take a chance on love again? You keep yourself so isolated, most of the young men around here don't even know you exist."

"You know why . . ."

"No, I know you truly believed you were safe here so your excuse doesn't hold water. You're just as afraid as I am, Lynn."

The sound of a door opening silenced both women.

By the time Grant joined them in the kitchen, to Jake's complete delight, Lynn was pouring batter onto the griddle . . .

. . . and pretending Nan wasn't right.

"Yes, I'm afraid," she agreed vehemently. "And I have a right to be."

"I don't deny that, but it's time for you to let go of the past."

"And how can I do that with Trey back in the picture?"

Nan shook her head. "I don't know, honey, but you have to find a way or it will eat you up completely."

Eleven

Grant smiled when he saw Nan. "You look terrific. I'm glad." Then unable to ignore the dog, he bent and gave Jake an enthusiastic greeting which was returned in kind.

Nan self-consciously touched her bruised cheek. "That's sweet of you to say, but I hardly look terrific. You're a kind man, Grant."

"Just telling the truth," he said, taking a turn at the sink to wash his hands. As he returned to the table, he touched her shoulder as he sat. "Thank you for helping me find Lynn. I meant to tell you that earlier, when we were in front of the store."

"You were too busy arguing with the deputy, who, I have to tell you, was not thrilled with you. But I, for one, think it's great you're so concerned."

He gave Nan a teasing grin. "And I'm guessing it's safe to say that a certain sheriff has been justifiably concerned about you?"

With a huff, Nan stood and tossed her fresh napkin down on the table. "What is it with everybody today? The sheriff is just doing his job. That's all." Slipping on her jacket, she marched to the door. "I'll call you later," she said to Lynn without looking back.

Lynn and Grant exchanged amused glances.

"Oops," he said. "I think I touched a nerve."

"It's my fault," she assured him. "Before you came in, I was teasing her about Ted and I think she's feeling self-conscious."

"Why? She's a beautiful woman and Ted's obviously noticed. The man may starch everything from his shirts to his shorts, but he seems intelligent, after all."

Lynn used her spatula to lift the edge of one of the pancakes before flipping it expertly. "Nan went through a nasty divorce when Jeremy was about ten. Her ex had been having affairs for years, but she didn't want to see it. Then when he left her, he tried to make her feel she was the reason he strayed."

"Give me a break," Grant muttered. "Please don't tell me she swallowed that."

"Hook, line and sinker."

Grant grimaced and shook his head. "That's really infuriating."

As the coffeepot sputtered its last drops into the carafe, Lynn pointed to a cabinet with the spatula. "Cups are in there. Help yourself."

He picked a mug from the shelf. "Do you want something?"

"No, thanks. And you're right, it makes me furious that Nan took his lies to heart. She believes she's too fat and too ugly for any man to love and stay faithful to."

"Fat? Ugly?" Grant poured his cup and returned to the table. "You've got to be kidding me. Nan's got a great figure. All the curves are in the right places as far as I can tell."

"I wish I was joking, but sadly, I'm not," she said as she slid two perfectly browned cakes onto a plate. She'd already set out squeeze butter and warmed syrup.

"You know," he said, taking a careful sip of hot coffee, "not all men want toothpicks. Some of us actually want a woman who is more in his arms than bones with a bit of skin stretched over them."

She gave him a long look, as if she was debating whether or not he was being truthful.

"I'm serious," he said, pulling the plate toward him, "but you don't seem to believe me."

"Let's just say you're the exception, not the rule."

"And I thought *I* was cynical," he said under his breath.

She waved her spatula at him when he didn't begin eating. "Don't you dare let those get cold. Mine'll be done in just a minute."

He didn't need to be asked twice. Slathering rich, dark maple syrup onto his pancakes, he dug in with relish. "Mmmm, delicious."

"No, you're just hungry," she demurred.

"No, they're delicious. Geez, woman, do you argue about everything?"

She tipped her head to the side, as though giving his question serious consideration. "No, come to think of it. I just haven't had anyone to argue with in so long I think I'm taking advantage of the opportunity."

Grant chuckled and shook his head. By the time Lynn sat down, he'd devoured his serving. He stood and moved to the stove to take over at the griddle.

"You don't have to do—"

"Yes, I do," he said firmly. "It's not exactly brain surgery to flip a pancake."

"True," she agreed, cutting her first bite, "but as a general rule I don't make my guests cook."

"Then don't think of me as a guest."

He noticed her fork paused on the way to her mouth, but she didn't respond. He let her eat without further conversation, resisting the temptation to tease her further. Once he'd polished off another helping, and Lynn had refused any more, he sat back contentedly. He felt sleepy despite the coffee he'd enjoyed with his meal.

"I—" he broke off his statement to yawn behind his hand. "Excuse me! I think it's nap time. Why don't you lock up and get to bed. I'll sprawl out on the couch."

Lynn stood abruptly and began clearing the table. She seemed inordinately careful as she rinsed the plates in the sink before placing them in the dishwasher. He watched her curiously, wondering what was going on behind those beautiful green eyes that she kept fixed on her task.

Finally, she dried her hands on a tea towel and turned to face him. "No, Grant, you'll sleep with me."

His amazement was so complete it startled her into a laugh.

"My couch is the most uncomfortable thing you can imagine and you deserve a chance to stretch out. Besides," she said, pulling her shoulders back as if to challenge him, "it's a little late for false modesty."

It was impossible to block the image of her body, slick with water, from flashing into his mind. If her fierce blush was any indication, she was remembering their conflagration by the stream, just as he was.

"Lynn, this isn't about modesty. It's about your peace of mind and I'm not about to impose on you," he said softly, moving to stand in front of her. "I've slept on worse. I'll be fine."

She looked up bravely. "Maybe I don't want you to."

"Lynn—"

"Maybe I want you near me. Maybe I'm feeling a little vulnerable and not quite as tough as I'd like everyone to believe."

He cocked his head to the side, and a soft smile played on his mouth. "Then I'd be honored to join you. You have my word of honor that you'll be safe."

She blushed deeply. "Maybe I don't want to be safe— from you."

Grant had no words to say to her invitation. He tried to ignore her evocative words, telling himself she would change her mind after she'd had some rest.

His body wouldn't listen.

He was caught up in the sight of her, looking sexier than a woman had a right to in denim and flannel with her skin scrubbed clean and pink. The scent of her, fresh and crisp, lingering on her still-damp hair. The sound of her, as her breath came a bit too fast. It left him wanting the taste of her . . . all of her.

It was no hardship to let her pull him by the hand through the living area to the bedroom that bore her stamp on every inch of space.

She was a neat woman, but there was a romantic in her trying to get out. It showed in the pastel colors she'd chosen for the quilt on the double bed, in the pure white curtains saved from sterility by a gathered ruffle and embroidered trim, in the candles in every conceivable shape and scent on the bookcases, the nightstands, the chest of drawers. Perfume bottles were lined up with military precision on the dresser, yet bore names like Gentle Rain and Morning Dew.

Everything about her caught his attention. And despite his vow to be a gentleman, his mouth went completely dry as she shed her clothes to reveal a bra of spun lace. The matching panties were hardly more than a vee of insubstantial silk with the sides riding high over the curves of her hips.

"Good God you're beautiful," he whispered, unable to take his eyes away. Not that any red-blooded American man would want to, of course, but this man in particular was bewitched, and had no wish for a counter-spell.

She seemed surprised by his observation, glancing down at the undergarments that had his full attention. Her chest flushed with a rush of heat that swept up to her cheeks.

"I . . . uh . . . like pretty lingerie," she stuttered as she shed her bra and slipped on a short, slinky gown of pale

green that was every bit as inviting as what she'd just
had on. He couldn't fathom how she thought she was
any less desirable in this scrap of come-hither. As he
stood rooted to the spot, it struck him that she really was
completely unaware of her allure. Her confusion at his
reaction was honest, and one of the sexiest things he
could imagine.

How could a woman so naturally beautiful, so unaf-
fectedly sensual, be oblivious to her effect on a man?
He didn't have to look down to know the evidence of
her effect on him was rather obvious and hardly denia-
ble.

Folding back the covers, she slipped in and eyed him
as he stood there a slight smile playing at the edges of
her mouth. Coming out of his zombie-state, he shed his
own jeans and shirt, then joined her between the cool
sheets.

He automatically held out his arm in invitation, and
sighed in bliss as she moved next to him and laid her
head upon his chest. Without hesitating, he kissed her
forehead and wrapped his arms around her possessively,
fitting their bodies as closely together as the laws of
physics would allow.

"For the first time," she said, yawning, "I feel like
I've come home."

He traced her spine with his fingertips. "A nice feeling," he agreed.

"Mmmmm . . ." Her voice trailed into a soft sigh.

"Sweet dreams," he said against the sweet-smelling
softness of her hair.

"You, too."

If asked, he would have sworn that sleep would be
impossible with her soft and nearly naked in his arms,
no matter how exhausted he felt.

He was wrong . . .

•   •   •

Lynn awoke by slow degrees. It took a moment to orient herself to the fact that she was in her own bed, and that her head rested on a broad, masculine chest.

She breathed in Grant's clean, male scent and smiled in the dimness. Her curtains blocked most of the light, so she couldn't tell what time it was, but she guessed they'd slept away most of the afternoon. She didn't raise her head to look at the clock on her nightstand for fear of disturbing him. This feeling was simply too precious to cut short out of curiosity.

Since she felt so rested, she'd be tempted to say she'd slept the clock around, but she doubted that was true. Surely she'd be stiff in that case, and yet all she felt was wondrously languorous.

And she absolutely, positively refused to think about how illogical she was being. There would be time for regrets later, but for today, she was going to live in the moment and be damned the consequences. She'd spent the last five years on pins and needles; she'd earned a day or two of peace and she intended to claim every last second of them.

Ever so slowly, she inched her way off the bed and stepped silently into the bathroom. She brushed her teeth and hair, and stared into the mirror. The woman who looked back didn't seem to be the same Lynn Powell who'd walked in a few hours ago. It would take more than a bit of rest to remove the shadows from under her eyes, but still her face seemed . . . younger.

Absently, she applied a dab of her favorite perfume to her throat and wrists. She hesitated a moment, then added a touch between her breasts. She wished she had a sexier nightgown to put on, but she hadn't exactly been stocking up on peignoir sets these past few years. She indulged in pretty underwear, but she somehow convinced herself that that was different.

She turned out the light before she opened the door again, and leaned her shoulder against the doorjamb.

Smiling in the semidarkness, she watched Grant dream.
She was reminded of a John Wayne movie she'd seen a
long time ago. His leading lady had told him he was
comfortable. Lynn liked that. It certainly fit Grant. He
was a comfortable man ... to be with, to snuggle
against.

And he certainly had all the Duke-like qualities a feminist like herself should brindle against. But she didn't.
She liked that he was strong, and capable, and wanted
to protect her. It wasn't that she *needed* his protection;
it was simply nice that it was an option.

To say he was amazingly sexy was stating the obvious. Though his features were softened in relaxation,
he'd lost none of his rugged sensuality. He had a face
that even in sleep drew a woman's eye and a sigh. Especially in sleep.

She was curious to note he wasn't the type of man
she'd been attracted to in years gone by. It was painful
to admit that she had made a surprising number of bad
choices in the past. She had picked men who were controlling because her own lack of self-esteem hadn't attracted men of character, of strength.

On the outside, she had appeared confident, stylish,
but it had all been a shell that hid a woman afraid to be
independent. It had seemed easier to let someone guide
her than to strike out on her own and accept the consequences that came, good or bad. She'd just begun to
make her own way when the nightmare had started.

But today, she'd chosen well. She was no longer that
woman afraid of herself, of life. And she'd chosen a man
who could be her equal, a man whose very strength allowed him to be gentle, to be a companion, not a master.

She unabashedly let her eyes roam down the expanse
of his chest until it sloped into a trim waist. The sheets
had slipped down to his narrow hips, and her smile widened as she noted the waistband of his snug, white
briefs.

She would have guessed he was a briefs kind of man.

Sadly, his long legs were hidden under the peach-colored sheet, but that was all right. She was confident she'd get to enjoy the view of his long, strong legs before the day progressed much farther.

Lynn loosed a silent sigh. It felt wonderful to indulge in such thoughts. In fact, this little trip down sensuality lane had done an amazing job of relaxing her. If anyone had predicted this moment even a week ago, she would have laughed out loud. Yet, here she was, standing in the dark. Smiling like a goof. Staring at an incredibly handsome man.

She shook her head. Truth truly was stranger than fiction . . .

"Is there anything I can do to accommodate your . . . perusal?" Grant asked, his voice deep and husky.

Lynn looked up to see he was watching her watch him. She let a slow, wicked smile tip her lips.

"Just what did you have in mind, sir?"

Grant sat up in one smooth move, tossing the covers off his legs. He stepped toward her with the confidence of a man comfortable with his body. And who could blame him? Most men would pay dearly to be so toned and fit, but she was somehow sure he'd gotten his physique the old-fashioned way—by working, not working out.

When he reached her, she waited expectantly for a kiss.

Instead, he pecked her on the forehead and swatted her rear as he slipped into the bathroom. She jumped, then danced away with a laugh as he shut the door.

Drawing her nightgown over her head, she dropped it onto the floor and slipped back under the sheet. She pulled it over her, not to play the seductress, but rather because it had been a long time since she'd waited in bed for a man. Waited anywhere for a man. She was nervous.

And full of anticipation.

She settled onto her side and slid one arm under her head to watch the door. It didn't take long for Grant to rejoin her, but she noted with amusement that he left on the light . . . and his briefs.

She patted the mattress.

"Lynn," he said, sitting beside her and brushing a strand of hair from her face, "before we go too far we have to talk. About consequences."

Smiling, she touched his cheek. "You engineer types. Always so logical."

"It's something we have to consid—"

"Grant, I haven't been with a man in a long, long time. I don't have any form of birth control here, but I've done some calculating in my head. While it's not foolproof, I'm pretty confident this is a safe time. And if it's not, I will gladly, gloriously accept the consequences."

She didn't want to think anymore, but knew in her heart of hearts she'd thank the heavens above to have his child, to have a part of him with her wherever she had to roam.

"Are you sure—"

"If I had even the tiniest doubt, I'd tell you. Come to me, Grant. Please."

In a ballet of movement, Lynn rolled to her back as Grant swept away his briefs and the sheet to cover her with his body. She wrapped her arms around his neck, welcoming him as he bent his head to kiss her.

His breath was minty as their lips met and parted. She teased him with her tongue, summoning him to a sensual dance. He obeyed willingly, eagerly, leaving no room for doubt that he had anticipated this moment as much as she had.

"You are so intoxicating," he breathed, raising his head to look down at her.

A blush suffused her face. "Don't—"

"Don't what? Watch you? Don't tell you that you are breathtakingly beautiful? I can't make that promise. Watching you is about the sexiest thing I can imagine."

Yanking his head back down, she distracted him with a fierce kiss, pressing her mouth to his in almost bruising force. In seconds she was light-headed with bliss as he gave back in equal measure. His lips trailed fire across her cheeks until he reached the curve of her neck. When he nuzzled under her ear, she moaned and tilted her head as far as she could to give him a bigger playground.

She couldn't keep her hands still. As his mouth explored her neck and shoulders, her hands traced the contours of muscles on his chest, his back. Her fingers dipped into the vee created by his spine, then splayed across the powerful roundness of his buttocks.

"Don't stop," he whispered, a mere rasp of words when her hands slowed their survey of his long frame.

Kneading, sliding, tantalizing. Her fingers danced along the heated satin of his skin . . .

. . . as his began to dance on hers. He trembled as his hand sculpted her waist, up her ribs, to cup her breast in his hot palm. She gasped and arched her back in pure, primal response. The tiny noises she made in the back of her throat drove him wild.

When he took her distended nipple into his mouth, she cried out as wave upon wave of desire consumed her. He wasted little time sliding his fingers down her leg, then up the sensitive inside of her thighs.

"Open for me," he begged against her neck.

Awash in a sea of sensation, she bent her knees and welcomed his tender invasion. His thumb found the impossibly sensitive nub hidden in her soft folds, and with skill and grace urged her to her pleasure.

Unable to resist the tide of bliss building inside her,

she stretched out her arms, clutching the sheets. She gasped for breath as her climax sent her arching off the bed in a maelstrom of pleasure.

It was a long moment before she floated back to earth. "Grant—"

"Shhh," he said, stopping her with a kiss. "Just lay back and enjoy."

"But—"

"No buts, Lynn. This time is for you. Just for you."

A parade of kisses down her stomach and beyond kept her heart racing and her breath ragged. Soon her fingers were buried in the sheets again as his tongue brought her to another pinnacle of pleasure. Then another.

When she could take no more, he kissed his way back up her body, giving her time to recover. She welcomed his weight as he positioned himself, making a soft mew deep in her throat when he stayed still.

"Are you ready?" he asked, his calm tone belying the trembling in his arms.

"Yes! Please, Grant . . ."

Gritting his teeth against the need to plunge into her and find release from this sweet torture, Grant sheathed himself in her velvet heat one slow inch at a time.

He groaned against her throat, praying he wouldn't spill himself like some untried boy. She was so tight. So hot. So perfectly matched to him.

Determined to make this moment magical for her, Grant ruthlessly controlled his need. He started slowly, drawing out each stroke to give them both the most pleasure possible from the joining. As her cries and her hands urged him on, he increased his rhythm, delighting in each response she gifted to him.

"Grant, please!" she begged, raking her nails down his back in demand.

Unable to deny her, or his body, any longer, he drove into her with all the passion he'd held in check. He threw back his head and cried out, just as she arched against

him. Her own cry mingled with his in the stillness of
the room.

Relieving her of his weight, he rolled onto his back
and pulled her to him, cradling her body against him as
they both fought to regain their breath. Grant used the
edge of the sheet to dry the sheen of sweat from her face
before doing the same to himself.

He smiled at the ceiling as he sucked in huge gasps
of air and tried to calm his racing pulse. He felt utterly
replete.

"Thank you," he said, his lips pressed against the top
of her head. With deep breaths, he filled his lungs with
the light floral scent that he would forever associate with
her.

Lynn lifted her head and looked at the man who had
just given her a gift beyond price. He'd given her physical satisfaction; that went without saying. But he'd
healed a place inside of her that had been desperately
lonely, a place she had been afraid would never be
whole again.

"Grant, I—"

Love you.

Lynn put her hand to her mouth in shock. Thank God
she had somehow stopped herself before the words
slipped out. She stayed frozen as he looked at her expectantly, but words would not come to cover her awkward silence.

"Yes?"

"I, uh, just wanted to tell you how wonderful . . . that
is, how good . . . I mean—"

Grant chuckled and tucked her back against his side.
"I know exactly what you mean. I hope you'll believe
me when I tell you I've never felt anything like this."

"Neither have I," she returned softly, grateful her position saved her from having to meet his eyes.

He tried to hide a yawn and she smiled against his
chest.

"Go to sleep, Grant. We'll talk more later."

As if her permission had flipped a switch, Grant's breathing became deep and even before she could tuck the sheet and quilt around him. He hardly moved when she slipped from the bed. She needed some time to explore what had just happened to her, and his nearness was too distracting, too exhilarating.

She shrugged into her favorite robe and closed the bedroom door behind her, wincing as it made a loud clicking sound. After shushing Jake's bark of greeting with a gentle reprimand, she listened for a long moment to be sure Grant was still asleep. With her faithful companion by her side, she headed for the living room and a pair of slippers waiting by the coat tree in the front hall.

Grabbing her coat from the rack, she stepped into her flannel slippers and made her way to the porch to settle onto the swing. Jake jumped up beside her as she snuggled into her jacket to create a cocoon of warmth. She hugged Jake and her emotions close. She had not offered Grant a trite phrase; she'd never, ever felt this way.

The sun had almost set. Early stars dotted the sky, and the moon hung low in the horizon. The breeze was temperate as the warm front that had spared her and Grant from harsh weather while they'd travelled held firm.

But her mind wasn't on the weather. It was on the words that had sprung into her mind, unbidden, as the afterglow of passion had surrounded her.

Dear heaven, of all the things she'd been expecting, love was not among them! She'd been prepared for, even invited, lust. Certainly passion. Tenderness. But love?

Love simply did not happen in a few simple revolutions of the earth. It took time. That was the rule.

Lynn buried her face in her free hand, the other still clutching Jake's warm fur, and shrugged her quilt over her shoulders. She wasn't even sure she knew what love was. She had cared deeply for Leonard, and had thought, years ago, that she had loved Trey. But now she doubted everything . . . what she used to feel, and certainly what she was feeling now.

In the end, though, what did it matter? Grant would return to his life, and she would be left with her memories.

She'd been a colossal fool to think she could be with him so blithely. But she'd wanted to believe, needed to believe, that she could have a few blessed minutes of intimacy without having her soul ripped out.

She'd been wrong. Joining with Grant had stripped her of the layers of protection she had painstakingly built around her heart. Now she was more vulnerable than the day she'd lain at the bottom of that ravine.

Lifting her head, she looked at the stars, concentrating on the brightest one in the sky. Not a star at all, of course, but Venus reflecting the powerful rays of the sun. She tried to remember the names of the constellations Leonard had tried to teach her, but astronomy had been her one weakness in her survival skills. He'd spent extra time teaching her how to use maps and compasses to compensate.

She just wished he'd been able to teach her about love.

Like how to recognize it. And how to deal with it.

A pair of headlights slashed the darkness, making Lynn jump to her feet and sending Jake into attention. Automatically, fear sent her pulse racing. Thankfully, there was enough twilight left to see that the car bore the logo of the county sheriff's office.

She calmed down as Ted stepped out and moved to the porch.

"Lynn," he said, tipping his hat. "I hope I haven't come at an inconvenient time?" He bent to give Jake a solid scratch behind the ears.

She thought about the man lying naked in her bed and was glad that the shadows hid her blush.

"Not at all," she fibbed. "What can I do for you?"

"I apologize for bothering you so soon, but I have to ask you some questions."

She nodded. "Do you need me to come to your office?"

"No, I can do it here, if you'd rather."

"Would you like to come inside? I can have some fresh coffee ready in no time."

"Thank you, I'd be grateful."

She led the way, depositing her quilt on the couch. Tightening her robe, she was acutely aware of her nakedness and changed directions to head for her room.

"Uh, Sheriff, please have a seat. I'll be right back."

She hurried to the bedroom and threw on some underclothes and the first pair of sweats she laid her hands on. Racing to the dresser, she dragged a brush through her hair and gathered it back into a gold clip.

Feeling more comfortable, she returned to the kitchen and busied herself at the sink with the coffeepot while Jake disappeared into the living room.

"What do we need to talk about?" she asked, keeping her eyes on her task. She was getting some decidedly cool vibes from the other side of the table, and couldn't figure out why.

"I understand that Lynn isn't your real name," he said, taking a notebook and pen from his pocket, keeping his eyes on the pages as he flipped to a clean sheet.

Her hands paused as she was about to start the coffee brewing. She had to force herself to reach the rest of the way and flip the switch. The seemingly inconsequential action took on major proportions.

With her palms suddenly a bit damp, she took a seat. "That's not entirely correct. The short version of the long story is that Leonard Powell and I married in Las Vegas before he died. We also got divorced so I could do a legal name change with the most minimal of fuss."

"So your marriage to Mr. Powell wasn't real."

"It was a marriage of . . . necessity. For my survival. And it was real enough."

As succinctly as she could, she told him of her beating at Trey's hands, and Leonard's rescue.

Ted made notes on his pad for several moments. When he looked up, his eyes were only marginally warmer.

"I need to let you know that Murdock is not in great shape. He's got serious internal injuries, and the doctor isn't sure he's going to make it."

Lynn grabbed onto the table ledge, feeling wobbly despite the fact that she was sitting down. Ted instantly reached out to steady her.

"Are you all right?"

"Just a little drop in blood sugar, probably. I'm fine."

He eyed her skeptically, but continued when she gestured to do so. "I'm not here about that, really. What I need to talk about is some of the other things he said."

"He's conscious?" she squeaked, her throat tight.

"Just sporadically. He went into surgery almost immediately, but afterwards he said some pretty wild things. The problem is, everything he said is inadmissible in court. He wasn't completely free from anesthesia."

"What did he say?"

"He confessed to attacking Nan, to the damage to your house, to hunting you down with his helicopter. And he confessed to trying to kill you."

She stared at Ted, unable to speak. Hardly able to breathe. Then she gave a fatalistic snort. "And not one word of it can be used against him."

Ted nodded. "That's right. But I want to get some details from you, so if he says something when he's fully cognizant, maybe I can trip him up."

"I appreciate the thought, but I feel he's too canny for that."

He speared her with a look. "I take it you don't have much faith in the justice system."

She met his eyes squarely. "Let's just say I believe that every day peace officers try to help women who are the victims of domestic violence. What I don't believe is that there are enough officers who make domestic violence a priority. And I don't believe in the legal system. I've seen it fail too many times, and not just in my own case."

"So you choose to be a vigilante?"

Ah, now she understood that undercurrent of anger.

"I hardly consider myself a vigilante. That would mean I strike out for revenge against abusers. Nothing could be further from the truth. I simply help the victims who find me to get away."

"And that's not a form of revenge?"

She cocked her head to the side. "Are you honestly sitting there defending the abusers of this world?"

"No, I'm sitting here saying I have a problem with people who circumvent the law, no matter how noble or just they believe their motives."

Lynn stood and backed against the counter, her arms crossed over her stomach. "I tell you what, Sheriff. The day some woman you know . . . say your sister, or a close friend . . . survives a beating that by all rights should have taken her life, you come talk to me again. And after the trial, when slick lawyers get any substantiated charges reduced or plea-bargained, then we'll discuss just how well the law works, or how dependable the legal system is."

Grant came into the kitchen dressed in Leonard's old clothes, taking the scene in at a glance. "What the hell is going on?"

Lynn looked at Ted. "The Sheriff and I seem to be having some philosophical differences about the necessity of some women running from their abusers."

Ted stood, his chair squeaking on the tile as he pushed it back. "I apologize for upsetting you, Lynn. The conversation took a turn I did not intend. If you'll call me tomorrow, we'll get together to finish writing down those details in case Murdock survives."

She nodded stiffly.

"I'll show myself out," he said, putting on his hat.

Lynn didn't move, even after she heard the front door shut. She'd been hoping to spend a few days in her own home before having to face any momentous decisions. She'd believed between his injuries, and being under guard, Trey was a neutralized threat. At least for a little while.

But now she knew.

He would live. Even semiconscious he was plotting and planning and scheming, setting up a way to beat the system. At most he'd get a few days in jail for his attack on Nan, maybe simple probation. The property destruction charges would probably be dismissed in the midst of a plea bargain.

All in all, he'd get a tap on the wrist.

Oh, she probably had a week or two before he'd strike. But once he was released from the hospital, and not under guard, the illusion of freedom would be over. She had no misconceptions that fear of the law would make Trey behave.

Which left her no choice. She had to run. In fact, she'd be a damned fool to waste any more time, no matter how tempting it was to grab some precious memories in Grant's arms. She'd explore her financial options tomorrow, and then pick a place on a far corner of the earth to hide.

And maybe, if she was lucky, she would forget the one man who had made her heart soar to a heaven she'd never dreamed possible, had made her body respond in ways she'd thought was only a figment of an author's imagination.

With her heart heavy, she twisted around and turned off the coffeepot.

Twelve

When he'd awakened and Lynn hadn't been in the bed, Grant had experienced a stabbing sense of panic. After scanning the bathroom, he'd heard voices filtering through the door and dressed with amazing speed. He'd hurried out to find Lynn and the sheriff locking horns.

The tension in the room wasn't lessened by the sheriff's departure. Lynn was wound so tight Grant was afraid she'd unravel like a frayed cord right there in front of him. Her fists were clenched so hard that her knuckles were white, and there was no mistaking the trembling she was trying desperately to contain. It was a picture that deeply upset him, especially after the evening they'd shared.

Grant stepped closer and reached out to gather her close. When she sidestepped and moved into the living room, he pulled back in stunned hurt. It was as if the passion they'd shared just hours ago had never happened.

"Lynn, what's the matter?" he asked, searching her face for the reason behind her stricken expression. He'd seen her frustrated, angry, and terrified, all in varying degrees. But he'd never seen her look so . . . lost.

And he'd never felt so afraid.

She shook her head. "Nothing I can't handle."

Grant reached out again, a sense of desperation eating at his stomach. "Lynn, don't do this. Don't block me out. Please, sweetheart."

She looked at him as if trying to memorize every nuance of his face. Then she slowly walked over and laid her cheek against his chest, wrapping her arms tightly around him.

Burying his nose in the soft curve of her shoulder, he held on for dear life. He couldn't dismiss the feeling that something precious was slipping away from him before he'd had the chance to fully grasp it.

"Come back to bed," she urged. Taking his hand, she led the way.

Twice he tried to talk to her, and twice she silenced him . . . once with the gentle touch of her fingertips, and then with her mouth. That small contact set him on fire, and they were still standing in the middle of the room.

Vowing that they would talk, and soon, he gave in to the riot of sensations she caused with her kisses, her touch. He'd never been prone to losing his head, but when it came to Lynn, he seemed unable to remain calm and practical.

They shed their clothes and came together again in a lovemaking so sweet it made his chest hurt with unreleased tears. She then rolled him onto his back and took control, giving him a gift of her passion once more.

This time, in the afterglow, it was she who fell asleep. Grant lay there in the dark, stroking her velvet soft skin, trying to come to terms with the words that had formed in his mind as he watched her, poised above him, taking her pleasure from his body.

Then she'd opened her eyes and looked down at him. Her skin was flushed, her mouth open in a satisfied smile—

—and he knew. *He loved her.*

It made no sense. Against all odds, against all logic,

he loved this beautiful woman who'd been so hurt, been
so scared, been alone for too long.

More than anything he'd ever known, he wanted to
invite her into his life and cherish her. He wanted to
make the fear go away. He wanted her to be his wife,
and the mother of his children.

The thought was enough to send his senses reeling.

Not that long ago he hadn't been sure he ever wanted
to marry again. And having children had seemed so remote that he rarely thought about it. Now, in a matter
of days, he'd not only decided he was in love, but he
was contemplating marriage? And a house full of kids?

But what about his dreams? He had been putting plans
into motion to run for public office and he didn't intend
to stop at the city council. He'd had a longing to start
a new career for some time, to do something that
made a difference. He'd conquered his current challenge,
and a new one was in order. That was the kind of man
he was, and he accepted that he would always need new
mountains to climb.

Yet Lynn had been abundantly clear about her feelings for the political and judicial systems, and Grant was
certain she had no desire to be a politician's wife. And
who could blame her?

Could he give up his dream? And what if these new
feelings were fleeting? In his heart he believed they were
deep and true, but was that enough? Enough to radically
change his whole vision of the future?

He rolled his eyes at his arrogance. Just what made
him think Lynn would even accept his suit? The sex had
been incredible, but he wasn't nearly so arrogant as to
think his prowess in bed was enough to sway a woman
of Lynn's strength. She was made of sterner stuff,
which, of course, was why he was so wildly attracted to
her. She knew her own mind and made her own way.

Which were the very obstacles he'd have to overcome
if he wanted to get his ring on her finger. But he wasn't

known as a "major" pain for nothing. When he set his
mind on a course of action, the devil take the hindmost
because Grant Major was going to succeed.

Turning his head slowly, he placed a kiss on her forehead. For now, it was unlined with worry. As soon as
she awoke, those tiny furrows would be back, but, she
was at peace for the moment. If he had his way, he'd
conquer her demons . . . or help her conquer them . . .
then that peace would no longer be fleeting.

Offering a silent prayer that he'd get the opportunity
to try, Grant let sleep come.

Lynn couldn't sleep one more minute. She and Grant
had spent the entire night alternating between glorious
lovemaking and vivid dreams. Now, with the faint glow
of sunrise teasing under the curtains, she knew she had
to get out of bed. She never slept late, and even with
Grant's body warm and comfortable beside her, she
couldn't be still any longer.

Conceding defeat, she eased out from under the
covers. If she was lucky, she could be gone before he
awoke. That would be the most preferable option because she didn't really want to face him this morning.

Not with her soul in a knot over her newly discovered,
very confusing feelings. She hoped being away from
him, even for a few hours, would help her get her head
on straight. Then she'd see these feelings for what they
were—sexual awakening, maybe infatuation, but nothing so extreme as love. Surely that had just been a passing thought brought on by sensual fulfillment.

And what incredible fulfillment it had been. Grant had
introduced her to a world she'd never even known existed. A world of passion, of pleasure, of gentleness, and
desire. What she'd thought was lovemaking had been a
mockery of what she had shared in these few, too-short
hours with Grant.

Lynn shut the door silently and hurried to the second

bedroom that doubled as her office and quilting center. It was also where she kept her extra clothes. It wasn't that she was a clothes horse and required so much space, but rather a matter of necessity. The closet in the master bedroom was so tiny it couldn't hold more than her basic wardrobe. A smile caught her unaware as she realized that, for this morning anyway, she was actually grateful for the inconvenience.

It only took a moment to locate her passport, birth certificate and Social Security card. The expired driver's license she'd take with her to the Department of Motor Vehicles. There was no point in trying to use her "new" name since the jig was up. She'd have to assume a new identity when she got to where she was going. Wherever that was . . .

Writing quickly, she penned a note to leave by the coffeepot, telling Grant her plans . . . and asking him to go home, to go back to his life and try to forget the woman who'd brought him nothing but trouble.

Dressing quickly in her winter uniform of jeans, a turtleneck, and a flannel shirt, she sat in her chair to tug on warm socks and thick boots. When she took her needle from the case and slipped it into her collar, she was surprised at how cold the metal felt. It was usually warm and comforting. Today it seemed cold and disapproving.

Scolding herself for being silly, she snuck into the kitchen and put her note by the coffeemaker, then furtively exited by the front door. She would have gone the logical way, out the back door, but it squeaked due to the damage.

She paused on the porch, shrugging into her coat and pulling it tightly against her. She breathed in her favorite part of the day. The dew was still wet on the ground, the night creatures were silent and those who ruled the day hadn't awakened yet. The sun was a sliver of gold out across the trees and the very air vibrated with the promise of new beginnings.

Drawing a breath of clean, cold air, she tried not to think about the man sleeping peacefully in her bed. He would be upset with her, she had no doubt, but this was something she had to do alone.

Hurrying around the side of the house, she headed for the barn with the surety of someone who'd made the walk hundreds of times. She didn't need a flashlight as she could find her way to Trouble's stall blindfolded.

She opened the door and flipped on the light switch. Then she screamed.

It only took her a second to recognize Grant leaning back against her workbench. His jeans were zipped but unsnapped, and his shirt unbuttoned. His stance was negligent, but his crossed arms and fierce frown gave other signals.

"Going somewhere?"

Nonplussed, she struggled to regain her composure. She hoped she looked cool when she raised an eyebrow. "Actually, I'm riding into town to see if I can access my settlement funds. Then I'm going to get a driver's license. But ultimately, yes, I'm leaving."

"If cash is an issue, I'll give you whatever you need."

"I don't need your money, Grant."

"That's the point, isn't it," he said, stating a fact more than asking a question.

"What is?"

"You don't need anyone. Or you won't allow yourself to need anyone."

She welcomed the surge of anger that coursed through her. In fact, she was grateful.

"You're absolutely right, Grant. I don't need anyone. I haven't needed anyone for a long time, and I'm not about to start now."

With renewed determination, she walked past him and gathered Trouble's tack.

"Isn't it a little early to be heading to the bank?"

"I planned on returning Hot Shot to Nan's stable and

checking on Sassy. Then I'll call the bank from Nan's house and see if the officer I worked with when I set up the account is still available."

"And you weren't going to wake me up?"

"I didn't need your permission, nor did I consider it your business."

"Then you'd prefer letting me worry myself sick that something had happened to you."

"I left you a note. In the kitchen."

"And that makes it all okay?"

She stopped short, ashamed by the truth. Running off with only a simple note of explanation was a betrayal of his concern. She stopped arranging Trouble's bridle and looked at the floor. He deserved better, and she knew it.

"Grant . . . I . . ." She raised her eyes to find his glare no less forbidding. "I didn't intend to worry you. I assumed you'd check the kitchen, then the stables, and see I'd ridden off. Then you'd get mad at me and leave."

"Leave? Just like that. After all we've been through, and most especially after yesterday, you honestly believe I'd get in a huff and just abandon you? Good God, Lynn, how shallow do you think I am?"

Not shallow at all. In fact, a depth of character ran through the man who managed to look sexy even though he was mad enough at her to chew nails.

"That is one word I'd never apply to you, Grant."

"Then what the hell were you thinking?"

She couldn't fight the tears welling in her eyes. "That I had to get away from you," she whispered honestly. "At least for a few hours. Until I can get my head on straight."

Turning her back to him, she coaxed Trouble into taking the bit and fit the straps over his ears. She needed to keep her hands busy. It was the perfect excuse not to look at Grant.

"I need you to go home, Grant. I'm as safe at this

moment as I can be, with Ted's watchful eye on Trey. Ted may be mad at me, but he's a damn good sheriff and will protect me."

"So now you're just dismissing me? Thank you for your services, but run along now?"

She blushed furiously at his jab, and whirled on him. "Don't you dare try and pull that on me. What we just shared was precious to me, but it does not give you rights."

"You'll have to forgive me, because I've never gone to bed with a woman, any woman, casually. I know that's not the macho thing to admit, but there you have it. I have to feel something before I take that step. And what I feel for you is a hell of a lot more than *something*."

Lynn tamped down the elation that surged through her. It didn't matter if the man fell to his knees and avowed his undying love. She couldn't let herself be swayed and weakened. Not now. She couldn't let him stay in harm's way.

It took every ounce of willpower to keep her heart from showing in her eyes. She kept her expression severe and her posture unbending as she turned away and saddled Trouble.

The ensuing silence would have led her to believe he'd left, except that her every nerve was attuned to him. As clearly as if she were looking at him instead of a girth strap, he still stood behind her, his handsome face troubled.

"I appreciate what you're saying," she said without turning, "but—"

"Let me help you, Lynn. Don't leave me here to pace."

If his voice had been arrogant and demanding, she could have kept her throat from closing. But he somehow knew to be gentle, coaxing, and hot tears streaked down her cheeks.

"Why are you doing this, Grant? Don't you understand—"

"No, I don't! I want to get it through that beautiful, stubborn head of yours that I can help. But you have to let me."

She sagged against Trouble's neck. "I can't take much more, Grant," she whispered brokenly. "I'm holding on by the edge of my fingernails and I simply can't deal with one more thing."

"Then let me drive you to town. While you're taking care of business, I'll get Nan's trailer and return Hot Shot to the barn. That will take care of one of the tasks you've got on your shoulders, yet give you some time by yourself."

She turned around, a teary smile playing on her lips. "And you'll know exactly where I am and keep me dependent on you for transportation."

He stepped forward and traced the track of a tear. "Is that so awful?"

Closing her eyes, she gave in. She didn't have the strength to fight anymore.

She set about unsaddling Trouble while Grant went in to finish dressing.

Nan locked the rear door of the shop behind her and set about her usual routine. When she was younger, she'd hated rising early. Now she loved getting to the store and having time to organize her thoughts and her day before shoppers arrived.

First, and most important, she started coffee for her customers . . . and maybe one certain sheriff. The gal from the pastry shop down the street would deliver croissants and doughnuts in a little while, but Nan vowed to stay away from the sweets. She'd been negligent about her diet lately, and she was determined to rectify that.

Never a small woman, she used to rail against the

vagaries of fate that had given her a body style that would never be fashionable. No matter how much weight she lost, she'd always be five-two, have full hips and short legs. When she'd finally accepted that her goal needed to be maintaining a healthy lifestyle instead of worrying about being thin, she'd become a much happier woman.

Of course, losing two hundred and ten pounds of ugly fat, named Jackson, had helped more than anything. In the beginning, it had crushed her to see her ex-husband with his very tall, very thin mistress. Now she could laugh. He was the fool who'd chosen a bimbo over his son.

But now that she thought about it, she wouldn't mind gaining about a hundred and eighty pounds of sheriff . . .

Nan smiled as she dusted a display of figurines, not minding the never-ending task for the first time in as long as she could remember. Everything seemed better this morning. Brighter. Hopeful.

A knock came at the back door. Surprised, she hurried over and flipped aside the curtain. Jeremy had a key, so she assumed it was Ted. She smiled to see she was right.

Tripping the dead bolt, she let him in. He hadn't been happy when she'd insisted on returning to her home yesterday, and she knew at least one deputy had spent part of the night outside her house. On one hand she had been grateful for the protection, while on the other she'd felt guilty about the preferential treatment.

When she'd taken Jeremy out to the ag farm long before the sun had risen, there had been no brown car with lights mounted on the roof in sight. She'd shrugged, assuming she'd caught them mid-shift change. Then again, maybe Ted had sent them on assignments more pressing than watching a sleeping house.

"Ted, good morning. Would you care for some coffee?"

"Thanks, I'd like that."

He removed his hat, but didn't return her smile. That made her nervous. "Is something wrong?"

He had been doing his lawman's survey of the room, cutting his eyes back to her when he heard the concern in her voice.

"Everything's status quo," he assured her. "Murdock's in and out of consciousness, but there's no real change in his condition. I just spoke with a nurse before I came over."

Nan relaxed marginally. "Oh, good. Your expression is so fierce, I—"

"How long have you known about Lynn Powell's activities?"

She turned around, a mug in each hand. "Pardon?" He looked both angry and troubled, and she wasn't sure how to respond.

"Lynn's work with an underground railroad. Did you know about it, and if so, for how long?"

Something inside her seemed to wither. Her hands began to shake, sloshing hot coffee over her fingers. She set the cups down with a hiss of pain and reached for a napkin. "Why are you asking?"

"Because I haven't slept a wink all night. I went out to Lynn's to talk to her about Murdock, and in the course of the conversation, I found out she's involved in something I'm having trouble wrapping my brain around. I want to know if you knew about it."

She placed the napkin on the counter with far more precision than necessary. "Why? Does it matter?"

Concern was at war with duty as he looked at her. "It does to me."

She moved around to the back side of her counter, for the first time needing some distance from the lanky, handsome man. The room was quiet as she studied his features.

"Yes, Ted, I knew. I've known from the beginning."

"And when exactly was the beginning?"

Thinking back, she tried to calculate. "A little over three years ago, but shouldn't you be asking Lynn these questions?"

"I'm asking you."

Nan lifted the cups one at a time to wipe the drops off the counter. "I take it there's a problem?"

"Yes, there's a problem. What she's doing is illegal."

Her stomach knotted painfully. "Illegal? Well, then, I guess I'm guilty too, Are you going to arrest me?" she asked, feeling the blood drain from her face. "Although I'm not sure exactly what for."

"Of course I'm not going to arrest you," he snapped. Then he put his hands on the counter and dropped his head, sighing. "Nan, I'm sorry."

"I just wish I knew what you're looking for. Is Lynn in trouble?"

"Outside this situation with her ex-husband? No, not that I'm aware of."

"Then . . . forgive me, but what's the problem?"

Ted turned his hat, brushing an imaginary speck of dust from the dark brim. "As a man, I have a certain admiration for her desire to help. As a sheriff, I can't tolerate anyone taking the law into their own hands."

She pulled back as if he'd physically slapped her. Carefully, so she didn't stumble on her suddenly weak knees, Nan sat in one of the rockers close by.

He immediately moved closer. "Are you all right?"

She waved him away, not wanting him near her until she sorted this through. "I'm confused, Ted. Are you telling me you think Lynn is a bad person, a criminal even, for helping people who are desperate?"

Ted rubbed his hand across his forehead. "No, I don't think she's a bad person. Misguided, maybe, but bad? No. As to whether her actions are criminal or not, that's pretty clear. She's helping people avoid the jurisdiction of the court, and the federal government."

"Wait a minute," Nan said, looking at him incredulously. "You're concerned because these women might be avoiding income tax? Don't you realize that most abused women have incomes well below the poverty line when they leave their abusers? A lot of them are at that level before they leave. And you've got your knickers in a twist because they might not be filing tax returns?"

It was Ted's turn to pull back, affronted. He tossed his hat on the counter. "I didn't say that. I'm not an I.R.S. agent so that's not really my concern. It's the overall issue of circumventing the law." He gave a huff of frustration. "I'm not arguing that the system is perfect. Only a fool would say otherwise. But no matter how you gussy it up, it's still illegal."

Anger restored her energy. Surging to her feet, she retreated behind the counter again. "We'll just have to disagree then. I find what Lynn is doing to be extremely honorable."

"I'll agree that her intentions are honorable, but I really didn't intend to argue about Lynn. I wanted to talk about you. About us."

She raised an eyebrow. "Is there an us?"

He stepped closer without crowding her. "I wanted there to be."

"Wanted? As in past tense?"

"Nan, these past few days have crystallized things for me. I've been attracted to you for a long while, but we haven't had a lot of opportunities to get together."

"We've both got jobs that don't allow much free time."

"That, and you've had a 'back off' sign over your head every time I see you."

She started in surprise. "I do?"

He nodded. "You have the most beautiful smile I've ever seen, but you don't let people get close. Well, me at least."

Some of the anger seeped out of her shoulders. "I never guessed you were interested. I mean, we've gone to lunch a few times, but that doesn't mean—"

"I have been interested for a long time. And having you and Jeremy with me for these couple of days just felt . . . right."

She struggled against hot tears threatening behind her eyes. "There's a giant 'but' at the end of that sentence."

Ted looked over her shoulder at the potpourri display. Somehow she doubted he found the bags of cinnamon delight and vanilla daydream all that interesting. He was just avoiding meeting her eyes.

"Yeah," he finally breathed. "There is a 'but.' I have to know how involved you are with these activities."

Nan nodded slowly, picking up a little stuffed lion. She stroked down his mane because she desperately needed something to do with her hands.

"The truth is, I'm not very involved at all—"

His face relaxed with relief.

"—but only because Lynn won't let me."

The tension returned.

"Ted, I'd be in there tooth and nail if Lynn would accept my assistance. But she is determined to protect me."

"I'm grateful for that—"

"Don't be. If I had more guts, I'd set up my own system, but I've never wanted to butt into her business. So I send money to the women's shelter in Austin and do what I can to help Lynn. But I should be doing more."

Ted slowly nodded.

Nan tried for a smile. And failed. "So I guess this means you'll be going to the dances at the fire hall more often."

His forehead furrowed in massive confusion. "What?"

"That was my very lame way of saying you'll be back on the market."

"I never considered myself on any market," he scoffed.

"Of course you didn't," she said, rolling her eyes. "You're only one of *the* most eligible bachelors in the county. Or are you oblivious to the entourage that follows you around when you deign to show up?"

A blush heated his cheeks. "That's enough, Nan."

It wasn't nearly enough, but he didn't seem to understand that taking a teasing tone was the only thing holding her together.

"Well," she said too brightly, taking up her dust rag again. "I guess we'd both better get back to work."

"Nan—"

She shook her head sharply. "No, Ted, don't say any more. It's pretty clear we have some major philosophical differences so I think it's best if we just get things back to the way they were."

"We can try to work this out—"

"No. No, I don't think so." Grabbing an ornament off the table at her elbow, she began to polish the crystal angel's spread wings. "It would be best if you left now."

Ted picked up his hat with obvious reluctance, but he moved toward the door without arguing. "I'll call you."

"Come by the shop any time," she said with forced cheerfulness. "There's always a pot of coffee ready."

As he closed the door quietly behind him, tears that would no longer stay dammed came rushing to the surface.

The crystal angel slipped from her fingers to the floor, smashing into pieces.

Thirteen

Grant waited until Lynn had gone into Nan's house before he allowed a determined frown to settle over his face. He'd had to work hard to keep his expression devoid of the fury roiling inside of him.

Now that Lynn had given him her word not to run off, he had something to do before he kept his promise to get Hot Shot home to his stall.

Grant hooked the trailer to avoid raising Lynn's suspicions and headed straight to town, not pausing until he was inside the hospital and waiting for the elevator. When he reached the fifth floor, he looked for the deputy outside Murdock's room, and was surprised instead to find the sheriff himself seated in the hard plastic chair.

"Sheriff," he said, tipping his head and offering his hand.

Ted stood and accepted the handshake. "What brings you here, Major?"

"I understand he's been conscious," Grant said, jerking his head toward the door.

"Off and on."

Grant nodded and gave the sheriff an assessing look. "Listen . . . Ted. I need to have a . . . little conversation with Mr. Murdock."

Ted returned the look with equal measure. "I may not like it, you understand, but his safety is my responsibility at the moment."

"Warning taken. I don't plan on inflicting any bodily harm."

Yet.

Ted looked down at the Styrofoam cup in his hand. "I suppose I do need to get some more coffee, and if someone, say, slipped into the room while I was gone, I couldn't do much about it."

His smile was small, but contained gratitude. Ted apparently understood that Grant had a few things to say to Murdock that couldn't be said in front of witnesses. "Thanks."

Ted stepped down the hall without responding. Grant opened the door and stepped inside the room, his eyes immediately seeking Murdock.

He didn't hesitate to move right next to the bed, resting the heels of his hands on the rails the nurses had pulled to their full height.

As if sensing him, Murdock's lashes fluttered open. His brown eyes were dulled by pain, but he appeared awake enough to understand what Grant was about to say.

"I'll cut right to the chase, Murdock. If you try to hurt Lynn again, or if you even threaten to hurt her, you won't have to worry about the law and any trial you're facing. I'll kill you."

"I've never been overly intimidated by threats," he answered, his throat raspy.

"You'd be wise to be this time," Grant said softly, but his voice was steely.

Murdock looked away and took several breaths. "Words at this point are pretty useless," he said crisply, "but I will tell you this. Things will be different from now on."

"You're damn straight they will. When you get out of prison, you're never going to be within a hundred miles of Lynn ever again. Do you understand me?"

"I understand you're feeling protective of the woman you love."

Grant's stare turned glacial. "If you plan on venting that jealousy, you'd better try it on someone your own size. And I'm your volunteer."

Murdock sighed. "I guess I am a bit jealous, but I don't owe you any explanations, Major. The only person I owe is Lynn." He turned his face toward the window.

Grant sensed he'd just been dismissed, but he wasn't through. "I'm watching you, Murdock. I'm going to be a shadow you can't escape. Just remember that and be looking over your shoulder."

With a negligible smile, Murdock met Grant's eyes again. "I may not like it, but it looks like Lynn has found a protector in you."

"Till my last breath," Grant vowed meaningfully.

Satisfied that he'd made his point, Grant pivoted on his heels and walked out.

Lynn moved through Nan's silent house, appreciating the stillness. The drive over hadn't been that long, but every second had seemed to stretch into an hour. Since she'd left Jake at home she didn't even have him for a distraction. But Grant had been true to his word. He'd left her at the door and headed for Nan's stables the minute they'd arrived.

Walking through the living room to the kitchen, Lynn took the cordless phone off the base as she went by. After scrounging up a phone book, she sat at the table to begin.

An hour later, she sat back and tossed down her pencil in disbelief. She'd been prepared to find out Trey had managed to steal her settlement funds. To her amazement, not only was the money still there, but her account representative had been investing for her by the power of a proxy she'd signed.

Lynn was stunned at her naivete. She vaguely remembered the barrage of questions thrown at her by the bank officer some eight years ago, but she had no idea the choices she'd made had put her money into an investment fund instead of a certificate of deposit.

As she looked down at the figure on the paper in front of her, she was, for once, grateful that she hadn't paid proper attention. While she was aware she could just as easily be flat broke, in this instance, she was the proud owner of a nice wad of cash and a stock portfolio that was beautifully balanced. She was no millionaire, but she could easily buy a vehicle, or a plane ticket to anywhere in the world.

She smiled as she realized getting to Australia was no longer a pipe dream.

Then her smile faded at the thought of actually going.

Before she could become distraught, she went out to the stable to rub Sassy's soft nose. The birth had to be imminent, but the mare was obviously glad to see her owner, and didn't appear to be in any distress.

As Lynn expected, it didn't take long for Grant to return. Hot Shot seemed glad to be home, and Sassy whickered at her new stablemate.

It took the better part of the rest of the day, but by evening, she followed Grant back to her house in a four-wheel drive Jeep of her own. She also had a driver's license, insurance, and a sizeable purse full of cash. And through it all, Grant had been beside her, quiet and supportive. She both appreciated his presence, and resented it, and he seemed to know it.

Feeling annoyed with herself, and irritated in general, she went inside the house first, knowing Grant would be straight behind. She laid the items she'd collected over the course of the day on the entryway table and headed for her bedroom for a long, hot shower and fresh clothes.

On the way, she paused by the narrow stairwell to the attic. The urge to go upstairs was instantaneous. And

inexplicable. She started to go on by when she felt a tug
at her collar. She reached up, thinking she had gotten
snagged on something, but there was nothing wrong.
Only the needle, almost hot against her thumb.

With a shrug, she gave in, flipping on a light switch
as she ascended. When she opened the door and stepped
inside, enough light filtered in from the tiny hallway to
let her find the string hanging from the single, bare bulb.

She glanced around at the room that seemed frozen
in time. She remembered the first time Leonard had
brought her up here when he'd been feeling nostalgic
and had wanted to share some of the things he'd been
unable to throw out or give away, things that had no
value to anyone but him.

It had been the day he'd given her the needle.

A fine layer of dust had settled on the furniture and
other flotsam and jetsam of several generations. In one
corner was his grandfather's favorite chair, the fabric
worn in the seat and faded all over. In another corner
sat his grandmother's antique sewing machine, its
wooden cover dry from years without polish.

Over here was an old dressmaker's form clothed in
Leonard's orange hunting jacket. Over there, a broken
birdcage was tilted on its side beside a cheval mirror
tilted drunkenly on a broken leg. An impossibly silly
straw hat decorrated with plastic cherries topped the hap-
hazard pile, and Lynn wondered who'd worn the bizarre
thing, and why.

As she scanned, a wooden chest caught her attention.
She'd been up here many times, but oddly, she couldn't
remember seeing it before. With a shrug, she moved a
pile of picture albums, done in the old scrapbook style,
that were blocking the trunk, and then knelt in front of
it. The hinges protested noisily when she lifted the lid,
and she wrinkled her nose at the dry, dusty smell that
wafted upward.

She gasped as she looked inside. A wedding dress lay

folded neatly, the once white fabric yellowed with age. Carefully, she pulled out the long gown, and with respectful fingers touched the astonishing number of seed pearls sewn onto the lace bodice. Someone had taken many hours doing the intensive detail required to make lace come alive like this. Then her fingers came to an abrupt edge where the seamstress had simply stopped, leaving the left side of the bodice unbeaded.

Inconsolable sadness overcame her and tears streamed down her cheeks. The dress was a symbol of love lost, or love unrealized.

She stood before the mirror in the corner and held the dress against her, marveling that it could have been made just for her. She constantly had to alter hems and sleeves, so it astonished her that she could find a creation of this magnitude in her proportions.

The dress cried out for a story, a telling of the whys and whens of a love waylaid before the altar. Feeling silly, she folded the gown over her arm before she did something foolish like try it on. Instead, she bent back over the chest to explore further. She found a simple satin headband, also beaded, which she guessed was part of, or intended to be part of, a veil. A lace-covered pillow, which she decided was for the ring-bearer, joined the headband on the floor. Gloves, a garter, a lace fan . . . all the accoutrements for a bride. All in perfect shape.

Then she saw it. A small notebook tucked into the corner tied with a frayed ribbon. She sensed a power in the yellowed pages bound in brittle leather. With hesitation, she picked up the diary she somehow, inexplicably, knew had been passed on with her needle.

She settled onto the floor and draped the dress over her lap. With reverent fingers, she untied the bow, opened the binding, and began to read . . .

Paris, 1702
   I do not know that I can abide my crippled state.

Mme. Duponne says, "Paulette, you must stop hiding in the shop all day, all night." But what have I except to finish dresses for those fashionable ladies who stroll along the Seine? I shall never stroll, only hobble like an old woman. Mme. Duponne says the butcher's son has asked her of me, but I do not encourage him. He deserves better. No, it is enough that I produce the finest seams in Paris with my special, golden needle. I am in much demand as a seamstress, and my volunteer work at the hospital occupies my time. That shall be sufficient. It has to be . . .

Madrid, 1821

My name is Hermalinda Vasquez de Torro. I am the daughter of the powerful Don Alejandro de Torro. My life in Madrid should be filled with gaiety, but I do not go down the grand staircase anymore. Not since my father refused the suit of my lover. I would have gone with him to this new place, this California, but my father caught me as I was about to board the ship. He slapped me, then took me home and threw me into the prison of my room. Even when his temper cools and he allows me out, I will never smile again. If I cannot have Joseph, then I will have no one. I will show my father. He will never obtain what he desires the most from me . . . grandchildren. I will do the work he says is for the lower classes: helping the orphans under Father Victor's care at the mission. Father says they are worthless peons who do not deserve the charity of their betters, that I embarrass him with my sewing for such as them. I say they are now my reason for living. Seeing their smiling faces as a pretty dress or embroidered shirt I have made with my perfect, golden needle brightens their days spent in poverty and adversity

*is a balm to my heart. I will share my love with
them. They are all I have . . .*

Berlin, 1895

*Herr Gunter came by after service today. He
knows it is a sin to toil on the Sabbath but he knows
I have no one, and there is much that needs to be
done. "Hilda," he says, "let me deal with God. You
take care of yourself. And a biscuit with your honey
butter wouldn't hurt . . ." I have to smile at his ir-
reverence, for I know his devotion is deep. And I accept because even though I am ashamed, I must find
a way to keep my small home in good repair. For
my son's sake. I try to show the elders my repen-
tance for my one foray into the temptations of the
flesh, but they are slow to forgive. I must be careful
that I do not tarnish Herr Gunter's reputation. But
I am so grateful for his help. And he is such a sweet
and handsome man. If only . . . But no, I must not
even think such thoughts. I must take up my golden
needle and finish the mending I have let overflow
my basket. Perhaps I shall work on a shirt for Herr
Gunter . . .*

San Francisco, 1945

*Margaret Fielding. Mrs. Herbert Fielding. Mrs.
Margaret Fielding . . . I cannot stop myself from
writing the name I should have had. Damn the war
and all its destruction! I will be punished for writing such blasphemy, I suppose, but these days even
quilting with my special, golden needle does not
ease my heart. I know he's gone but I cannot let
go. Mr. Caldwell, the druggist, has been asking
me to dinner. Maybe I should go. I don't know.
I've been so busy at the USO, greeting soldiers
with a smile and a cup of joe. The ladies at the
church have formed a quilting bee, and asked me*

*to join. I think I will. That young pilot looked so
much like my Herbert. Maybe it wouldn't hurt to
have one Coke date . . .*

Lynn snapped the book shut and fell back on her
hands, gasping. As she'd flipped through the pages, each
story she'd read had seemed so real, as if she were
watching Paulette, Hermalinda, Hilda and Margaret as
they wrote their entries, each in their distinctive hand.
A voice in the back of her mind asked Lynn when she'd
learned French, Spanish and German. She was willing
to believe it was all part of the magic, but the question
faded as she saw these fellow owners of the needle in
her mind.

Paulette was tiny, barely five feet tall with beautiful
brown hair and soulful eyes. Her long gown covered her
misshapen leg as she sat at a secretary and dipped her
quill to write.

Hermalinda was of medium height, but exceedingly
thin. Her raven black hair was dressed with a lace man-
tilla, and her piercing brown eyes sparked with anger.
Each stroke of the pen revealed her strong will and stubborn spirit.

Hilda was a tall woman, solidly built. Her blonde hair
was so pale it was flaxen in color, but her blue eyes
were gentle. Her hands were calloused from long hours
of work, but her fingers were nimble with both pen and
needle.

Margaret was—

"I was wondering when you'd come see me."

Lynn scuttled back, staring at the woman with steel
gray hair pulled back in a low ponytail, dressed in blue
jeans and flannel shirt.

"Who—how—" Lynn stuttered. "I didn't hear you
come in."

"Oh, I've been here awhile. Why haven't you been
up before?"

"Up where?" Lynn wondered if she had a neighbor with dementia who'd wandered away and didn't realize she wasn't in her own home.

The woman smiled indulgently. "Here. To the attic. Weren't you curious?"

Lynn struggled for a reply. "Uh, well, I've been up before—"

"That was years ago, when Leonard was alive."

"How did you—"

The woman straightened from where she leaned against the door and strolled around the small room, touching a dust-covered item here and there. "I miss Leonard terribly," she whispered as she stroked the bright orange jacket Leonard had always worn during hunting season.

Lynn didn't have time to wonder that the woman's touch wasn't disturbing any dust. Too many other thoughts were whirring through her head, like how to get this woman home and that maybe she'd better change the locks . . . or be more careful about setting them in the first place.

"Um, my name's Lynn Powell—"

"I know who you are, honey. I'm Dora. Dora Darrington." A far-off look overcame her. "Should have been Dora Powell, but I was too scared, too busy running . . ."

"You knew Leonard?"

"My, yes. Didn't he tell you about me?"

Leonard had been a wonderful man, but he had never been anxious to talk about his past. And she hadn't wanted to pry. Or more truthfully, and to her shame, she'd been too absorbed in her own problems to encourage Leonard to reveal his. It seemed this was someone who'd turned an infatuation with Leonard into something more in her mind.

"Dora, is there someone I can call—"

"Don't run from love, Lynn. You'll regret it."

Lynn stood slowly, hoping she didn't startle the woman.

"Don't worry about me, dear. It's you I'm concerned about. You're the whole reason I'm here."

Had she said her thought aloud? She didn't think she had, but obviously she hadn't guarded her tongue as well as she should have.

"Um . . . you're worried about *me*, Dora? Why?"

Dora completed her circuit of the room and returned to the trunk. Lynn made the absent note that Dora moved smoothly for a woman her age. She was further baffled when Dora gestured toward the open lid of the trunk and it fell shut with an abrupt thunk.

Lynn hadn't realized there was a draft in the room or that the truck was so unsteady . . .

"I see you making the same mistake I did. That all of us did," she said, nodding at the diary.

Staying rooted where she stood, Lynn wasn't sure what to say to this kind but obviously lost woman.

"Dora—"

"No, Lynn, listen to me. Please listen. Stop running. Face what is in front of you or you'll run forever."

Lynn struggled to keep her concern off her face. She had to get this woman home.

"I am home! At least, it should have been my home. But I was too scared to see, to try, to trust."

Lynn was about to reply when Grant's voice floated up the stairs. "Hey, are you all right up there?"

Turning her head, she made the mistake of stepping without looking. Something caught under her heel and rolled. Her foot went flying. Down she went, cursing as the back of her head struck something.

Then there was only darkness.

Grant heard the crash and went pounding up the stairs two at a time. Bursting through the door, he saw Lynn on the floor and his heart nearly stopped. Racing to her side, he didn't hesitate; he hefted her to his chest and hurried down the stairs and out to his SUV to lay her on the backseat. She was breathing, so he strapped a seat belt around her waist and vaulted into the driver's seat, gunning the engine to life.

By the time he pulled under the covered emergency entrance at the local hospital Lynn was beginning to stir.

"Don't move," he ordered, jumping out to meet the attendants rushing from the building.

She protested as they helped her onto a gurney and wheeled her inside.

"I'm fine," she insisted, trying to sit up.

"Please stay down, miss," the male nurse said, putting a gentle but insistent hand on her shoulder.

Grant finished giving the succinct version of the facts as he knew them to the petite blonde walking beside him, or rather jogging to keep up with his hurried steps.

"Are you family, sir?" she asked as they stopped the gurney in a curtained area.

"No, I—"

"Then I'm afraid you'll have to wait outside."

And just like that, Grant found himself waiting on the opposite side of a Plexiglas wall. A curtain was twitched shut, blocking his view of Lynn.

His stomach was a churning mass of acid by the time the same nurse came out to the desk a little while later. He jumped to his feet and rushed to her.

"Is she all right?"

"Miss Powell? Yes, she's going to be fine. She took a blow to her head, but there's no concussion. Her electrolytes are very low, though. We're going to give her some fluids and watch her for a bit, but she should be ready to go home in a few hours."

"Can I see her?"

The nurse looked him over. "I'll check."

It seemed an eternity before she returned. "Miss Powell said she'll see you."

Grant hurried to the cubicle and stepped around the curtain. She looked lost against the sterile white of the sheets. Her eyes were closed and her breathing was even. She was much too pale, by his definition, and he prayed that the liquid dripping evenly down the tubing into her arm would restore the color to her cheeks.

"Lynn?" he asked quietly, not wanting to wake her if she was asleep.

She opened her eyes, then quickly closed them again. "I feel like such an idiot."

He frowned. "Why? You fell is all."

"I've never been such a dunderhead before."

"You've never fallen?"

"I've never knocked myself out." She looked at him, startled. "Did you get Dora home?"

"Dora? Dora who?"

"The woman in the attic. In the flannel shirt."

"Lynn," Grant said gently, "you were the only woman in the attic, flannel shirt or not."

"But—" She stopped herself short.

"You must have seen yourself in the mirror as you fell," he offered reasonably.

She frowned, and stared at the striped curtain. "Yes . . . that must be it. Either that or it was something my brain cooked up when I knocked myself out."

Grant took a seat in the vinyl chair beside the bed and hoped he hid his concern that she'd done more damage to her head than they'd thought. But his concern at the moment wasn't an imaginary woman in the attic. He wanted to know exactly what she was planning.

"We didn't get a chance to talk when we got home. Now doesn't seem like the appropriate time to have a conversation, but I've got this feeling you're plotting something in that gorgeous head of yours." He met her eyes calmly, hoping she didn't see the gut-wrenching stress he was trying to hide.

"No, no plans yet. I've just been resting."

"Will you at least let me know before you leave this time?"

She slowly raised her eyes to his. "I truly am sorry about this morning, Grant. You deserved better of me."

"I didn't say that to throw a guilt trip on you. I just want to be sure I have a chance to say . . . good-bye."

She dropped her head to her pillow and studied the ceiling. He was afraid she wasn't going to offer him any promises when she finally nodded. "Yes, I'll tell you."

He released a sigh. "Thank you." He stood and wiped his hands down his thighs. "Is there anything I can do for you? The doctor said he wanted to keep you here for a few hours."

"You could check on Nan at the store instead of being bored stiff sitting here all evening. I don't want her to worry about me."

"I'll do that." Now that he was satisfied she was all right, he'd check on Murdock first. He wasn't leaving her side until he was satisfied she was safe.

As if she'd read his thoughts, she cleared her throat and said, "Do you know where he . . . where Trey is?"

Grant nodded. "He's up on the fifth floor." He tilted his head to the left a bit. "Lynn, I'd be happy to stay with you. I just had a sense I'm making you uncomfortable."

She blushed guiltily, but took a deep breath. "Truth is, I need some time to think. I just don't like not knowing where he is."

"I'll find out and tell you."

She nodded as he left. Grant found the information easily, and after checking personally with the deputy outside the door four floors up, he returned to the emergency room cubicle and reported what he knew to a grateful Lynn.

"Murdock's still on the fifth floor. He regained consciousness around noon, but only for a few minutes," Grant said. "The nurse told me something wild. He was clutching your quilt when they brought him in, and when they tried to take it from him, he became uncontrollable. They cut a square off the quilt and let him keep that, and he hasn't let go of it the entire time."

She frowned, as if trying to make sense of what he'd said. Then she became agitated. "I've got to get out of here."

"Lynn, if you're not going to stay in that bed until the doctor releases you, then I'm not leaving."

She sighed in resignation. "I'll behave. Do you at least understand why I don't feel particularly comfortable here?"

"I do. Which is why I'd really rather stay—"

"Please, Grant, go. I've got to get my thoughts together and to be honest, you're a rather powerful distraction."

Well, he was certainly glad to know he wasn't the only one affected by the energy between them. Not that he wanted her to be bothered, but dammit, he needed to know that what had transpired had been more than two bodies achieving sexual satisfaction.

As he headed for Nan's store, Grant struggled with the picture of Lynn lying in that hospital bed, looking wan. It was a picture he never wanted to see again. She certainly could make him fume with anger when she was in Valkyrie mode, but that was a thousand times better than seeing her sad and weak.

God above, how was he going to convince that stubborn woman to let him help her, love her? It was enough to drive a man crazy!

Grant looked in his rearview mirror back toward the hospital.

"You're going to stop running, Lynn Powell. Some how, some way, I'm going to show you there's another way."

Fourteen

Her hands stacked under her head, Lynn stared at the ceiling. The room was amazingly quiet considering she was in an emergency ward. She was lucky she'd made a fool of herself on such a slow day.

What the heck had happened in the attic? Surely she had dreamed all that stuff about Dora after she'd fallen. Grant hadn't seen anyone, and the room was much too small and crowded for anyone to hide, but Dora had seemed so real. Lynn would have sworn a woman in her fifties, her face lined with life and regret, had been in that room with her, reproving her gently, yet with an urgency that stayed with her.

It must have been those stories, thought Lynn. Her overstimulated imagination had taken hold of the stories she'd been reading, and when her blood sugar had dropped . . . or whatever physiological explanation there was for her dream . . . she'd already had the premise imprinted on her mind. To imagine the women in the stories was one thing. To think she'd seen one was another entirely.

There did seem to be a sorrowful theme following the stories of the women who'd possessed the needle. Each of them had had a chance for romance and happiness,

and yet ended up lonely. They had hidden behind fear,
or arrogance, or pride. They had spent their lives sharing
their love through their talents with the needle, but it
had never been enough to make up for a life without a
husband and children, especially in the centuries when
a woman was defined by those two things.

Of course, *she* didn't fit the scenario because she was
a woman of the new millennium. She wasn't bound by
the restrictions society had placed on Paulette or Hilda
or even Margaret. She could be anything she chose to
be, and as a modern woman, she didn't need a man to
complete her life.

What she found the most amazing was that the needle
could possibly be so old, and still be in perfect condition.
In fact, it could be much older. She wondered if there
was a journal somewhere with stories from the sixteenth
century, the fifteenth . . . and possibly even before.

The possibility was mind-boggling, but equally fas-
cinating. She had held an instrument in her hand that
had been touched by countless women over hundreds of
years. No wonder it felt almost alive at times. Certainly
it carried the energy of those talented artists who'd come
before her.

And to never have broken, or dulled? Well, that was
the kind of proof she needed to finally accept Nan's
magic theory.

Attendant with her fascination was sadness at the
thought of so many women never knowing true love.
Lynn wished some of them had stated in the journal that
they'd followed their hearts in the end. There were so
many entries, but none had returned to the journal to say
if a miracle had occurred in their own lives, or if the
needle was only meant to help others.

But, she reminded herself, her situation was entirely
different. She didn't have the luxury of following her
heart, even if she had the inclination. If she gave in to

the urge to tell Grant how she felt, she would put him at grave risk.

As it was, she was going to have a hard time making him go away. She felt sure that he would feel compelled to stay if he thought her heart was involved. Not because he returned her feelings in kind she was sure, but because he was the embodiment of chivalry. In many ways, Grant was a man born in the wrong time. She could easily imagine him mounted on a destrier, his armor polished to a brilliant gleam as he prepared to defend a damsel or a castle in distress.

No, she couldn't be so selfish. Loving Grant meant getting as far away from him as possible before he did something foolish and got himself killed.

The monitor at her right side began to beep. She was amazed that she had been lost in her thoughts long enough for the bag of fluids to run dry. As the nurse, whose name tag said Molly, removed the needle and tubing, she promised Lynn the doctor would be in shortly to sign the release forms.

When she was sure the nurse had left her room, Lynn didn't hesitate in taking off the horrid hospital gown, and pulling on her clothes. She had a visit to make, and she had to do it before Grant returned. For the sake of her own soul, she would face down her demon, alone this time. Then she had to leave . . . for good.

After glancing furtively around the edge of the curtain, Lynn walked silently down the hall to the stairwell and made her way up to the fifth floor. She was plotting how she could get the guard to let her in to see Trey when she noticed the chair outside his room was empty. A glance at the nurse's station showed a man of medium build in a tan uniform talking with a nurse at the central station.

She should have been surprised, she supposed, but now that she had accepted the fact that she had help from an . . . outside . . . source, she was merely grateful for the divine intervention. She slipped silently through the door and stood there at his bedside, staring down at him.

As she tried to breathe, she reminded herself that she needed to do this. She had to face him, even if he was asleep.

"I'm not going to be afraid of you forever," she whispered in the quiet. "I'm going to disappear for good this time, and build a new life. A life where you won't find me."

"Is running really the answer?"

She jumped backward at his voice. He didn't open his eyes until he'd finished his question, and then he looked at her. She was so frightened by how clear, how sharp he seemed . . . not at all dopey as he should have been. Twisting for the door, she intended to run, but something stopped her.

Turning back, she took deep, gasping breaths and struggled for calm. She had the upper hand here. She wasn't stitched up and drugged up and wired up. And while she didn't have any weapons on her, she still had her training. Against a wounded man, she figured she had a shot.

Then she considered his question. "It's not like I have any options, Trey," she said harshly.

"There are always options," he said reasonably, wincing as he shifted on the bed.

Lynn pulled her shoulders back. "I didn't come here to have a conversation with you."

"Then why did you come?"

"To take one last look at the man who had made my life miserable, and to tell you that I won't give you that power ever again."

"Even as you plan to run away?"

How could this man lay there and sound so damned reasonable? It made her blood boil and she had to use all her will to keep from lashing out at him.

"I'll never let you find me. You got lucky this time. I won't make the same mistakes again."

Trey let his head drop back against his pillow as though gathering strength and she was struck once more by the difference between the man who'd been wrapped in her quilt on the open ground, and this one who was clean and bandaged. It was dangerous to even entertain the notion that he was somehow different, but she could not deny that he seemed . . . calm.

It was just a result of the pain medication, of that she had no doubt.

"I won't try to hurt you again, Lynn."

She snorted. Loudly.

He smiled, a small, sad movement of his lips. "I didn't expect you to believe me. Just as I don't expect you to accept my apologies."

"Your apologies?" she squeaked, shocked almost beyond belief. "You're apologizing to me?"

Trey nodded. "For everything. Not that you have any obligation to let me make amends, but I'd like to try."

"You are out of your mind," she whispered, thunderstruck.

"No, actually, I'm in it for the first time in a long while."

"Yeah, well, forgive me for not jumping for joy."

He made a gesture with his hand not bound with tubes and white tape. "I know words are useless, so I intend to prove to you that I've changed."

"Changed? Um hmmm. And when did this miraculous transformation occur?"

"When you wrapped me up in this quilt and saved my life." He opened his hand and showed her the square of fabric he'd been clutching.

"Oh, I'm really going to believe that one. You are one evil son of a bitch, you know that?"

He nodded. "Yes, I know that I was. And I'm hardly an angel all of a sudden, but I am sorry that I hurt you.

More than physically. Hopefully not irreparably."

Lynn sneered. "Don't give yourself too much credit. I'm going to be just fine."

"I hope so."

She whirled to leave again.

"Lynn, I'm dying."

She took her hand off the door handle. "That's incredibly sick, even for you, Trey."

"I'm telling you the truth. When they had me open, they discovered I'm eaten up with cancer. They gave me the name of it, but I can't remember. The long and short of it is, it's a fast growth type. I've got a year at the outside."

"And I'm supposed to say . . . what?"

"Nothing. I just wanted you to know that you truly don't have anything to worry about. And I'm glad I got to thank you."

She shook her head, trying to clear the befuddlement. "Now you're thanking me?"

"For the gift of a chance to make things right. I would have died without this quilt. Then you would never have been free of me because you would always have been plagued by guilt, wondering if you tried hard enough."

"I'm going to be free of you now," she snarled, not wanting to hear anything more he had to say.

"Soon," he agreed. "I have some things to take care of, and she promised me I'd be able to get it all done."

"She?"

"The angel."

Lynn just stared, mouth agape. Now she knew he really was drugged to high heaven. But that's what she deserved for talking to a man on morphine or heaven only knew what painkillers, and a consummate liar on top of that.

"Jolly for you, Trey. I hope you had a good talk."

He just kept his eyes on hers, calmly. "It doesn't matter if you believe me, Lynn. Just . . . don't run away."

"Oh, sure, you seeing angels is gonna keep me glued here."

"I'm going to make a statement to the sheriff. If I'm released from the hospital, I'll be spending some time in jail."

"Yeah, like the statement of a man under anesthesia will hold up in court."

What little color Trey had drained from his face. He closed his eyes and took short, shallow breaths. When he looked at her again, pain glazed his features.

"I've got to go back to sleep for a while. But, please, Lynn. Don't run away. If you do, you'll be running forever, and you deserve so much more."

Which was what Dora had said. Or rather, what the figment of her imagination she'd named Dora had said . . .

Lynn left the room without a backward glance. It had been insane to have the conversation with him in the first place. Now, instead of bolstering her confidence, her need to face him down had caused her more confusion, making her the crazy one. Why had she listened to one word coming out of that man's mouth—

"Miss! What are you doing in there?"

The deputy hurried forward and Lynn read the name on his tag. "You might tell the doctor he was awake, Deputy Goodwin," she said, heading down the hall with quick steps.

"Wait!"

But she didn't. Out of the corner of her eye she saw Goodwin go into Trey's room, and took advantage of his distraction to make her escape back to the emergency room. She stopped by the nurses' station to let them know she was leaving, then found a pay phone. She felt bad charging the toll to Nan, but she had nothing in her pockets but a bit of lint and a receipt from the feed store.

"Nan? Is Grant there?"

Nan's surprise was clear, even over the wire. "He was. Hey, are you all right?"

"I'm fine. I'm just ready to go, and I promised Grant I'd wait for him."

"He's gone to Ted's office. I mean, Ted came by here and asked to talk to Grant. I'll come get you."

"Thanks. If the hospital was closer in, I'd just walk."

"Don't you even think about it. I'll be right there."

By the time Lynn talked to the doctor and told the office she'd be by later to pay the bill in cash, Nan was rushing through the automatic doors.

"I told Sylvia to let Grant know I'd gone to pick you up, and that I'd get you home," she said breathlessly.

Lynn knew the helpers in the store, and Sylvia was one of the most personable assistants Nan had ever hired. Lynn had no doubt Sylvia would be happy to pass along a message to Grant . . . and a good dose of flirtation as well.

Which did *not* make her jealous, she assured herself fiercely.

As they walked out, Lynn noticed the sadness on her friend's face. "Hey, what's up?" she asked as they settled themselves in the cab of Nan's truck.

Nan shrugged as she started the engine and flipped on the headlights. The sad darkness in her eyes wasn't anything Lynn had seen before.

"Nothing you need to worry about, Lynn. You've got enough on your plate right now."

"Just a minute," Lynn said hotly. "You are upset and you're gonna 'fess up."

Nan drove for a while in silence, but Lynn wasn't about to let her off the hook.

"Ted and I won't be seeing each other."

Lynn pursed her lips. "Okay, why?"

"Because we have a difference of philosophy."

Slapping a hand on the dashboard, Lynn snapped, "Stop this truck. Right now."

Surprised, Nan did as directed, pulling into the parking lot of the little cafe that served the best Mexican food in the county. Not that it was apparent by the exterior, but inside the tiny house converted into a restaurant. Maria Santiago mixed the best margarita this side of Guadalajara.

"Find a spot to park. It's time for some girl talk."

Nan pulled into one of the few empty slots and by silent agreement, they didn't speak again until they were seated at a booth with chips and salsa in front of them.

"Okay, now tell me about this difference of philosophy," Lynn said, dipping a crispy tortilla into the spicy red sauce. "I'm guessing this has something to do with me."

"Why would you guess that?"

"Because Ted came to see me, to talk about Trey. And then our conversation devolved into a discussion about whether or not I toe the line of legality with what I've been doing."

"But he said you weren't in any trouble."

Lynn stirred the salsa in a lazy circle. "I don't think I am, in the strictest sense. I think someone would have to file charges against me for me to be in any trouble, but that's not the point, is it?"

"No," Nan sighed. "It's not. But I have to give Ted some benefit of the doubt. He's a lawman, after all. It's all he's ever been. All he's ever wanted to be. And it must have thrown him for a loop to have the woman he was considering dating to be mixed up in something potentially illegal."

"But you're not involved! At least, not until Betsy, and there's nothing that could be remotely considered illegal in that situation."

Nan took a sip from her glass of water and tried for a smile. "It's sweet of you to try and defend me, but it's not what I've actually done or not done that's the problem. It's the intent. You know I'd have done more before now, and would do more in the future, if you'd let me."

Lynn wiped a drop of salsa from the table with more vehemence than necessary. "Which is exactly why I haven't wanted you to be in on any of this!"

"It doesn't matter—"

"It does, too! Things were looking great between you two, and I've fouled everything up."

Chuckling, Nan took Lynn's hand. "It's so like you to try and take the blame. I look at it that it's a good thing we found this out before my heart got more involved than it already is."

Lynn sat back, staring at her friend. "You love him, don't you."

"Is it so obvious?"

"Maybe just to me."

"I hope so. I'd hate to think I'm walking around like a moonstruck idiot, all calf-eyed over a man who doesn't want me, and have everyone notice."

"Hey, I wouldn't go that far. It sounds like he's just trying to work things out."

"The problem is, I don't see how things can."

"Have faith, Nan."

Nan gave her a comical, gape-mouthed look. "Would you repeat what you just said?"

Lynn blushed. "Come off it, Nan. I'm just telling you what you've told me a thousand times."

"Yeah, I know, but this is—"

"Different?"

It was Nan's turn to blush. "Yeah." She toyed with another chip as their frosty glasses arrived. "It sure feels different on this side of advice."

Lynn just wiggled an eyebrow as she took a lick of salt from the rim of her glass. "Oh, cripes," she said when she saw a waitress present a bill to the table next to them, "I keep forgetting I don't have my wallet with me. Grant didn't think to pick it up when he took me to the hospital."

Nan rolled her eyes dramatically. "I think I can cover it. You pay next time."

Would there be a next time? Lynn stared at the table as she savored a salty/sweet sip of lime and tequila.

A gusty sigh emanated from across the table. "I sure miss the temporal body sometimes."

Lynn's attention darted up. "Dora!"

Nan raised an eyebrow. "Dora?"

"Um . . . nothing," Lynn said, covering her goof by taking a healthy sip of margarita.

Dora eyed the glass with envy. Lynn gave her a look she hoped conveyed sympathy.

"So," Dora said, folding her hands on the table. "Do you believe in me now?"

Lynn risked a nod, hoping Nan wouldn't notice.

"So," Dora said, running her finger longingly against the icy condensation on Lynn's glass, "is there going to be?"

Lynn cast a glance at Nan, then raised a questioning eyebrow at the ghost.

"A next time. Nan said you could pick up the tab next time, and I was just wondering if you'll be around to pay up."

Thankfully, Nan excused herself to go to the ladies' room, freeing Lynn to talk.

"I don't know," Lynn said, wiping her mouth to cover her words.

"Well, honey, you're the only one who does!"

"Dora, I have to go away. I have to—"

"Yeah, yeah, protect the world. I know."

Lynn scowled. "Why are you being flip about this? There are lives at stake here."

"Because you're using it as an excuse to run away."

"What?!"

"You're using—"

"I heard. I just don't understand how you can say that."

"Lynn, if there's one thing I know, it's about running away. You can dress this up however you want, but you're making excuses to avoid your heart."

She sat, stunned, as Dora finished her lecture. She'd never had anyone take quite that tone with her and she wasn't sure how to respond. "Dora, I—"

"Don't run, Lynn. Stay. Fight. Face it. And for the love of God, don't run away from Grant."

Lynn's attention was diverted as Nan returned. When she looked back across the table, Dora was gone.

Releasing a disappointed sigh, Lynn signaled the waitress and ordered another round.

Nan seemed as lost in her own thoughts as Lynn was, so while her friend was pondering about one certain county sheriff, Lynn pondered her other-wordly scolding.

Sometimes, she decided as she dipped another chip, the truth hurts. She was using the situation, dire as it was, as an excuse to avoid emotions and commitments that scared the hell out of her. Using a noble excuse, she had given herself an easy out.

Toying with a chip, she finally put it down without taking a bite.

Well, Dora, there will be another time.

Because she wasn't going to run. Not because of Dora. Not because of what Trey had said. Not even because of Grant.

But because of who she'd become over the course of a week.

She didn't believe for one minute that Trey was dying or repentant. She was absolutely certain that his claims were another of his elaborate ploys to destroy her confidence. He wanted her to have hope again, so he could crush it.

Well, she wasn't going to let him. She was going to stop him. Not only for herself, but for any woman he might hurt in the future. Running away might protect

Nan and Grant, but there were more people out there who needed her to find the courage to stay.

As to Dora's admonition about Grant, she wasn't sure she had the fortitude to face that issue yet. For now it had to be enough that she'd crossed one major hurdle. Her personal life was just going to have to wait.

Lynn sat back as the power of her epiphany sank in. She glanced around the room and had to admit that she hadn't been prepared for a dramatic revelation while poised over a chipped bowl of spicy red sauce. Epiphanies were usually reserved for places of quiet contemplation, places of majestic beauty like old cathedrals or secluded spots in nature overlooking the rugged beauty of the hills.

A smile tipped her lips as she shifted on the plastic-covered bench and decided that this was the perfect place after all. The irony couldn't help but strike her funny bone.

"Earth to Lynn, come in Lynn."

Snapping out of her thoughts, she gave Nan an apologetic smile. "Sorry, little trip off-planet there."

"See anything interesting?"

"Just made a surprising discovery."

"Care to share it with me?"

"I'm not going to run away this time."

Fear suffused Nan's face. "What? Why?" She held up a hand. "I didn't mean that the way it sounds. I don't want you to leave, but you're in so much danger."

Lynn planted her palms on the table and studied her splayed fingers. "I know, but I've been a prisoner ever since the day Leonard found me. A prisoner to fear, to uncertainty, to the rules of hiding."

"But isn't it better than dead?"

"I'm not so sure anymore."

"Lynn—"

"Listen, I made the decision to face Trey down when I left the last time, and while things didn't end up as I'd thought, I'm not going to go backward. I was tempted, I admit it, but I won't let him ruin my life again."

"That's awfully brave."

"No, it's not bravery. I'm tired of running, hiding in shadows. I want to live in the sunlight again."

"Well, whatever you need from me, you know you've got it."

Lynn put her fingers over Nan's. "Your love and friendship gave me some of the strength I needed to make this decision. You've held faith for me for a long time, when I couldn't."

"So, what are you going to do?"

Sighing, Lynn sat back. "I'm going to start living. For however long that is. There are no guarantees in this life . . . I could get hit by a bus tomorrow. But as far as Trey is concerned, I'm going to do my best to put him behind bars. I won't give him the chance to hurt another woman, anyone, ever again."

Nan touched her still tender cheek. "I'll be glad to help you."

Lynn frowned. "You may want to think that through, Nan. He's not the kind of man you want to anger. You have a child and much more at stake than I do."

"I don't think Jeremy wants a coward for a mother."

"The last thing I'd think you are is a coward."

"Oh, I don't know about that. Just as you've spent these last few years hiding, I've been doing some hiding of my own. Hiding from myself, from my needs. I only valued myself as a mother and a businesswoman. I forgot about me as a woman, as a person. I'm going to change that, and it starts with not being afraid to do the right thing."

"The statistics are full of women who did the right thing, and paid high prices."

"If push comes to shove, I'll send Jeremy to live with my aunt in Alaska. Hell, I'd even send him to his father's in Washington State to keep him safe. But I'm staying right here, Lynn. I need to. For my own sake as much as yours."

"I have to admit that I'm glad. I know that's selfish, but having a friend like you will make this all easier."

"And a friend like Grant . . . ?"

Pain sliced through her heart. "I have to make him go away. Somehow, some way."

"But, why? You're crazy about him. I can tell."

"I know. It's insane, isn't it? I've just met him, and yet . . ."

"And yet you love him."

Lynn grimaced. "It's that obvious, huh?"

"About as much as my feelings for Ted, I guess. Hopefully we can see it in each other because we're so close and it's not as obvious as neon signs on our foreheads."

"Amen to that."

"Have you considered that Grant might be willing to take whatever risks there are to stay with you?"

"And offer him what? He has a bright future in politics. He'd be good at it. He doesn't want to live in a little town where we roll up the sidewalks at seven o'clock with a woman whose most exciting attribute is that she can sew a pretty blanket or two."

"Have you asked him?"

"No, and I'm not going to because the point is moot. Whatever my future holds, I want it to be filled with peace."

"And you assume that Grant and peace are mutually exclusive?"

"I don't see a compromise. I cannot ask him to put his future on hold until my life smooths out. That would be grossly unfair. I can't plan a future at all right now, so there's no sense in dreaming . . . or pretending."

Nan nodded. "Yeah, dreams hurt sometimes."

"Oh, honey, I'm sorry. I'm being an insensitive clod. We're supposed to be talking about you, not me."

"As far as I know, there's no rules about the ebb and flow of this conversation. Besides, I rather like talking about something positive, like your staying here instead of the demise of my little daydream concerning a certain lawman's affections."

"You sound as if there's no hope with our illustrious sheriff."

"Nope, and as you said, there's no sense in dreaming about what you can't have."

"He might come around."

"And he might not. I'm not going to lay my heart on the ground to be stomped on. Either he accepts me for me, or we have nothing to work from."

"I'll be here for you no matter what, but I do think he's just conflicted. Give him time."

Nan shrugged. "We'll see. Now, let's order some food and eat. All this talking has made me hungry."

Lynn watched her friend bury her nose in the menu to effectively end the conversation for the moment. She could understand Nan's reluctance; Lynn was in the same place herself. But in Nan's case, she had a man who was crazy about her. As for Lynn, she had little doubt that once she put some distance between herself and Grant, he would be grateful to escape the whole situation. Right now he was too busy being protective, but when he was back in his own life, he'd be glad he'd gotten away from her.

God knew she'd be delighted when the drama ended. There was nothing she wanted more fervently than for this to all be over.

Fifteen

Grant was waiting on the porch when Nan dropped Lynn
off. He'd been waiting for hours. He wasn't exactly worried. Nan's assistant had let him know the change in
plans, and besides, it had given him a chance to think.

There hadn't been much pondering time since this all
began. His thoughts had started out jumbled and confused, but as the evening had grown cooler, and he'd
gone inside to get a quilt, things had become much
clearer.

The bottom line was, he loved Lynn. No, it didn't
make sense. No, it wasn't logical. No, it didn't fit into
his well-laid plans.

And that was just fine.

Well, it would be fine if he could get one very stubborn woman to listen to him.

The women said their good-byes in the yard, and
Grant returned Nan's wave as she drove off. Then, finally, after a hectic day, he was alone with Lynn.

"How was your evening?" he asked as she ascended
the stairs.

"Great. I see you got my message."

"Yes, and I've put the time to good use."

"Really?"

"Um hmm," he said. Taking a chance, he held open his arms, the quilt spread over his back like wings. To his immense relief, and joy, she stepped into his embrace to lay her head on his chest and wrap her arms around his waist.

Enfolding her in the cocoon of warmth, he held on and simply absorbed her as they stood in the quiet darkness. Everything about her was precious to him. Nothing before had ever felt as incredible to him as the feel of her silky hair against his cheek, or the curve of her luscious body melded so perfectly against his, or the clean, faintly floral scent of her in his nose. Simple things, yet elemental, like sunshine and oxygen.

"We need to talk," he said against her temple, placing a kiss there as he finished speaking.

"You're right," she sighed.

They moved as one to the swing and it seemed as natural as breathing for Grant to sit down and Lynn to curl up against him. It was tempting just to stay that way for the rest of the night, but he knew he couldn't give in to the urge.

"We need to talk."

"You already said that."

"I guess I'm just nervous."

"You don't feel nervous. You feel marvelous."

"Thanks, but I'm not going to let you distract me."

"Darn. I thought that was rather clever of me."

"I'll give you credit for ingenuity, but take points away for stalling."

"Okay, I'm listening."

"Lynn, I love you."

She didn't speak. Instead, as if he'd stung her, she bolted off the swing and took refuge across the porch. "Grant—"

Grant stood as well, letting the quilt slide to the seat. "Don't. Don't interrupt. You stopped me last night, but I won't let you run away from me again."

Lynn laughed uncomfortably. "But it's what I'm good at."

"I know, honey, and it's why I want to change the future. For us. Marry me, Lynn."

She closed her eyes tightly. "I can't."

"Then live with me."

Her steady gaze was etched with sadness. "Grant, you have to know that you are precious to me. But there can't be an us. There are too many factors up in the air for me to make any plans. Not to mention that you have an entire life waiting for you back in Austin. A life I'm mucking up."

"I think I'm the one who gets to decide if my life is mucked up or not. And I just might like the changes that come about."

"Not if you're dead. Not if Trey takes revenge on your family."

"Forgive me for being blunt, but isn't it a tad arrogant to think that you alone could cause Murdock to go after me? I was going to cancel any business dealings with him whether or not you came into the picture. He has plenty of reasons to be angry with me and want revenge. Reasons that have absolutely nothing to do with you."

"You're rushing me, Grant."

"I don't have a choice! I know you. If I'm not careful, I'll blink and you'll be gone."

"You know me? Don't you understand? *I* don't know me! I spent the first part of my life being shallow and stupid and driven by greed to try and bolster a low self-esteem. Then I've spent the last eight years in fear . . . and growing up. I know who Elizabeth Murdock was more than I know who Lynn Powell is. How can I be with you, when I've never been with me?"

"We can discover those things together."

She shook her head. "What if you don't like the Lynn Powell I discover? Worse, what if I don't like her?"

"I think it's a safe bet that I'll love you no matter

what. Nothing you find out about yourself is going to change the person who is innately you."

"I'm not so sure. Grant, I know how to be lonely, but I don't know how to be alone. And I need to know that before I make any decisions."

Grant's cell phone chirped, and he snarled in frustration. He checked the caller display and gave her an apologetic look as he took the call.

"Hi, Mom, what's up?"

Lynn wrapped her arms around herself and sat in the wicker rocker, trying to be unobtrusive. She didn't begrudge him taking the call, but she was determined to finish this all-important conversation.

"What?! How'd it happen?"

Her eyes darted to his stricken face as he sat down woodenly on the swing. She hurried to his side and placed a hand on his arm, trying to be patient but sensing his tension level had gone from high to astronomical. When he disconnected the call, his hands hung limply between his knees.

"My dad and Betsy were in an accident," he said, his eyes distant. "A six-car pileup on IH-35. They're both hurt."

"Go," she said, instantly. "Your mother needs you and so will your dad and Betsy."

"I can't believe this . . ."

"Don't worry about me, Grant. I'm fine. I'm going to stay fine."

"Come with me," he said urgently. "I'd feel better—"

Lynn put her hand gently against his face. "I wish I could, but we both know that's not a good idea. You've got your family to take care of, and you don't need me there distracting you. Besides, I've got some things of my own to take care of. I promise you, I'll be here when you get a chance to let me know how everyone is."

He finally nodded, reluctantly. "Here, keep my cell

phone. I'll call from a pay phone at the hospital." He wrote down his home information, the hospital's name and phone number, and an emergency number that would reach his secretary.

"Grant, I can't—"

But he wasn't listening. He jogged to his SUV and pulled the charger for the cell phone out of the dash. Deciding arguing was futile, she accepted the equipment with a nod.

Then she stiffened. "Grant, wait right here. I'll be right back."

Racing into the house, she went straight to the armoire that housed quilts in progress, and the finished pieces she had never been able to put in Nan's shop. There was no explanation, but she'd just known these few were meant to be gifts, not sold.

Her hands searched instinctively for two lap quilts she'd done years ago. When she'd felt the urge to do these particular patterns, she hadn't understood why. Now she knew.

She rushed back and handed Grant the quilts. "Here, these are for your dad and Betsy."

He took her chin in his hand and pulled her to him for a deep, soul-stirring kiss. "Thank you. This means a lot to me."

She smiled against his mouth. "You're welcome. Now go."

He was so torn, it was palpable. She took his hand and walked with him to the truck.

"Drive safely. The streets are going to be slick."

He enfolded her in a fierce hug, then dipped his head to plant one last, searing kiss on her lips. She welcomed him, telling him with her soul what her mouth could not say.

Then he was gone.

As the SUV's taillights disappeared from view, Lynn felt a void such as she'd never known. Despite her brave

words, she had not wanted him to leave. Now she faced
the terrifying challenge of self-discovery. So much had
changed, in so short a time. Monumental changes. Irrev-
ocable changes.

Terrifying changes.

Heading for the house, she picked up the quilt from
the swing and went inside. As she locked the door, she
smiled at the futility of the gesture. A simple dead bolt
wouldn't protect her. She had only herself for that. Still,
it would be foolish to leave her house open without even
the illusion of safety.

It wasn't until she sat down on the couch and had
only the silence of the house for company that she realized how much she missed Grant.

And how safe he'd made her feel.

And how desperately she loved him . . .

Lynn awoke bleary-eyed the next morning. She was still
on the couch, wrapped in the quilt, with an arsenal
around her—nun-chaku on her left, throwing stars on
her right, her curved staff at her feet. She'd been setting
up her defense perimeter when Grant had called to say
his father and sister were going to be all right. They were
both in serious condition, but would make it.

She'd cried. Out of the blue and surprising them both,
she was sure. She hadn't realized how worried she'd
been about Betsy, and by association Mr. Major, but
there it was. Certainly her emotions were near the surface, but tears had never been common for Lynn. Grant
had been touched, and that made her display something
she could live with.

He'd told her he loved her, and would be back as soon
as he could. That had made the tears come faster, but
she'd hidden them . . . or tried to. He had no way of
knowing he was reinforcing her dilemma. His family
needed him. He had too much at stake for her to give
in to the raging need to be with him, to run away and

live forever on some deserted island. Not out of fear, but because she loved him. She wanted to spend every waking moment beside him, and every sleeping one in his arms.

But that wasn't her destiny.

Wiping away her tears, she'd made herself eat a snack, even though she wasn't hungry, and she'd returned to her nest on the couch. She'd worked on the binding of her current project until exhaustion sent her into a restless slumber.

Now the sun was up, she was so stiff she could hardly move, and she felt particularly foolish. Her neck cracked as she straightened, letting her know she was going to pay for her evening on a couch meant for sitting, not sleeping.

With a groan, she went to her room and drew a full, as hot-as-she-could-stand-it bath and settled in. Her back fairly sighed with pleasure. She stayed in until the water turned tepid, and only then, reluctantly, did she climb out. Once she was dressed, though, the old Lynn was back. She headed for her office with renewed determination. Jake followed and immediately laid down on his favorite, worn spot in the rug.

With a smile at the framed photo of Leonard she always kept on the corner of her desk, she settled into her chair. First thing on her list of things to do was a trip to the phone company. For the first time in five years, she was going to have a phone. A real phone. Then she'd get a cellular for backup so Grant could find her while his family was in crisis and until the phone company could come and install her new phone lines.

After that, she planned to call several contractors to get bids on fixing her garage. And she'd need an electric door opener so she could pull straight in on the days of awful weather. It was a luxury, sure, but she deserved it.

Lynn tapped her pencil against her lip and studied the

ceiling. What next? Oh, the grocery store! She was going to go into town and buy super-sized portions so big
it would take her forever to use them up. She was going
to stock up on everything from soap to rice to soup. As
long as it was nonperishable, she intended to buy at least
a six-month supply. And dog food. She was buying Jake
the biggest, heaviest bag in the feed store.

Another two taps of the pencil and she added a trip
to the Western shop. She needed a snappy new outfit . . .
and a new pair of Luccheses. Next dance at the fire hall,
she would be there. Maybe not with bells on, but certainly with new boots.

Lynn sat back as a grin formed. A slightly terrified
one, but a bright one nonetheless. She had no idea freedom would be so exhilarating. Exhaustion notwithstanding, she felt more alive than she had in years. There was
still real danger around her, no doubt, but for the first
time, she felt in control of her destiny.

A coolness came over the room and for a moment,
she thought Dora was back. Then Leonard's picture fell
over, and Jake jumped to his feet, woofing softly. His
tail wagged happily as he looked at a spot off to Lynn's
left.

As she straightened the picture, her smiled softened.

"Hello, Leonard. I wish I could see you, but I guess
that's not meant to be."

She had no way of knowing, of course, but she felt
he could hear her. It made her feel good to pretend,
anyway.

"I'm going to be fine, Len. Just fine. I finally get what
you tried to teach me all along. Surviving isn't enough.
I need to live. And that means taking chances . . . with
my heart."

Jake danced in place and Lynn laughed at his antics.

"Is Len smiling, Jake? I hope so." She looked around
the room. "I love you, Len. Thank you. For everything."

Jake whined, and his tail slowly stopped. Calling him

over, Lynn ruffled his ears. "He couldn't stay, boy. My guess is one certain lady ghost was waiting for them to head out on a hot date. At least, I sure hope so."

With another soft woof, Jake returned to his snoozing post.

Lynn went back to her list-making, realizing how completely the burden of hiding had hung like a pall over every single day of her life. She'd lived with it so long she hadn't realized how pervasive the miasma had been. Now, the insecure woman who made poor choices in life and in men was gone forever. The person she was becoming bore little to no resemblance to the misguided female who had sought fulfillment outside of herself.

Lynn knew, in the depths of her heart, that the only place to find happiness and contentment was within.

She laughed at the rather hoity, intellectual tone to her thoughts, but they were true. No person could make her whole, and no one thing could make her happy.

Not that she didn't long for companionship . . . with one very special companion . . . but for now she could be content with her newfound freedom. Although she had changed, shifted, the circumstances that threatened her had not. Her willingness to face the future head-on did not mean she could be any less vigilant in protecting the people she loved.

She shook her head as she thought about the frustration on Grant's face as they'd argued. And he called her stubborn! The man could give lessons in stubborn.

Which was probably why she loved him so much. He was so rock solid, so . . . so . . . comfortable. She'd never been this content with a man before. And it was just one more reason she loved him . . . and why it hurt so much to let him go.

Pushing back from the desk, she pushed aside the encroaching melancholy and gathered her things for the trip into town. Once outside, she looked at the shiny, new, black Jeep and her smile returned.

Freedom. How incredible.

A thought occurred to her and she raced inside and up the stairs to the attic. She picked up the journal and wrapped it in a soft cloth before placing it carefully in her purse. She owed each of them a debt of gratitude for sharing their stories with her, and it seemed right somehow to share these seemingly mundane, but life-altering moments with them.

Her errands ended up taking the better part of the day, but each stop felt connected with the ladies from the past. Even with the skies heavy with an impending storm, she came home invigorated. To spend an entire afternoon shopping and not being afraid to meet people's eyes, of not trying to be invisible, had been an awesome experience.

As she dragged groceries and packages into the house, she laughed at the urge to jump right back into the Jeep and find another store. She realized she was going a bit overboard, but figured she could be forgiven, all things considered.

In the quiet stillness, though, the ache of missing Grant returned, just as she knew it would. She'd reveled in the day even though she'd been preparing for the pendulum to swing back. Tonight she'd sleep alone, without Grant's tall, warm body curved around hers, his big, gentle hands on her breasts, his mouth placing kisses on her face, her neck, her shoulders. He would not be there to pull her close while he slept, unconsciously making sure he fit exactly so against her back.

Lynn looked at the bed as she hung up her new purchases. A tear formed, and slowly rolled down her cheek.

She didn't want to lose the excitement the day had brought her, but she was helpless against the flood of memories as she stared at the place where she'd known such happiness. It may have been fleeting, but it had been life-altering.

Sitting on the bed, she stroked the quilt that had covered two lovers immersed in each other, discovering each other, absorbing each other.

With her eyes bleary, she laid down and fell into another fatigued sleep. When she awakened a few hours later, the storm raged outside. She was too antsy to sleep, and the urge to start stitching a quilt top she'd completed some months before became overwhelming.

It took her until the wee hours of the morning to get the top, batting and backing sandwiched to her satisfaction, then even longer to get it basted. But once she was in her favorite chair, the center stretched taut over her hoop and her needle poised for that first stitch, it was all worth it.

She wasn't aware of the passage of time. Now and then she grabbed a bite to eat, stoked the fire she'd started, or napped with her new creation over her lap. Her attention was completely absorbed in the rhythm of rocking her needle in and out of the fabric to create the tiny stitches she was so proud of. As she stretched her arm to pull the thread through, her pride grew. Stitch, pull. Stitch, pull. Until her shoulders ached. Until even the hard calluses she'd built up on her fingers were sore. Until her eyes burned.

When she pulled the hoop from the quilt for the last time, she stretched her arms above her head and gave a Cheshire cat grin of satisfaction.

It was beautiful. Muted hues of red, blue, purple, with accents of ecru, white and eggshell, formed a series of hearts entwined with green vines. The combination of piecing and applique were the most intricate she'd ever done, but with the basic design quilted, she knew she'd been right to put in the time and effort. She'd go back and finish the detail work later, but for now, it was enough.

After carefully folding her newest creation and setting it on the couch, she planned to take a long, hot shower.

Instead, the urge to return to the journal was as strong
as if a hand were pulling her arm. After all that had
happened lately she didn't dare question it, and retrieved
the volume from her purse.

Stoking the fire, she wrapped herself in her new quilt
and settled in to read. Starting at the beginning, she devoured each entry slowly, carefully. It took hours to finish and by the end her eyes were burning from fatigue
as much as tears.

As she shut the binding, her fingers stroked the aged
leather and the brittle string that held it together. Her
thoughts were filled with the women who had possessed
this tiny bit of metal she kept in her collar. She no longer
doubted it was magic, or at least divinely guided, for
there could be no logical explanation for writings this
old staying together, or with the needle itself. It was
amazing that some collector hadn't gotten his hands on
these precious words that were a glimpse into the lives
of women from centuries past. She would have expected
the diary to be in a museum somewhere, under glass,
untouchable.

But that was the point. The miracle was in the touching, the needing, the using. And each of these women
had something in common: they had all known passion
and lost it, either by death, or by running from their
lover, or driving him away. Each woman had had a full
heart they had needed to share, to give away, but each
time fear had won and love had lost.

The feeling that these women were waiting for her to
bring the circle to a close nearly floored her. Being chosen to be the one to break the cycle was a responsibility
she wasn't sure she was prepared, or able, to fulfill.

As clearly as if Dora had reappeared, Lynn heard her
voice. "Don't run from love, Lynn. You'll regret it."

"But I can't put him in danger. That's not right, no
matter how much I might want things to be different."

A cool breeze danced over her spine and Lynn knew

Dora had returned. "Isn't that his right to choose? Haven't you railed against the fact that choices were stripped from you, that you've had to live in reaction, not action, for a long time?"

"But—"

"No buts. You're making choices for him, Lynn. How have you felt, having choices made for you?"

She chose not to answer.

"He won't force his way into your life. He's a good man, an honorable one. And one who loves you."

Lynn looked down at the diary and nodded. When she glanced up again, Dora was gone, the storm had passed, and the sun was beginning to poke through the clouds.

And she knew what she had to do.

But before she could leave, a certain tan patrol car drove into her yard, and once again Lynn found herself facing the lanky sheriff over her kitchen table.

"Ted, you just caught me on my way out."

"I won't keep you long. I just wanted to let you know that Murdock made a confession."

"I thought it couldn't count with the medication and all."

"He insisted that the doctors scale the meds back, and even called in his attorney. The lawyer was totally ticked off, but there wasn't much he could do about it. It's not foolproof, considering the situation, but it's about the best we can hope for right now."

As she looked at the dedicated lawman, whose lean face was haggard, she realized that whatever Trey had said was irrelevant. Truth or not, admissible in court or not, it didn't matter. She'd see this through and hope that justice would prevail. Her faith was a bit shaky in this particular area but with the help of her friends, both heavenly and earth-bound, it was time to give the legal system a chance.

And in the meantime, she was going to grab onto life with both hands and not let go.

"Thank you for driving all the way out here to tell me."

"You need to know that he's going to be released from the hospital within the next week or so, and it's highly likely that his attorney will get him bond. That means he'll be free until the trial."

"I understand. I'll watch my back."

Ted nodded. "I wish I could throw his butt in jail and toss the key down a storm drain."

She smiled at the vehemence in his normally even tone. "I do, too, but we both know you can't."

"Doesn't stop me from wishin'."

Cocking her head to the side, she said, "May I offer you a piece of advice, Sheriff? Principle is a cold bed-mate. Nan's convictions don't have to be antithetical to you. Find a way to compromise or you'll regret it for the rest of your life. And so will she."

Nodding again, he put his hat on his head. "Thanks. I'll think about it."

"Don't think, Ted. Act. Go to her. Talk this out. Life is precious and sometimes much too short. Don't lose another minute."

"You take care, Lynn. Call me if you need me."

"I will. Let me know what I need to do about Trey. I should have phone service of my own any day now."

"The district attorney will want to meet with you as soon as you can. We'll get all our ducks in a row so Murdock doesn't slip away on some technicality."

"You don't know him very well, Ted. He won't be an easy case."

"He doesn't know me, Lynn. He will pay."

She put her hand on his arm as they walked outside together to the porch. They stood side-by-side for a moment, looking out over the yard. "You're a good man, Ted. And a fine sheriff. Thank you for all you've done for me."

"Just my job—"

"No, you've gone above and beyond just a job. And I thank you. We may have some differences of opinion, but it doesn't lessen my esteem in the slightest."

He tipped his hat. "I appreciate that. I'd best be off."

She nodded as well, and turned to lock her door. When she turned back around, Ted had already reached his cruiser. She only hoped his next stop was to see a certain store owner whose heart was in pieces.

With a bolstering breath, Lynn headed for her Jeep and hoped her heart didn't end up the same way.

Sixteen

Grant sat in the hospital garden as the sun began its early descent. He'd been out there for hours, trying to come to terms with the bombshell his father had dropped.

His father wanted to retire from the bench and had asked Grant to reactivate his license. Then, the elder Major had said, they could go into private practice together.

While Grant had thought many times about going into practice, it had never occurred to him that his father would ever retire, much less that he had any desire to return to civil law. It had gotten him thinking, though, and ideas were popping like popcorn in his head.

There was so much he could do if he practiced law. Whole new horizons opened up that dovetailed nicely into a future with Lynn. If he could just get her to listen. Now that he had something to offer, some common goal, he might just sway her after all.

The door squeaked, and he looked over his shoulder to see who was joining him on the rather damp, cold patio. He stood, almost afraid to believe his eyes.

"Lynn?"

"Hello, Grant. How are you?"

"Tired, but hanging in there."

"And your dad? Betsy?"

"They're great. It was the most amazing thing. The very minute I put your quilts on their beds, they started improving at astonishing rates. The doctor says he doesn't understand it, and the nurses say it's miraculous."

She took a tentative step closer. "I'm glad. Very glad."

Grant closed the distance another stride. "And I'm glad you're here."

Smiling hesitantly, she held out the quilt. "I have something for you this time."

"Me?"

She nodded. "It's called Hearts Entwined."

Holding it up to the bright light spilling from the glass door, he ran his hand over the pattern and stitches.

"It's beautiful, exquisite. But you didn't have to drive all the way into Austin to bring this to me."

"Yes, I did. I—" she paused for a moment, taking a deep breath, making Grant wonder exactly what it was that she was about to say.

"Lynn—"

"Let me finish before I lose my courage." Stepping behind one of the wrought-iron chairs, she held on to the cold metal back with both hands. "Grant, I've been through a lot these last few weeks. And I've run a gamut of emotions. But if nothing else, I've figured out one thing. I can't run anymore."

"You said you were staying, no matter what."

"Yes, but that's not what I mean. I'm not running from my heart any longer. I love you, with all my being. And if you still want me, I'm yours. I'll move to Austin. I'll help you with your political career. I'll do anything I have to, to be with you."

Grant hauled her into his arms, quilt and all, and swung her around in a circle, a whoop of joy escaping from his lips to echo off the brick walls.

He kissed her with all the hope, all the unbridled bliss her words had brought him. "There, does that answer your question?"

She laughed, tipping her head back to look at him. "I guess so."

"And I've been doing a lot of thinking. What would you say if I started practicing law?"

"I'd say that's great, but why the change?"

He told her of his dad's revelation, and how his mind had been in a whirl all day because of it. "I don't think it's quite what my dad had in mind, but I'm thinking the victims of domestic violence in this area could use another advocate. With a mentor like my dad, I'll be a hot shot attorney in no time."

"Grant, there's not much money in representing these women."

"I'm not in this for money. I've already got plenty of it. What I *need* is to build a life with a certain beautiful redhead, and to help her fulfill her dreams while I pursue a few of my own."

"I can't believe this is working out," she said with weak relief. "Even as I was driving over here, I was so afraid that I'd be adding my own journal entry soon."

"What?"

"I'll explain it all later."

"Come on. Let's go see Betsy and tell her the news. She's been wanting to be a bridesmaid for years."

She touched her fingers to his face. "I love you, Grant. Thank you for coming into my life."

"I love you, Lynn. With all my heart. It's been a wild ride, but the future looks amazing from here."

Grinning, he turned her around and gave her a gentle push toward the door. "Come on. I want to get you into my bed."

She returned the smile. "Now that's a future I'm ready for."

Epilogue

One year and seven months later, Lynn and Grant Major stood on one side of an oversized red ribbon. The building on the other was the final construction project of Major Builders, Incorporated. The sign above the limestone facade said, HILL COUNTRY WOMEN'S CENTER, in huge letters.

Lynn placed a loving hand on her bulging stomach and snuggled into the curve of Grant's arms. With a dynamic plan for the future, the Majors had been unstoppable. The success of their efforts was in no small part due to Grant's mother's talent for hosting galas, something she had become adept at over the years as a judge's wife, and everyone agreed that Betsy had found her calling in charity fund-raising.

And the law firm of Major and Major already had more clients than they could handle.

But the real surprise had come when a letter had arrived from an attorney, referencing the Estate of Vernon Tremaine Murdock, III, Deceased. Trey had done the jail time adjudged in his plea bargain, and had not bothered her again. She and Grant had never let down their guard, but it seemed Trey had truly experienced a transformation in the hospital, just as he'd said. He hadn't turned into Mr. Warm and Fuzzy, but he had kept his word, and his distance.

Lynn would always have doubts about his true motivation. Whether he'd been trying to buy his way into heaven, or if indeed his desire to make amends had been sincere, she'd never know. But there was an entire wing of the women's shelter that would not have been possible without his bequeathal.

Despite the intensity of the summer heat, a cool breeze danced down Lynn's spine. Glancing behind her, she smiled.

In a semicircle were a few of those who'd shared the magic needle with her. Dora, Hilda, Margert, Hermalinda, Paulette. And a lady who was dressed in what looked like a medieval coathardie.

As Lynn scanned the faces of generations past, the baby kicked. And as one, the women smiled.

The group slowly moved to surround a young woman standing a bit apart from the rest of the crowd. If Lynn's memory served her, the woman's name was Marta, and she'd arrived at the center as a much-needed volunteer just a few weeks before. Marta shivered, unaware her sudden chill came from Dora placing a ghostly hand on her shoulder. Dora, Hilda, and all the rest looked at Lynn, nodding.

She hadn't been anxious for the day to come, but Lynn knew her tenure as keeper of the needle was over. Love had triumphed, and it was time for the needle to reach another woman in danger of spending her life without a love. As it should be.

"What are you looking at, honey?" Grant asked curiously.

"Oh, just saying good-bye."

"Good-bye?" He scanned the crowd gathered behind them. "To whom?"

"Just some old friends."

"Nan and Ted?" he asked, a bit incredulous.

"Heavens, no," Lynn laughed, looking across the way at her confidante as she stood under the protective arm of the sheriff. "Can you believe Ted decided against running for re-election?"

"Of course I can believe it. He was afraid he'd lose Nan, and no job was worth that."

Lynn snuggled closer, smiling against Grant's shirt. Nan had realized the depth of Ted's commitment to the law, and promised to find a way to work within the system, thereby meeting both their needs . . . and saving the love of a lifetime.

"Well, my love," Grant said, kissing her temple, "if you've finished your good-byes, it's now time to say hello."

She nodded and faced forward again, ready for the next stage, the next adventure. Healing had taken a long time, but as she looked at the Center, she was grateful. No one wished for tragedy, but she could say that this time, tragedy had become triumph.

She accepted the huge scissors from the mayor, and reached for Grant. With their hands entwined, they cut the ribbon, and the applause was deafening.

"To our future," she said, for his ears alone. "Safe. Whole."

"Together."

"Forever."

"Well, girls, maybe, just maybe, the cycle is broken," Dora said to the entourage.

Hilda nodded. "Please, Gott, let it be so. All of us who came before Lynn were foolish. She was wise enough to follow her heart."

"Oui," Paulette agreed. "And now we must hope zhat Marta will continue ze trend and love again."

"On the other hand," Hermalinda said pragmatically, "she could be one stubborn señorita and share our fate."

"Well, I will hope for the best," Margaret said, putting a hand on her hip. "Besides, she'll have us to help her!"

Jeanette's face was serene. "I leave her in your capable hands, my friends."

As one, they looked at Jeanette and offered her a wave good-bye. They sighed as Justin came out of the glare of the blazing sun, and offered his hand to his love.

The ladies joined hands, as their number decreased by one, and, for now, faded into bright sunshine . . .